*The naked yearning in her face
twisted something deep inside him*

"What were you doing at the bank?" he
asked gently.

Roseanne flinched. Her eyes widened, and her
mouth opened, but nothing came out.

"Easy," MacAlister murmured. "I just
wondered why you'd gone there. Did you
remember something about the bank?"

Reflected firelight shimmered in his eyes,
mesmerizing her. She wanted to trust him,
wanted to with all her heart. But something held
her back. "I . . . I don't know."

"Another one of those things you sense,"
he grumbled.

Roseanne looked away, unable to face his
unspoken censure.

"Can you explain it to me?"

A shudder shook her as she turned back to face
him, her eyes filled with misery. "I want to,"
she whispered. "But I . . . I can't . . . not
yet, anyway."

"You will," he said steadily, eyes locked
on hers. "You'll trust me, then you'll tell
me everything. . . ."

Dear Reader,

It may still be winter outside, but here at Intimate Moments, things couldn't be hotter. Take our American Hero title, for instance: Paula Detmer Riggs's *Firebrand*. Judd Calhoun left his Oregon home—and his first love, Darcy Kerrigan—in disgrace. Now he's back—as the new fire chief—and the heat that sizzled between the two of them is as powerful as ever. But there are still old wounds to heal and new dangers to face. Talk about the flames of passion...!

Rachel Lee is on tap with the third of her Conard County series, *Miss Emmaline and the Archangel*. It seems the town spinster has a darker past than anyone suspects, and now it's catching up to her. With no one to turn to except Gage Dalton, the man they call Hell's Own Archangel, her future looks grim. But there's more to this man than his forbidding looks would indicate—much more—and Miss Emmaline is about to learn just what it means to be a woman in love. Marilyn Pappano's *Memories of Laura* takes place in the quintessential small town—Nowhere, Montana—where a woman without a memory meets a man who's sure he knows her past. And it's not a pretty one. So why does sheriff Buck Logan find himself falling for her all over again? In her second book, *Dixon's Bluff*, Sally Tyler Hayes mixes danger and desire and love for a small girl and comes up with a novel you won't want to miss. Harlequin Historical author Suzanne Barclay enters the contemporary arena with *Man with a Mission*, a suspense-filled and highly romantic tale linking two seemingly mismatched people who actually have one very important thing in common: love. Finally, welcome new author Raine Hollister. In *Exception to the Rule*, heroine Layne Taylor finds herself running afoul of the law when she tries to defend her brother against a murder charge. But with Texas Ranger Brant Wade as her opponent, things soon start to get extremely personal.

As always, enjoy!

Leslie Wainger
Senior Editor and Editorial Coordinator

MAN WITH A MISSION

Suzanne Barclay

Published by Silhouette Books New York

America's Publisher of Contemporary Romance

SILHOUETTE BOOKS
300 East 42nd St., New York, N.Y. 10017

MAN WITH A MISSION

ISBN: 0-373-07483-2

First Silhouette Books printing March 1993

Printed in the U.S.A.

SUZANNE BARCLAY

makes her home on a mountain in New York State's answer to the Napa Valley...the lush wine country of upstate New York's Finger Lakes region. "It is the perfect setting for a writer, miles from the temptations of friends and shopping malls," she says. When not working at her computer, Suzanne enjoys making miniature furniture and trying out new recipes on her husband. The family pets, Tasha and Max, a miniature schnauzer and Airedale respectively, lure her outside for a daily walk just to make certain she keeps her perspective in order.

To Wendy and Bruce,
in memory of all the great times Ken and I had
exploring the Napa Valley with you

Prologue

The night was cold and wet and...dangerous. But not as dangerous as what she had left behind.

Fighting down a surge of panic, the slender young woman dashed out the door of the mansion and hurried along the side of the building. Her heart beat a frantic tattoo against her ribs, but she dared not run. The fog that had stolen in from New York City's East River completely shrouded the landscape, turning shrubbery and pavement into potentially deadly traps.

At the corner of the building she paused to catch her breath, glancing nervously over her shoulder, then ahead to the faint glimmer of street lights on First Avenue. If she could just reach it before—

Behind her, the door was wrenched opened again, briefly spilling hazy yellow light into the fog before a man's broad silhouette filled the space. He stood still, waiting, his gun a natural extension of his hand.

He was hunting for her.

Stifling a gasp of terror, she lurched around the corner and flattened herself against the slick gray stone. Breathing raggedly, she reached up to touch the gold-and-diamond necklet resting in the valley between her breasts. Despite the clammy chill of her skin, it felt warm . . . almost reassuring. But it was a false sense of security.

Lucien was dead. There was no way she could talk herself out of this mess. When the gunman caught her, he would kill her.

Driven by the image of Lucien's lifeless body and the blood—his blood—spattered across the white walls, she jerked the edges of the heavy fur coat around her shivering body and darted down the long, fog-shrouded driveway.

Over the pounding of her pulse, she heard the soft squish of crepe-soled shoes coming after her.

Panicked, she broke into a run, the long sides of the ankle-length sable caught high in her sweaty fists. Panting, sobbing, she swept through the wrought-iron gates that marked the edge of the property and hurtled across the street without a thought for oncoming traffic.

Behind her, the screech of brakes and a muffled curse told her the man was gaining.

She dragged air into her burning lungs and ran on, her desperate eyes searching the fog-clogged shadows for someone, anyone, to help her. But the streets were empty, and she was tiring fast.

The angry, determined slap of rubber on wet pavement came closer, so close she thought she heard her pursuer's hoarse breathing. Any second she expected to feel his touch . . . or the bite of cold steel.

Ahead and across the street, she spotted the faint glow of a lighted window, the first she had seen. Lights meant people, safety. With a gasp of desperation, she forced a burst of speed from her aching muscles and headed for it. In the dark, she stumbled over the curb, struggled to regain her balance, but it was too late, she was falling.

"No!" she screamed. As her knees and palms struck the slick pavement, she heard a muffled *thunk!*

Pain exploded in her head. Pain and darkness. She never felt her body hit the cold, wet sidewalk, nor heard the insistent wail of police sirens drawing nearer.

But the gunman did. With a savage curse, he melted back into the shadows to watch. And wait. There was every chance the woman was dead. If she wasn't . . . there would be other chances to kill her and take the key.

Chapter 1

Upton Bank and Trust. The words, chiseled in stone above the entrance to the stately old New York City bank, matched those on the key in her pocket.

This was it. Against all odds, she'd found it.

Pushing open the ornately carved door, Roseanne stepped inside and stared up two stories of gray-veined marble to the domed ceiling. The bank looked more like a mausoleum than a financial institution. Appropriate, since buried somewhere inside it were the answers to her questions. She hoped.

Roseanne's heart jumped and stuck behind the lump in her throat. What if she was wrong? What if she had slipped away from the clinic, risked crossing the dangerous city for nothing? What if the box was empty? What if she never remembered who she was?

The fear grew stronger; her stomach rolled, raw with it. Despite her best efforts to remain calm, she swayed, caught the cold marble doorframe and clung to it through a wave of dizziness that reminded her this was her first day out of bed.

One week ago, a bullet—fired by persons unknown, according to the police report—had creased her skull and stolen her memories, her identity, everything she was. The only ties she had to her past life were a fur coat, a diamond necklace and the key to a safe-deposit box tagged with the name of this bank.

What would she do if the box didn't solve the mystery of her identity? She couldn't go on living in limbo like this much longer without losing what little remained of her mind.

Shivering despite the swath of sable covering her from neck to ankles, Roseanne pushed away from the door and slowly started across the stately lobby. Her icy hands were thrust deep in the velvet-lined pockets, one clenched around the key. Beneath the heavy fur, she wore faded jeans and a nubby green sweater, courtesy of one of the nurses.

"Probably not as grand as you're used to," the young woman had apologized when she'd offered the clothes.

"I don't know what I'm used to, but these are very welcome," Roseanne had replied, grateful to be spared the humiliation of the backless hospital gown. "I don't even know if Roseanne is really my name."

"It was stitched into your coat," the nurse had pointed out. "You're lucky your assailant didn't take it or your necklace." With a sigh of yearning, she had petted the luxurious dark fur thrown across the foot of the bed.

The police had told her she was lucky to be alive; the doctors claimed she'd had a close call and was lucky to have regained consciousness. She didn't feel lucky; she felt angry and frustrated. "The man who shot me took something far more valuable than possessions," she had muttered.

"Your memory. I know how lost you must feel."

No you don't, Roseanne had wanted to scream. No one understood what it was like to wake up each day to nothing. To look in the mirror and not recognize the delicate, too-pale face staring back. To be torn from sleep night after night by the same nightmare—a man chasing her through the fog. She would awaken drenched in sweat, heart pounding in terror, with no idea who the man was, or why he wanted her dead, or even if he was the same man who had shot her.

The detective assigned to her case had grilled her for days without shaking loose a clue. Neither the name Roseanne, nor the diamond initials RED hanging from a gold chain around her neck, had meant anything to her.

The staff at Norwood Medical Clinic, where she had been taken following the shooting, had been equally stymied. If they just had more to go on, the doctors had said, they might be able to jar her memory.

Yesterday, Roseanne had found the key pinned deep inside the pocket of the sable. The nurse had told her it was probably a bank safe-deposit box key and explained that people kept their valuables in such boxes... like jewelry or important papers.

For a full minute, Roseanne had stared at the key, sensing she would find important information about her past inside the bank box. She'd started to call the detective, but some deep-seated instinct had cautioned her to visit the bank alone. So, instead of alerting the police, Roseanne had asked the nurse for a telephone book, looked up the address of the main branch of Upton Bank and Trust, then awaited a chance to slip away from the clinic.

She clenched her fist a little tighter around the key as she crossed the interminable stretch of gleaming marble. The click of her borrowed shoes echoed alarmingly off the slick stone, drawing stares from the few patrons still in the bank at six o'clock on this dark, bitter Friday night in November. Self-conscious, she forced herself to walk slowly to the safe-deposit section. None of them could possibly know why she was here.

"May I help?" The thin, well-dressed young man behind the counter frowned at her through thick glasses.

It was now or never. "I need access to my safe-deposit box." Roseanne was startled by her cool, assured voice. Had she come here often? Was this man or this situation familiar to her on some level? For the first time since regaining consciousness, she didn't feel like a mass of raw, quivering nerves.

The clerk gave the fur coat a second glance and his shoulders straightened. "Of course... madame." He smiled as he whipped out a form and proffered a pen.

Roseanne's cautious optimism plunged as she read the form. They expected the box number, her name and signature. Nibbling on her lower lip, she eased the key from her pocket. The letters *DCT* were engraved on the key itself. The attached tag had Upton Bank and Trust on one side and the number 103 on the other.

Feeling the clerk's eyes on her, she wrote the number down, moved to the next line and wrote *Roseanne*. Her hand trembled as it hovered over the blank space marked Last Name. No memory flickered. Tears of despair burned the backs of her eyes.

"That box is not at this office," the clerk warned.

"Oh. I didn't know. My... my husband opened the account," she stammered. *Why had she said that?*

The clerk gazed pointedly at her ringless left hand. "I see. Well, the DCT on the key means your... husband... opened it for you at the Danbury, Connecticut, branch of our bank."

Roseanne's shoulders slumped. Where was Danbury? How was she going to get there? *Not by standing here,* an inner voice rebuked. *Right.* Stiffening her spine, Roseanne politely thanked the clerk and recrossed the bank.

Well, at least she was not a cowerer, Roseanne thought, sighing as she pushed open the heavy door and stepped out onto the street. Every day she learned something new about herself. Heights terrified her; she was a fussy eater and overly sentimental—she had cried through *Old Yeller* and *Little Women* on the late-night movie. On the plus side, she did not whine, brood or cower.

Roseanne sighed again and scuffed her toe against a crack in the pavement. It bothered her that she'd hidden the key from the police and gone to the bank by herself. Was she a private person anxious to face the disappointment of an empty box alone? Or did her subconscious know it contained something bad about her?

An old bum lurched past, brushing her shoulder with his as he stumbled. Automatically, she reached out to help him, then hastily pulled her hands back, burned by the memory of Detective Farley's list of the suspects who might have fired the bullet that had nearly killed her.

Thief. Drug addict. Pimp. Had she been part of the city's criminal population? Was that why she'd been shot? Was that why she trusted no one but herself near the box?

No! She was not a criminal. Roseanne fought down a wave of revulsion. Both the detective and the doctors had said she was a sensitive, well-educated person. The contents of the Danbury bank box would prove it. She had to believe that. *She had to.*

A gust of wind whistled around the skyscrapers, biting into Roseanne's neck. Shivering, she pulled the fur collar up around her ears and hastily glanced around at the string of lighted storefronts and towering buildings. The need to find a place to hide while she searched for a way to reach this Danbury was sharper even than the ugly smells of the city. She had no money for a hotel room, but returning to the clinic wasn't an option. The police were bound to ask questions about her little jaunt.

Half a block away, she saw a man in a dark overcoat emerge from an equally dark sedan. Leaving the door open, he moved toward her. Something in his manner and the intent expression on his florid face as he approached her made her skin crawl. *He was coming for her.*

Roseanne turned and fled, the leaden taste of panic in her mouth. The heavy coat flew out behind her, slowing her down. She filled her fists with fur, hiked the coat up and ran for all she was worth. A dozen yards ahead, the sidewalk was blocked for construction.

Whimpering, she veered left, only to find herself on an unlit side street. *Trapped.* She paused for an instant, unable to go back, unwilling to go ahead. But she had no choice. Gasping for breath, she began to run again, struggling to pour on enough speed to reach the next lighted street. It was a futile effort, she realized with a spurt of primitive fear. Her legs were weak from the days spent in bed; she'd never make it.

Roseanne risked a quick glance over her shoulder, saw her pursuer turn and dash down the alley after her. Her stomach clenched. He was still half a block behind, but gaining fast.

God, it was her nightmare come to life. Her mouth went dry, and her feet tangled. Even as she put out her arms to catch herself, a hand suddenly snaked out from the shadows, snagged her forearm and dragged her back into the inky recess of a narrow alley. Her scream was muffled by a wide, callused palm, her frantic struggles subdued between a rock-hard chest and steely arms.

"Shh. Not a sound, and he'll pass us by," whispered a voice as deep and rich as velvet.

She couldn't see him in the pitch black, but he sounded cultured and he smelled clean. Acting on instinct again, Roseanne surrendered, sagging in his viselike grip. Dizzy with relief and exertion, she fought to catch her breath.

"Easy. If you promise not to make a sound, I'll take my hand away so you can breathe better."

Numbly, she nodded. When the hand moved, she licked her lips and gratefully drew in gulps of the cold, sour air. It tasted like heaven. Pulse slowing, she tipped her head back to get a look at the man who held her, but he blended with the night.

Roseanne tensed as the heavy footsteps of her pursuer approached, then pounded past them.

"Come on...we have to get moving," her rescuer whispered. He turned her away from the fading sounds, herding her toward the back of the alley where it was even darker.

"I can't go with you," she said, but quietly, in case the other man came back.

"You haven't got much choice."

Roseanne hesitated. Suppose the man who had been chasing her was a policeman? Suppose this man was...

"Move it, princess," he hissed, his hands tightening painfully on her arms as he propelled her before him.

Roseanne dug in her heels. "You're hurting me."

"Christ!"

The shadowy world tilted as he slung her over his shoulder; the impact knocked the remaining breath from her body. She hung there, terrified and nearly senseless as the man trotted off into the night.

He ran a block or two. Roseanne lost count because she kept slipping in and out of consciousness. The whole thing reminded her of the way Tarzan had carried Jane off into the jungle on the afternoon movie two days ago. She stifled a hysterical bubble of laughter. Fear and lack of oxygen were making her giddy when she needed all her faculties to figure a way out of this situation. Pulling herself together, she raised her head a fraction and noticed that the area they were in now was lighted.

"Stand here a minute while I unlock the car."

Roseanne staggered as her feet were abruptly dropped on the ground, and she was leaned up against a cold, gritty metal surface. Before she could recover enough to run, he scooped her up again, stuffed her into the car and slid in behind the wheel.

The interior of the car smelled stale and sweaty, and the cracked leather seat snagged at her coat. Roseanne lifted her bottom to free the fur, and one foot nearly went through the squishy floorboards.

"That does it. I'm getting out." She pushed at the door on her side. When it refused to budge, hysteria reared its ugly head again, and she pounded on the door with her fist.

"What the hell do you think you're doing?" he growled.

Roseanne swallowed and turned, expecting the man who had so ruthlessly carried her off to resemble the Hunchback of Notre Dame. By the eery glow of an overhead streetlight, she saw her assumption was wrong. He was not exactly handsome, more like arresting. His hair was longish, dark as the night. Shadows and light played over his strong, rugged features, glinting off the hard lines of his cheekbones and jaw, emphasizing the grim set of a mouth that might be sensual under other circumstances.

A shiver went through Roseanne as she raised her eyes to his. They were amber, as intense and hungry as a hunting cat's, but crowded with ghosts that reminded her too vividly of her own nightmares. She was suddenly certain he had suffered.

She was just as certain he was dangerous.

The breath caught in her throat. "I would like to get out."

"No thanks for saving you from that guy?"

The low, rough timbre of his voice made her skin tingle and her stomach flutter oddly. Fine, she was coming down with that flu the TV ads harped on. "Thank you very much." Not caring that she sounded ridiculous, like Shirley Temple at a tea party, Roseanne reached for the door. It still refused to budge.

"Helps to unlatch it first," he said as the engine growled to life.

"They don't show how it's done in TV commercials."

He blinked once, then his gaze narrowed. "I don't know what the hell your game is, princess, but for your own good, we're getting the hell out of here before that punk shows up again." Without waiting for her consent, he moved a lever and the car shot forward.

As the car surged around a corner and rocketed out into a stream of other cars, Roseanne screamed and braced her feet on the rotten floor to keep her balance. She clutched the split leather seat with both hands as a kaleidoscope of stores, lights and people flew by, faster and faster. Then they were skidding to a stop, and she screamed again as her body was thrown forward, toward the windshield.

A hard arm flashed across her midsection and slammed her back against the seat. "Jeez! What's wrong with you? Haven't you ever ridden in a car before?"

Panting a little, Roseanne turned on him. "I have no idea. I don't even know who—"

Behind them, someone laid on the horn.

Her rescuer snarled something under his breath, and the car rocketed off again, surrounded by a shifting herd of cars and trucks. The speed and proximity of the other vehicles was terrifying. Roseanne gasped and flinched as a yellow car flashed by a scant inch from her door.

"Stifle the screams, princess," he warned. "You're setting my nerves on edge, and I don't need the distraction."

Roseanne risked peeking at him and saw he was hunched over the wheel, his head and eyes moving as he raked the rolling traffic. He looked tense and ruthless.

"I want out. I—I'll jump if I have to," she warned, one hand reaching for the lever she hoped opened the door.

"Okay. Give me a sec." He glanced in the small mirror near his head. "I'll pull over, and we can talk."

He was as good as his word, and a few hair-raising seconds later he made a heart-stopping dash across the line of oncoming cars and screeched to a halt near the sidewalk.

Roseanne moaned and leaned her head back, eyes closed.

"So what's with you?"

Roseanne rolled her head so she could see him. He looked just as severe as he had fighting the traffic. Licking her lips, she forced her trembling body upright. "Th-thank you for helping me get away from that man. If you will show me how to operate the door, I will let you go about your business." Her voice trailed off as she belatedly wondered what kind of business a man conducted in a dark alley.

His frown deepened. "It's dangerous to wander around alone."

This man and this car were dangerous. "I'll be fine."

"You have a place to go?" He sounded sure she didn't.

Roseanne wished she was better at lying. "I—I . . . yes."

"Where?" his low voice had the same whiplike bite as the police detective's.

It was the final straw. Roseanne had been questioned, prodded and hounded beyond the endurance of the fragile shell she had grown these seven days to cover her fears. "I have no idea where you can take me," she snapped. "I have no idea who I am, or where I belong. So . . . so just let me get out and—"

His image blurred, and she broke off abruptly, surprised and thoroughly embarrassed to find she was crying. Turning her face to the window, she savagely dashed the moisture from her eyes.

She expected words of pity; he offered none. "I'm taking you to my place." He shifted the car into gear again.

"No!" Roseanne spun back around. "I—I can't. I don't even know who you are."

"MacAlister," he growled and began searching the small mirror outside the car.

"I don't know anything about you."

Snorting, he raked her with a cold, contemptuous glance. "Yeah? Too bad the situation isn't mutual." His tone was low and ripe with innuendo.

"What is that supposed to mean?"

He raised one eyebrow, insinuating she knew perfectly well what he meant. "You're good," he said grudgingly.

Roseanne froze. "Do you know me?" she whispered.

Something flickered briefly behind his shuttered gaze, then disappeared. "No," he said in a clipped voice.

He lied. *But why?* And how could a man met by chance in a dark alley know her?

MacAlister exhaled sharply and raked a wide hand through his hair. "Look, I know I'm not what you're used to, princess," he muttered, his tone gentler, almost soothing, as though he'd just sensed her confusion and wanted to relieve it. "But I'm a hell of a lot safer than what you'll find out on the streets."

"Mmm." Head cocked as though considering his words, Roseanne studied her rescuer. What was going on behind those carefully shuttered eyes? Maybe because she had lost her own identity, the people she met interested her. She'd driven the clinic staff nuts wanting to know everything about them. What they thought, what they liked, what they disliked. Despite his rough exterior and earlier hostility, MacAlister fascinated her. "Why are you suddenly being nice to me?"

If her question surprised him, it didn't show in his rugged features, but then, MacAlister didn't seem the type to give much away. *Intriguing.* When he shrugged, she pressed. "If you don't know me, why do you call me 'princess'?" she demanded. "And why did you help me when you don't seem to like me?"

He stared at her for a moment. "I don't like your type."

"What type?"

"Rich little bitch."

"That's what they call the women on the soap operas who cause all the trouble," Roseanne said, hurt that she couldn't even defend herself, because it might be true.

"What are you, some kind of TV nut?" he grumbled.

"I was in an...accident. I don't remember much about...things. The doctors at the clinic suggested I watch television and read magazines to learn about things."

He raked her with another scathing, disbelieving glance. "People who suffer from amnesia forget their names, their personal history, not...not everything."

"I still remember how to walk and talk."

"Lucky me." He took a swipe at his hair again. *Nervous gesture?* she wondered, encouraged because it made him seem more human. "We can't sit here all night. Either I'm taking you home with me, or to this clinic of yours." He said it as though he knew she couldn't go back there.

Which she couldn't. If the doctors locked her up, she'd never get to the bank in Danbury. "I'll go with you."

MacAlister nodded and relaxed a little. "I hate hospitals, too. I think it's the smell."

Roseanne kept quiet. Actually the smells didn't bother her. They seemed . . . familiar. The police had speculated that she might have worked at a hospital.

"Okay. Let's get the hell out of here."

Roseanne clung to the seat as they surged away from the curb, hoping she'd done the right thing in following her instincts about MacAlister. With her memory gone, she was forced to rely heavily on her other faculties. She sensed he wasn't the man from her nightmares—sensed, too, that he wouldn't harm her, despite his animosity. God help her if she was wrong.

"Why are you helping me?" she asked again.

"I'm a sucker for a woman in distress," he grumbled as he deftly slipped in and out of the stream of speeding vehicles.

"Did you have a bad day?"

He shot her a narrowed glare. "What the hell is that supposed to mean?"

Roseanne studied him in the otherworldly glow of the dash lights, thinking he reminded her of an ancient warrior—rough, tough and slightly uncivilized, but with a hint of weariness and sorrow. A gladiator, or maybe a knight, who'd seen too much of death and dying.

"Maybe you had a bad day and are taking it out on me," she said slowly. "Kicking the pet, as they say."

"Kicking the what? Oh. It's dog, not pet. I don't kick dogs," he muttered.

"Just rich bitches?" She couldn't resist teasing.

He growled something under his breath and took the corner fast, tires squealing in the best Miami Vice tradition.

Among other things, MacAlister definitely lacked a sense of humor, she thought as she clung to the cracked seat. Why couldn't he have turned out to be someone she could trust with her secrets? Why did he say things that threw her off balance, played on her doubts and fears about who she was?

Because this was reality, not some TV program.

* * *

Roseanne's feet sank into the thick gray carpet as she stepped to the floor-to-ceiling window and turned to survey the enormous living room of MacAlister's luxury high-rise apartment.

His furniture was modern. A low burgundy-and-gray sofa and two burgundy leather chairs were grouped together with a smoked-glass coffee table. Twin floor lamps cast circles of light at either end of the couch, and three huge paintings provided a splash of color against the stark white walls. The place screamed subdued elegance.

"Are you sure you live here?"

"What's wrong with it?" he snapped.

"Oh, it's beautiful," she said hastily. *No sense of humor and defensive. Fun combination.* "It's like something out of Lifestyles of the Rich and Famous, but it doesn't fit with that car of yours. And it's so sterile . . . no pictures of loved ones, no personal items scattered around. It could belong to anyone."

MacAlister strolled closer, his hands shoved into the back pockets of tight, faded black jeans, his gaze intense. "Did you watch a program on psychoanalysis?"

In the light, he appeared more formidable than he had earlier in the shadows. He was lean and tough-looking, his jaw darkly stubbled, his black T-shirt revealing the hard, smooth shoulder muscles as clearly as the jeans emphasized his powerful thighs. Dark, lean and uncomfortably big.

Roseanne wanted to step back, but the condemnation glittering in his yellow eyes angered her, steadied her. He had no right to judge her. "No. I did *not* learn that from a program. There are just some things I . . . sense."

"Well, leave off sensing things about me," he growled.

"Fine." She wrapped her hands around her mug of hot instant coffee for support. It had been like this since he'd parked the car in the underground garage and dragged her into the elevator for the stomach-wrenching ride to his twentieth-floor apartment. He was back to being hostile, and she couldn't seem to resist testing the limits of his barely restrained temper.

It was all his fault for being so frustratingly cryptic and annoyingly scornful, she decided. She had been quiet and polite with the clinic staff and the police. But there was something about MacAlister that made her pulse beat a little faster, her skin feel too warm and a size too small. Drat. If she was getting the flu, she hoped it held off until she got away from him. MacAlister would be as gentle a nurse as Hulk Hogan.

"Perhaps I should go back to the clinic after all," Roseanne said, setting her mug down on the table.

Before she could draw a breath, MacAlister was standing over her. He moved with the lazy, deceptive speed of the panther on that nature program. Despite her earlier resolve to remain unaffected by his size and brooding temper, she stepped back until her legs bumped up against the couch.

He followed, standing so close she could feel the warmth of his body, feel his breath stir the hair at her temple. This time his nearness made her heart beat wildly, sent a fission of fire racing across her skin. Drat, it was getting worse.

"I wouldn't think of sending you out...especially dressed as you are," he said. "Think of the embarrassment."

Roseanne blinked herself free of his strange spell and looked down. "What's wrong with my clothes?"

"You look like a bag lady."

She frowned, searching her small store of knowledge. "Ah, a homeless person who carries her possessions in a shopping bag." She cocked her head to one side. "But I have no bag, and you are looking at everything I own." *Except the key.*

"What about the coat hanging in my closet?" he bit out. "Suppose I said I was keeping the coat if you didn't stay?"

Her mouth fell open in surprise. "You'd steal my coat?"

"Think of it as a fee...a fee for rescuing you."

"Oh, you can't do that." Roseanne's temper soared as the mocking triumph in his eyes assured her he could, and would, keep the coat. "You're a...a..." She fumbled for a swear word bad enough to suit him.

"Bastard." MacAlister smiled. A slow, predatory smile. "A genuine bastard, princess, and I'm keeping you right here where I can keep an eye on you."

"Why? Why are you doing this to me?"

"You're staying here because that's the way I want it. What's the matter, afraid I'll jump you?"

"No," Roseanne said slowly. "You don't have that funny look in your eyes that the murderers on those police programs get before they strangle the victim."

"Jesus Christ!" MacAlister raked a hand through his hair again and paced to the window. "It's a wonder you made it as far as the bank."

Roseanne's head came up. "How did you know I was there?"

"I was up the street...saw that guy mark you," he said coolly, leaning one wide shoulder against the window frame, his expression as impenetrable as the night sky behind him.

Suddenly Roseanne felt the weight of all the terrible things that had happened to her today, and her shoulders sagged. There was no use covering her feelings with false bravado. She was frightened, exhausted and she had nowhere else to go.

As though he'd sensed her weakness, MacAlister's voice suddenly turned gentle. "Drink your coffee."

Tears welled up in Roseanne's eyes, but she quickly blinked them back. She would *not* cry in front of Mister Hard-As-Nails MacAlister. "I'd like to go to bed," she said tightly.

"Fine by me." MacAlister straightened from the window with fluid grace. If he'd noticed how close she was to losing control, it hadn't affected him. No surprise. She'd decided he didn't have any nerves or any feelings. "There's only one bed, but you can have it, *princess.*" He made the word a curse.

Roseanne welcomed the anger that stiffened her backbone. Chin high, teeth clenched, she followed him down the hallway to the bedroom, watched in furious silence as he grabbed a pillow and blanket for himself. She'd stay tonight and be up before he awoke and on her way to the bank in Connecticut.

If she was forced to endure MacAlister's cordial hospitality for any longer, she would likely find out whether she was capable of murder. Catching a glimpse of his hard, closed profile as he turned to leave the bedroom, she saw that his nose had been broken once and mended off-center. Good. If he gave her any more trouble, she'd straighten it out for him.

MacAlister slammed the door on Roseanne Danforth Deets and stomped down the hall. *Damn. Damn.* This wasn't going to be as easy as Stone had promised. Why did she have to look softer, more fragile than the photos in her file? Why did she have to act more like a victim than the murdering little bitch he'd been assigned to tail?

She was good, he'd have to give her that, MacAlister thought as he poured himself a Scotch. Recalling the sad, dazed look in her eyes when she'd told him about her amnesia, he felt an unwelcome fission of compassion.

A man could get sucked in by vulnerability like that, deluded into sacrificing his goals.

Another man, maybe, but not him. He was smarter than that, and tougher. He'd get the contents of that safe-deposit box away from her before she even realized what he was after.

Chapter 2

The shadow rose out of the fog, as black and deadly and unstoppable as death. She turned, ran, but the shadow followed. It slipped closer every time she looked back. Closer, closer... Its hot breath fanned her, searing the air in her lungs. She tried to run faster, but her legs had turned to stone. A hand brushed her shoulder.

Roseanne sat up, a scream lodged in her throat. Heart pounding, she looked around and realized she had been dreaming. The same terrible nightmare that had haunted her all week.

The door to the room opened. "Roseanne?"

By the gray light filtering in through the window, she recognized MacAlister. "Nightmare," she croaked, automatically reaching for the bedside lamp. As the light clicked on and she got a good look at him, Roseanne longed for the darkness again.

Naked but for snug black briefs and a lethal-looking gun, MacAlister glided across the threshold. His harsh glance touched her briefly, then flickered around the room. Apparently satisfied, he lowered the gun and clicked on the safety.

"Nightmare, huh?" His muscles bunched and coiled as he crossed to the bed and stood over her. "I'm not surprised . . . considering."

Roseanne tried to meet his gaze, but found she couldn't drag her eyes away from his nearly nude body. There was so much of him. Miles of bronzed skin, smooth except for a few faded scars and the whirls of dark hair covering his chest. Looking at him fascinated her on one level, frightened her on another.

"Stop staring at me like you've never seen a naked man before—we both know different."

Still wearing her jeans and sweater, Roseanne sat up and glared at him. "If you know something about me . . ."

"Shh." He cocked his head. "Douse the light. Now!" he gritted, already moving out the door and down the hall.

"Now what?" Roseanne glanced at the bedside clock. A little after two. No wonder she felt like she'd been run down by a truck. Groaning, she turned off the light and hurried into the living room in time to see MacAlister zipping up his jeans in the shadow-filled room. When she opened her mouth to question him, he clamped his palm over it as he had in the alley.

"Not a sound," he breathed in her ear. "Go into the kitchen and don't come out until I call you. Be ready to move in a second if I do." His tone demanded obedience, and she turned to go, but a soft scraping noise at the door leading into the apartment stopped her dead in her tracks. The grimness of MacAlister's expression told her more than she wanted to know.

Someone was breaking into his apartment.

Weak-kneed, she tottered into the kitchen and crouched in the narrow alley between the oak cupboards. Straining to hear over the frantic beat of her heart was more than she could bear. Creeping forward, she peeked around the corner. Two shapes blocked out the thin strip of light visible under the door. *Feet.* Her stomach rolled.

A soft click was all the warning she had before the door opened. Inch by inch, the slice of light widened. The blue-steel muzzle of a gun intruded, followed closely by a dark figure. The hair on Roseanne's nape stirred. Oh, God. Where was MacAlister? Why wasn't he doing something?

A shadow detached itself from the wall and leaped into the air, one foot extended in a kick that struck the gunman's arm with a sickening crack. The intruder crumpled to the floor, writhing and moaning.

"Shut up. It's not broken . . . yet," MacAlister growled, pinning the man to the floor as he retrieved the gun.

Damn. He must be getting old, MacAlister thought. Either that, or six months of retirement from the Bureau had sapped his reflexes. His instincts were still razor-sharp, thank God, but he had landed the blow a second too late and a fraction too high. It hadn't made much difference—this time. But he'd have to be more careful from now on.

Jamming a knee into the small of the gunman's back, he methodically rifled the thug's pockets. Fifty bucks in small bills. No change. No credit cards. A thin wallet identified the man as Harvey Shaw. Brooklyn address on his driver's license.

"Local talent," MacAlister mused. It seemed unlikely, then, that this little intrusion was linked to his past life. Players in the international arena where he'd operated when he'd worked for the Bureau used imported help. Which meant the present situation was heating up fast. A hell of a lot faster than Stone had led him to believe when MacAlister had agreed to take on this assignment.

"Roseanne. Get out here—now," MacAlister barked. His admiration for her rose another unwilling notch when she came without hesitation. Her eyes were wide with fear, but her steps were as steady as the gaze she leveled at his captive.

"Recognize our friend?" MacAlister demanded, his hands clenched in the man's greasy hair as he forced his head up. "Was he the one who came after you at the bank?"

Roseanne swallowed. The jowly, pockmarked face was contorted with pain. "N-no." Her voice cracked. She cleared her throat and tried again. "That man was taller, thinner, I think. What . . . ?"

"There's a coil of rope in the closet behind you. Get it," MacAlister ordered without looking at her.

Roseanne wanted to object, but his fierce expression stopped her. It took her a minute to locate the rope. When she came back with it, the gunman looked like he'd been put through a wringer.

"You have two seconds to get your shoes on and get back here," MacAlister told her.

"Shouldn't I call the police?"

"No." Curtly. A man of few words, MacAlister.

Roseanne wasn't satisfied. "But..."

"Shaw didn't come here alone. He's got friends waiting downstairs," he said so ominously Roseanne shivered.

"All the more reason to call the police."

"Just get your shoes," MacAlister growled.

Roseanne heaved a sigh and obeyed with a curious sense of detachment. *This is not really happening. Any moment I'll wake up and find this was all part of my nightmare.* But the sudden thud and grunt of pain from the living room told her this nightmare was all too real.

"What happens now?" she asked MacAlister moments later, skirting the trussed-up gunman.

"We get the hell out of here." His words were muffled as he shimmied into a black sweatshirt. Both guns were stuck in the waistband of his low-riding jeans. As his head emerged from the shirt, MacAlister glanced up to find Roseanne staring at the guns. His stomach muscles contracted sharply. Was she planning to make a play for one of them?

Shaw had refused to say who'd sent him, but MacAlister figured it was the same person who'd ordered Lucien Deets killed. If Stone was right about Roseanne Deets's involvement in her husband's murder, then Shaw could be working for her. She'd shown no hint of recognition when she'd looked at Shaw, but...

"Do you think he meant to shoot us?" she murmured, her face so white and chalky he decided she wasn't going for the gun.

Relaxing a hair, MacAlister pulled on his boots. Damn, he wished he could make up his mind about her. The files told him one thing, his gut another. He hated it when things didn't add up the way they were supposed to. And Roseanne sure didn't.

"MacAlister?" She sounded worried, looked terrified.

"Probably not." Now, where had that come from? It shook him that he'd lied to ease her fears. "But we'd better get out of here before his friends come looking for him."

Roseanne nibbled at her lower lip as she took the fur from the closet. "Have you called the police?"

"No time," he lied smoothly. Deets's death—and whatever had gotten him killed—were strictly Bureau business. Stone had made that very clear. MacAlister drew the stiletto from under his pillow and tucked it into his boot top. "The coat stays."

She argued with him, but MacAlister won that round, too. "Stubborn, arrogant man," Roseanne seethed under her breath as she stepped into the hallway without the fur. Thankfully she'd put the key in her jeans pocket the night before.

MacAlister ignored Roseanne's mutterings and hurried her down the hall toward the Exit sign. He snatched open a metal door and pulled her into the stairwell after him. "Keep quiet," he whispered. "Sound travels in—"

Behind her, the metal door closed with a clang that reverberated up and down the stairwell.

"Ah, hell." MacAlister's lips thinned to a grim line. "Why not send out a damned map to let them know where we are?"

"It was an accident." Her chin trembled ominously.

"Okay, okay," he muttered in exasperation. "Just don't start bawling again." He prodded her back into the corridor. Hugging the wall, he moved stealthily toward the elevators.

Roseanne stalked after him, the anger he kindled burning through her fear. "I did not cry before, and I won't cry now."

No, she hadn't cried. Given all she'd been through, her control had surprised him. Usually women cried and clung and made demands. Which was a good reason not to get entangled with them, as far as MacAlister was concerned. Except for the obvious physical stuff, of course, and that could be achieved without making a commitment if a guy was careful in choosing his bed partners. Hell, he was an expert at avoiding commitment. Just ask Lily. His irresponsibility had gotten her killed.

MacAlister hit the Down button with unwarranted viciousness and raised the gun. As the elevator motors whined to life, he barked, "Stay down and out of the way."

Roseanne glowered at him. *You were expecting Mister Warmth to give you a medal for not crying?* She sighed loudly.

"Shh," he hissed as the hum stopped and the nearest set of doors opened with a whoosh. He whipped into the car so quickly the lines of his body blurred. "Empty. Get in," he growled. When she didn't move quickly enough, he grabbed her arm and hauled her in. "Stay alert," he cautioned as the car began to move. "We're going to bail out of here in a second." As he spoke, he threw the red button marked Stop. The car lurched to a halt.

Roseanne staggered, catching the slim metal handrail at the back of the car for balance. "What are you doing?"

"Laying a false trail." Tucking the gun into his jeans, he jumped up and pushed open a panel in the ceiling.

Apprehension reared its ugly head. "Where are we?"

"Between the fourth and fifth floors."

"What?" She tightened her grip on the rail.

Ignoring her, MacAlister jumped up again, caught the edges of the opening and effortlessly hauled himself through it. "Give me your hands, and I'll pull you up." Below the pushed-up sleeves of his sweatshirt, long tan arms covered with dark hair and corded with muscles stretched toward her. When she hesitated, he snapped his fingers. "I'll come down after you."

He'd do it, too. Reluctantly, she raised her hands. He snagged her wrists in a bruising grip, but she didn't groan until he jerked her up off her feet.

"Quiet. Sound travels in these shafts just like it did in the stairwell." He sat her down on the top of the car, her legs still dangling through the trapdoor.

"Well, excuse me for being human," she muttered.

His lips twitched, then softened. "Okay, stand up."

His gentler tone brought Roseanne's head up. In the stream of light pouring up from the car, she could make out dozens of heavy steel ropes hanging all around her. Instinctively, she tipped her head back, looking up... and up...

"Come on." MacAlister put his hands under her armpits and forced her to stand. The light disappeared as he quietly closed the trapdoor.

The realization that she was trapped atop a stalled elevator with five floors of empty space yawning below her swept through Roseanne like chain lightning, wrenching the bottom out of her stomach. With a muffled shriek, she threw herself at MacAlister.

He absorbed her weight without flinching, but cursed under his breath. "Damned woman. Do you want to send us over the side?"

"Oh, please," Roseanne whimpered, clinging to the reassuring strength of his solid body. "I hate heights. I couldn't even look out the fifth-floor window at the clinic without feeling like I was going to faint."

"Don't faint." He stopped trying to pry her fingers loose from the death grip they had on his neck. "Hey, I'm not crazy about heights myself," he gruffly admitted.

"Hold me . . . I feel like I'm going to fall." She was shaking so hard her teeth chattered.

MacAlister sighed, then slid his hands around her back and patted it awkwardly. He hadn't held a woman like this in a long time . . . not since Lily had walked out of his life. Oh, there had been women, but they had been looking for something more exciting than reassurance.

Comfort might be all Roseanne wanted, but she felt good in his arms. Damned good, all warm and soft and feminine. The delicious feel of her breasts against his chest, rising and falling with each panicky breath she took, sent a wave of pure desire jolting through him.

Damn. This was insane. He didn't want a woman in his life. Especially not one who was suspected of murdering her husband, MacAlister's business partner.

He fought for control and won. "I'll get you out of here," he said through clenched teeth. "But you have to do exactly as I say." It took tremendous willpower to ease her out of his arms, even more to pitch his voice low and file the harsh edge off it. "If there was another way out of here, I'd find it, but there isn't. And those men mean business. If they catch us..."

"I—I know. I've watched 'Miami Vice.'"

"Being here isn't nearly as much fun as watching on TV."
She chuckled. "I can certainly see that," she said dryly.

He squeezed her shoulder. "Back in control?"

"No. I'm terrified. But I don't feel like I'm going to black out any longer."

"That's a start." MacAlister felt another, less unwelcome spurt of respect for Roseanne Deets. Most women would be screaming by now. Still, they had a long way to go before they were safe. "Stay calm, follow instructions, and I'll get us out." He took his arms away, mentally crossing his fingers. "Sit down, take off your shoes and tuck them in your back pockets if you can. Then stay put until I get back."

Roseanne swallowed. "Back from where?"

"I'm going to climb up and open the doors to the fifth floor. Then I'll come down for you." He gently pried her hands loose, giving her a rusty smile when she let him go without a struggle. "Stay calm. Don't think about falling."

"Oh, God." Roseanne sat down immediately.

"Exactly," MacAlister muttered. Then he was gone.

It was the worst thing she had done in a week of terrible things. Roseanne prayed she'd live to put her shoes on again. When it occurred to her that she had to live long enough to find out what name went on her tombstone, a hysterical bubble of laughter rose in her throat.

Above her, the doors whooshed open, flooding the shaft with light. That made everything worse, illuminated her small metal island and the writhing silver cables. Moaning softly, she drew in deep breaths and tried to hang on to her sanity.

MacAlister dropped down beside her. In the gray half-light, he looked rock-strong and very capable. "Ready?"

His confidence sparked her own. "Ready." She swallowed again to settle her queasy stomach and stood.

"When I lift you up, grab hold of the floor. Do you see where I mean?"

Roseanne nodded. The projection stretched out into the shaft perhaps four feet above her head.

"All you have to do is hang on for a minute while I get above and pull you up."

"What...what about that space between the car and the wall of the shaft? If I can't hang on...?"

"Trust me. I won't let you fall."

Strangely enough, she *did* trust him. Despite his hostility, he was very good at getting them out of tight spots.

"Don't think about it—just do it."

"Right." She wiped her sweaty palms on her thighs and straightened. "Ready."

MacAlister looked at the fear shimmering in her wide green eyes, knew what it cost her to master it. As his lips curved into what looked suspiciously like another smile, she wished she were in a position to better appreciate the change it made in his rough-hewn features.

"Okay, brave lady. Let's get out of here." Slipping his hands around her slender waist, he hoisted her up until his arms were fully extended. "Can you reach it?"

"Yes." Quickly sliding her cold hands over the slick metal, she caught the edge where it met the carpet. "Okay. Got it."

"Hang tight for a sec." MacAlister took his hands away, and Roseanne's arms felt like they were being torn from the sockets as they bore the weight of her body. She groaned. The metal edge bit into her fingers; her muscles cried for release. Teeth locked against the pain, she fought to hang on. Just when she thought she couldn't stand it another second, his hard hands wrapped around her wrists and jerked her up to safety.

"Thank God." She sank to the floor, all but kissing the short-napped carpet. "Until now, I hadn't realized how precious life is...even one with no past."

"Cut the philosophy and let me see your hands."

"Ah, MacAlister. I can always count on you for a warm word of encouragement," she mumbled as he seized her hands. "Ouch."

"This isn't kindergarten," he snapped. "You cut the hell out of your fingers." He levered her into a sitting position and pulled a white handkerchief from his back pocket. Who would have suspected MacAlister was the type to carry a hankie?

The cloth came away red, and Roseanne sobered instantly, staring at the ugly red lines on the middle two fingers of her left hand. As the temporary numbness wore off, her fingers throbbed in time with her pulse.

"Not too bad." He tore the cloth in half and wrapped one around each finger with a gentleness that surprised her. "Hurt?"

"Of course it hurts," she began, then noticed the jagged gash in his left forearm. "Oh . . . let me see."

"It's nothing." He shook off the hand she extended.

Apparently he didn't *receive* compassion, either. "Your nothing is bleeding all over the floor," she said crisply.

That got his attention. He glared at the wound, then stuck a corner of his T-shirt in his mouth and tore a strip from it.

"What are you doing?"

"Binding it up. Can't afford to leave a trail of blood."

"Is that Rule Number Two in the Agent's Handbook?"

That startled him. "What do you mean?" he asked sharply.

She shrugged, feeling suddenly uncomfortable, as though she'd opened someone else's mail and read something she shouldn't. "Well, 'don't smile' is obviously the first Rule," she quipped, trying to make light of her comment. "So I thought . . ."

MacAlister grunted and bent to tie the cloth around his arm, but working one-handed proved more than even he could manage.

"Maybe I could get a better angle on that," she suggested after a moment.

"Why?" he asked with all the suspicion of a . . . a . . .

In that instant, Roseanne knew exactly what he reminded her of. Not a panther—a wolf. A lone wolf. Wary, aloof, self-sufficient. Needing no one, wanting no one. Only, she knew, better than most, that everyone needed someone sometime. "Because you helped me," she said without a trace of empathy.

His scowl deepened, and for a second she thought he might refuse. Then he handed her the cloth and extended his arm. "All right, and be quick about it. Watch you don't tie it too tight and cut off my circulation." He looked away, already scanning the area around them, obviously anxious to get going.

Gracious to the end, Roseanne silently muttered, but it saddened her that it was so hard for him to accept even such a small, necessary thing as her help bandaging his arm. What did he do when something major happened? Drew farther inside himself, she guessed. She'd be willing to bet he didn't have a wife. Or a family. No, he wouldn't let anyone get close to him. Roseanne knew how empty his life must be, even if he didn't.

Her hair was the first thing MacAlister noticed when he looked down to see how she was doing. Free now of the clip that had held it at the nape of her neck, her hair floated around her pale oval face like a cloud of copper silk. Would it feel as soft? He balled his fingers into a fist to keep from reaching out and touching it. She raised her head just then, her gaze locking with his. The smile she gave him was sweet and gentle.

Against his will, his body tightened with a surge of desire, surprising in its intensity. MacAlister groaned. God, he didn't need any complications. He'd been through hell these past seven months. Watched his best friend die in his arms, found his former lover dead on his front steps, learned he had a daughter by her, burned out of the Bureau, and finally, just when he'd thought he had things turned around, his new partner, Lucien Deets, had been murdered. It was enough to sour a guy on life. All he wanted was a chance to solve Deets's murder and put his own life into some kind of order.

He did not need more trouble...and Roseanne Deets was trouble. That she wasn't what he'd expected was part of it. That she intrigued him on several levels made it worse. No way was he getting any closer to her than he had to.

"Get up," he barked, steeling himself to ignore the shock in her wide green eyes. "We have to get moving, princess."

She hadn't expected gratitude from a wolf, but did he have to be so hostile? "Stop calling me princess."

"That's it, princess. Get angry and stay that way...the adrenaline'll keep you going." Ignoring his wound, he hauled her up by her arms and herded her toward the stairway.

"Do you have to keep mauling me?" she gritted.

"It's either me or Shaw's friends," he said ominously. "With luck, they think we're in the elevator. In case I didn't fool them, I want absolute silence on the stairs this time."

Roseanne started to put her shoes back on, but MacAlister said they'd make too much noise. And he was right, damn him.

She ground her teeth together as she followed him down the concrete steps. Even wearing his boots, MacAlister moved as soundlessly as the wind, while her stocking feet slapped on the stairs as she hurried to keep up with him.

When he shushed her, she glowered at him and gave serious consideration to bopping his dark, arrogant head with one of her shoes. Next time she needed rescuing, she'd be more careful whom she allowed to do it.

He stopped, and she snuck a peek at her fingers. They burned like fire, but the bleeding had almost stopped. Her pulse had slowed, and she suddenly felt incredibly tired.

"Stay here while I take a look around for the other two goons," MacAlister muttered, gesturing toward the metal door marked Parking Garage. He kept his gun at shoulder height as he eased the door open.

His sure, almost practiced movements had Roseanne wondering, not for the first time that night, what MacAlister did for a living. His speech was educated, even when he was being harsh. His apartment probably cost a fortune. Yet he drove an old heap and had the quickness and ruthless dexterity of a street fighter. Even when he wasn't in motion, there was an alertness, a wariness about him that made her tense. At times, it almost seemed he was waiting for her to do something that would confirm his bad opinion of her. He'd denied knowing her, yet she wondered...

"Bingo," he breathed.

Roseanne came away from the wall she had been leaning against and joined him, her heart racing again, her questions vanishing along with her exhaustion.

Two men stood watching the indicator over the elevators, their shabby black raincoats contrasting sharply with the soft peach-and-ivory wall tiles. They held their long-snouted guns as efficiently as MacAlister held his.

"The tall one looks like the man outside the bank," she murmured before MacAlister angrily shushed her.

"I got a bad feeling Harvey's run into trouble," a male voice whined. "That car's been stuck on five too long."

"It's his own damn fault, always wantin' to handle things himself," said a second, rougher voice. "Guess we'd better go up and save his ass. You take the stairs...I'll ride the other car up. And be careful . . . the boss'll kill us if we screw up.''

"Get behind the door," MacAlister mouthed to Roseanne.

She stood motionless, trapped in a thin wedge behind the door as it opened. The grunt and thud from the other side made her flinch. Then the door swung shut again, revealing Mac- Alister in a stance straight from the flickering screen. He had the guy mashed up against the wall, the muzzle of his gun bur- ied in the soft flesh below the gunman's ear. "Hand over your gun. Nice and easy," he warned tightly.

The tall man who'd accosted her outside the bank put his gun in MacAlister's palm, but his dark eyes were on Roseanne. The ruthlessness in them made her shiver.

MacAlister's features were set in a savage mask, his eyes cold and hard. "Who sent you and why?"

The gunman's nostrils flared, his gaze narrowing as it slid to Roseanne. "That's for me to know...ain't it?"

Her. He had come here for her. Roseanne went cold all over.

"I don't have time for games," MacAlister growled. His hand tightened on the man's neck. The thug's dark eyes bugged out, and he made sickening gurgling sounds.

Roseanne gasped and turned away. She wouldn't watch an- other TV cop show, she vowed. A soft thud brought her back around in time to see MacAlister lowering the man to the floor.

"Dead?" she whispered.

MacAlister scowled blackly. "I don't murder people in cold blood...if I can help it." He calmly added the gunman's weapon to the collection in his waistband. He was fast amass- ing quite an arsenal. The dreadful suspicion that he antici- pated needing them in the near future—*their* near future— made her stomach roll, made her wish she'd never met Mac- Alister.

He cracked open the door, took a look outside and mo- tioned to her. "Let's go."

She hesitated. With the gunman disabled, maybe she no longer needed MacAlister.

"Thinking of jumping ship, princess?"

"As a matter of fact..." Roseanne raised her chin, accept- ing the challenge that glittered in his eyes.

"Forget it." He grabbed her arm and propelled her through the doorway ahead of him. "We're in this together until I say differently. Got that?"

"Why are you doing this? You don't even like me."

She could hear his teeth grinding together, feel the heat from the anger burning in him as he hauled her up against him. "Liking you has nothing to do with it. Whether you realize it or not, you're in deep trouble, princess."

"I don't need your help," she snapped, her own temper fueled by his.

MacAlister sighed and shook his head, the anger fading from his amber eyes. "You're far too intelligent to believe that. And we're both dumb to stand around here arguing about it." He started across the garage, propelling her in front of him.

Roseanne ignored the grit biting into her stocking feet, but had to ask, "Why are you doing this?"

"I'm a sucker for a woman in distress." He glanced over his shoulder. "Keep moving, follow orders and stay on my left."

"Why?"

"I shoot best with my right hand."

Roseanne's soft, agonized groan was lost in the reverberating clang of the elevator doors opening.

"Down." MacAlister shoved her behind a large black car and placed his big body between her and the elevators.

As she peered around his wide shoulder, two men erupted from the elevator, guns raised and seeking. Instinctively, she shrank back behind MacAlister.

"Check the stairs," ordered Shaw.

Still hunkered down, MacAlister guided her through the rows of cars. She heard an explosion of muffled curses, knew they'd found the man in the stairwell, but MacAlister kept her busy learning to crab-walk and follow his nonverbal instructions. They stopped beside a low shape draped in a light green cover. He pulled the fabric away, revealing a sleek black car.

"Stay here," he mouthed and disappeared. A moment later she heard a faint clink, and a harsh light flooded the car's interior; it went out again as quickly as it had come on.

"Get in. Don't close the door," he hissed.

Once inside, the supple leather seat wrapped itself around her. With a grateful sigh she slumped against it.

From the other side of the car, she heard MacAlister curse under his breath and turned to see him wrestling with something under the dash.

"What are you doing?" she whispered.

"Starting the car."

An ugly suspicion struck her. "Whose car is this, anyway?"

"Mine. Ah." The motor caught with a low, pulsing growl. He grinned at her, his teeth a white blur in the darkness. "Left the keys upstairs, so I had to jimmy the lock and hot-wire it," he added. "Shut your door and hang on—this could get rough."

Roseanne barely had time to close the door before he engaged the lever in the console between them and the car shot forward. Oblivious to the pain in her fingers, she clutched the armrest as the car rounded a sharp curve, tires squealing and roared toward the elevator banks.

Suddenly, one of the dark-coated gunmen stepped directly into their path, gun raised.

"Duck," MacAlister yelled. He kept the car on a steady course, bearing down on the man. At the last second, the man jumped aside, his gun swinging to follow them. But as they pulled even with him, MacAlister shoved his door open. There was a horrible crunch as flesh made contact with the speeding car.

Roseanne gasped and tried to look back to see if the man was moving, but MacAlister took the next corner on two wheels, and she was fighting to stay in her seat. "Why did you do that?" she demanded as the car barreled down the straightaway.

"To keep from getting the tires shot out from under us...or worse," MacAlister replied, his grin demonic. If this is what it took to wring a smile out of him, she was content to do without.

The white exit sign gleamed up ahead of them, a beacon of hope in this vast, dark nightmare. Roseanne was enjoying a rare moment of optimism when shots rang out behind them. There was an ominous *thuk* as one caught the fleeing car.

"Ah, hell. There goes my new paint job. Stay down," MacAlister yelled, gunning the motor. Fishtailing, tires smoking, the car raced up the exit ramp and hurtled out onto a dark narrow street. He eased off on the gas long enough to jerk the wheel to the right, sending them into a controlled slide as far as the next corner and out into a sparse stream of traffic.

Roseanne clung to the armrest, her heart in her mouth as MacAlister dodged through the city, cutting off cars, turning from street to street seemingly at random, like a desperate rat seeking to escape a maze. But the cool determination carved into his rugged face owed little to panic. As usual, MacAlister looked like a man who knew exactly what he was doing.

"What now?" she asked hesitantly when he finally pulled over to the curb.

"I've got a call to make." With no more explanation than that, he opened the console, pulled out a phone and stepped from the car. Obviously wolves kept their conversations private, too.

Dimly, Roseanne wondered if she could escape while MacAlister was busy on the phone, but she was too exhausted, too numb to try. With curious detachment she watched the lights of the nearby bridge flicker and dance in the river's light chop.

"Okay. We're set," MacAlister announced as he slid in and replaced the phone.

"Set?" Her lethargy disappeared in a wave of dread.

"Yeah." He glanced over his shoulder, then pulled into traffic. "We have a safe place to stay."

Roseanne had grave reservations about remaining part of his "we." "You called the police?"

"No. A guy I used to work for." He cast her a quick glance, his usually harsh, unreadable expression softer. "Take it easy, princess. Stone's with the Bureau. They do this kind of thing all the time—find safehouses for people in trouble."

They were climbing up the approach to the bridge now, and MacAlister had slowed for the large truck they were following. Roseanne considered jumping out and running like hell. "W-where is this house?"

"Connecticut."

Of all the incredible luck. MacAlister was taking her to Connecticut, playing right into her hands without even realizing it. As the powerful car surged across the bridge, she relaxed in the seat. She felt a little guilty for using him after he had saved her life. Maybe she should tell him the truth. *No*. She couldn't do that. Not until she was certain she could trust him.

MacAlister gauged her mood out of the corner of his eye. She didn't trust him, which was his own damned fault. Fury at what she'd done to Lucien, and at the lies she'd told to avoid paying the price for her actions, kept burning through his control. And every time he let his emotions get the better of him, he scared her off and screwed up his game plan.

Better cool it, hotshot, he reminded himself. He wasn't here to judge her, he was here to gain her trust…and then betray it.

Chapter 3

The Bureau's Headquarters for Northeastern Operations was housed in an ordinary-looking gray building on Manhattan's Lower East Side. To avoid arousing suspicion, the agent seated at a desk on the second floor waited an hour after MacAlister's call before making one of his own. Normally he didn't work the night shift, but his presence shouldn't cause comment.

Since Crenshaw's retirement had been announced, everyone had been working late. Michael Stone, head of Field Operatives, and Andy Thompson, head of Internal Affairs, were the likely bets to replace the Chief. Both sections were taking the contest seriously. Assignments were attacked with the thoroughness and zeal usually reserved for presidential assassinations, each side hoping the other would blunder and earn a black eye with the review commission in charge of selecting Crenshaw's successor.

Unfortunately, half of the eight people who knew about the Deets case had also been in the office when MacAlister called. Since the four of them were the only ones who knew Mac-Alister and the girl had been sent to the safehouse in Connecticut, they had to stay *safe*.

Thick fingers drummed on the papers scattered over his desk as he waited for a series of clicks to switch his call through the elaborate maze of fiber-optic cables designed to protect its ultimate destination. Trust the Frog to trust no one. Not that he blamed the guy; in this business, security was everything.

"Yeah?"

Recognizing Peck's rough voice on the other end of the line, he replied, "I have some information." No names; names were dangerous. He was pretty sure his line wasn't tapped, but a man in his position couldn't be too careful.

"Rousseau's been waiting," Peck growled in a tone that told the agent Rousseau already knew his thugs hadn't killed MacAlister and the girl or gotten the key.

"What went wrong?" Rousseau demanded, anger accentuating the French heritage that had earned him his by-name . . . the Frog.

"Your men underestimated him. I told you he was good."

Rousseau swore softly. "Do you know where they are?" Beneath his cultured tones lurked the hard edge of tempered steel.

"Yes," the agent reluctantly admitted.

"I'll have them picked up."

"No! Don't do that."

"You dare to question my orders?"

"Yes, there'd be *questions*," the agent exclaimed. Jeez, if Rousseau's men showed up at the safehouse, there'd be hell to pay. "They are *safe* where they are," he stressed.

Rousseau's irritated sigh said he'd gotten the message. "How much does MacAlister know?"

"Only what he's been told."

"Hmm. How long will they be there?"

Letting out the breath he'd been holding, the agent looked around, saw no one nearby, but lowered his voice, anyway. "He'll stay as long as it takes for him to gain access to the box."

"*Non* . . . that is insupportable. I applaud your caution, but there is too much at stake, too great a risk that he might seize the contents and turn it over to your Bureau."

"He's calling in before he makes the pickup."

"Hmm. That is something." Rousseau still sounded skeptical. "But I cannot wait much longer in any case. I will give you three days. If he does not get the key from the girl by Monday, we will do this my way. Is that understood?"

"Understood." As he slipped the phone back in place, the agent pinched the skin at the bridge of his nose. Damn. He'd give anything to get out of this, but no one crossed a man like Rousseau. Deets had been a fool to try.

MacAlister walked to the side of the bed and looked down at Roseanne. It was midafternoon, but she was still sleeping so soundly she hadn't heard his knock. Both hands were tucked under her chin like a child, tearstains tracking her pale cheeks. Why had she cried herself to sleep?

It shouldn't have mattered to him. Hell, he'd learned to be immune to other people's problems long ago, only she had begun to crawl under his skin when she'd told him she had amnesia. Not that it came as a surprise. Stone had told him Roseanne Deets was faking amnesia to escape prosecution, but now MacAlister wasn't so sure. If she didn't have amnesia, she was the world's greatest actress. She'd have to be to fool him; he'd had years of experience in reading beneath the masks people wore to hide the truth.

What he saw when he looked deep into her slanted green eyes was bleakness, loneliness and pain. They'd gotten to him quicker than any calculated sob story. He understood all three, had lived in their shadow too long himself to remain unaffected by her suffering. Not that he had amnesia. Just the reverse. He had a lifetime of things he was doing his best to forget.

Gaze narrowing, he studied her, looking for the truth. Though he and the late Lucien Deets had been partners since MacAlister's retirement from the Bureau, he had never met Roseanne. She hadn't come to the office, and the few times MacAlister had gone to Deets's Upper East Side mansion, Roseanne had been out partying with her fast-living society friends.

What he knew about her came from reading the tabloid clippings in the Bureau files locked in his truck. Two failed marriages to rich older men by the time she was twenty-three. Followed by four years of wild parties and torrid affairs. A year ago, she'd married Deets, a man twenty years her senior.

She looked so damned young, so wrenchingly guileless lying there, it was hard to believe she was the same woman he'd read about. Okay, so maybe he was a sucker for a pretty face, but he knew there was more to her than that. The compassion, the fragility, the deep-seated current of emotions that had her swinging from prim to angry in a heartbeat, touched things inside him he hadn't known existed, made him want to tap into that current, feel it race hot with desire.

MacAlister felt his body swell and tighten, as it had last night, only swifter, sharper. He wanted to lie down beside her, pull her beneath him and drive into her until they were both mindless with pleasure. His body leaped at the thought; his mind remembered Stone's warning that Roseanne would do anything to dodge the murder rap and escape to some safe haven with the fortune the Bureau supposed Deets had hidden in his bank box.

MacAlister exhaled a ripe curse.

Roseanne's eyes flew open. "Oh," she cried, scooting up in the bed until her back was against the headboard.

"Hey. It's just me," he soothed, remembering last night's vow to be more persuasive, less caustic. Besides, he no longer felt angry; he felt...wary and confused. Which made them even.

She blinked rapidly. "W-what's wrong?"

"Nothing," he said blandly. "You've slept a long time."

MacAlister concerned about her? This was a switch. "I had a rather tough day...and night."

"Tell me about it," he replied dryly.

Could that be an attempt at humor? Roseanne cocked her head. There was something softer about MacAlister this morning, more accessible. "You seem more...relaxed. Why is that?"

"'Cause there's no one chasing us, I guess," he said off-handedly, feeling anything but casual as his gaze moved surreptitiously from her tumbled hair down to where her breasts lifted the front of the oversize flannel shirt he'd found for her in the closet.

Something flared in MacAlister's eyes. Her mind couldn't put a name to the emotion glittering in them, but it drove all her senses haywire. Her mouth went dry and her heart hammered so wildly she felt breathless. He wanted to touch her; her skin tingled as though he had. Still he didn't move, just continued to stare at her. "What is it?" she whispered.

Her question snapped him back from the sensual fantasy he'd been enjoying, reminded him instantly why he was standing here in the shadowy bedroom—and it wasn't for a roll in the hay. "It's nothing," he lied, his voice tight and hard. "I came to tell you I'm going to check on things outside."

"Oh." Roseanne berated herself for being hurt by his returning coldness. At least he was being curt instead of hostile. "I . . . er, what about breakfast?"

"It's four-thirty in the afternoon. You've slept through breakfast and lunch. I left you some of the stuff I bought last night if you're hungry."

"Where are you going?"

"Just to have a look around. Make sure . . . everything's okay." The harsh line of his mouth softened for an instant. "I didn't want you to wake up and find me gone."

Roseanne blinked. At times like this, she came very close to trusting MacAlister. "That was kind of you."

"I'm never kind," he growled. Damn. There was that smile of hers, the one that threatened to turn him inside out.

Roseanne thought about the time he'd taken to soothe her fears when they'd stood atop the elevator, the gentleness with which he'd bandaged her fingers last night, and started to disagree with him. His glowering expression stopped her. "How long will you be away?" she asked instead.

"Thinking of sneaking off while I'm gone?"

"No." *Not yet, anyway.* "I was planning on making dinner for us," she replied sweetly.

"How do you know you can cook? Suddenly regain your memory?"

It all came together. "You...you think I'm lying. You don't think I've lost my memory, do you? That's why you act so...so...hateful sometimes."

"Is it?" he said, cryptically. "I'll be back in an hour. Don't try to take off. This place is in the middle of nowhere. Besides, you might run into our friends from last night."

Don't leave me alone, Roseanne wanted to cry, but she forced herself to sit still until she heard the front door close. Then she bolted from the bed and flew through the house, arriving in the living room just in time to see MacAlister's sporty black car disappear through the trees. A quick, frantic check out the rest of the windows revealed nothing but dry grass and barren trees on all four sides. The place sat in the middle of a forest. No wonder MacAlister's former boss considered this such a safe place.

So why didn't she feel safe? Roseanne wondered, turning from the window and wrapping her arms around her suddenly chilled body. Because MacAlister wasn't here. In the short space of a few hours, she had come to depend on him. Strange, because he was the exact opposite of what she needed—cold, arrogant and unemotional, when what she craved was warmth and compassion. Still, she had no choice but to remain with him for the time being. He was all she had.

Roseanne sighed. At least he hadn't seemed as hostile today, and despite his gruffness, he had given her glimpses of gentleness. Besides, MacAlister might be her only chance of reaching the Danbury bank...provided she could bring herself to trust him with her secrets.

Her grumbling stomach reminded her of a more immediate problem. One she had more hope of solving.

She opened the refrigerator and prowled the shelves. A six-pack of imported beer shared the top one with a carton of milk. As she sipped a glass of milk, she riffled through the paper-wrapped deli packages on the lower shelves, rejecting the ham on sight. At the clinic, she had balked at eating red meat. Alarmed, the doctors had immediately called in the dietitian, who was delighted to arrange a "healthy diet" of poultry, veggies and carbohydrates for her.

Nibbling on some cheese, Roseanne turned her attention to the cupboards, found six kinds of chips and four open jars of peanuts—all stale. Obviously men on the lam didn't waste time cleaning out the culinary deadwood, she mused. Another cupboard yielded pasta, a jumble of spices and herbs, canned fruit, cookies and staples like oil and vinegar. Nothing to satisfy her hunger pangs.

On the counter, she found a box of doughnuts. They smelled reasonably fresh, but greasy. Probably part of MacAlister's haul, she thought as she bit into an unfrosted chocolate one. Even washed down with another glass of milk, the doughnut was so sweet it made her teeth itch.

The clinic's dietitian had commented on her culinary knowledge, Roseanne recalled as she sought solace under a long, hot shower. "Maybe you worked in the restaurant business," the woman had speculated. If so, perhaps she could make something out of the things in the kitchen, Roseanne thought.

Dressed in another large flannel shirt, black-and-green plaid this time, Roseanne studied her face critically in the vanity mirror, wondering what MacAlister saw in her that sometimes made him lash out.

On the surface, she supposed she was pretty enough. Her cheekbones were high, her nose straight over a full mouth. But it was the wide green eyes, tilted mysteriously at the corners, that dominated the face. *Her face.* What kind of person lived behind it? Suppose she never found out?

Suddenly, the image blurred. Oh, God, she was so frightened, so lonely. Inside, she felt as cold and empty as the barren fields surrounding the house. The enormity of her loss made her knees shake. She started to crumple, caught a glimpse of her haunted expression and stopped. Self-pity, she thought distastefully. Giving in to it would solve nothing.

Dragging in a ragged breath, Roseanne dashed the tears away and straightened again. She was alive, and grateful for it. The rest would come—when she got into the bank box. Another deep breath nearly broke the band of tension in her chest.

She bent to gather the dirty clothes she had worn the day before. Since she could hardly leave here wearing one of the flannel shirts, she'd best channel her energies into seeing if she remembered how to use the washer and dryer.

It was quite amazing, she thought a few minutes later as she watched the clothes slosh in the washer, how some hidden instinct seemed to take over when she attempted certain tasks. If only the rest of her memory were that easily tapped.

A glance at the clock showed her MacAlister should be back soon, and she had promised him dinner. She opened the cupboards and began stacking things on the white countertops. When she had everything out, she stood back and waited for inspiration to strike. If she really was a great cook, surely there was a recipe lurking somewhere in her brain. It was simply a matter of triggering the memory.

Though it was nearly dark, there were no lights on in the front of the house when MacAlister pulled into the garage. Swearing under his breath, he killed the ignition and flung out of the car. If she'd taken off... As he jerked open the kitchen door, warmth, light and tantalizing smells poured out to greet him. She was here. The anger left his body in a rush. Grocery bag dangling from one hand, he stepped inside and immediately saw her standing on the other side of the breakfast bar shredding lettuce.

"Well, I see you're still here," he muttered.

Her head snapped up. Her eyes caught his, and she smiled. The look on her face drove the air from his lungs with the jolt of an iron fist. For a dizzy second the world shifted, and he had a sense of coming home—to his house, his woman. He had to clench his fist to keep from reaching for her. She was a mirage, he sternly reminded himself.

"MacAlister? Are you all right? You look very strange." She stepped out into the open, and he nearly lost it again.

"Where the hell are your clothes?"

"In the dryer." She looked down at the narrow expanse of skin left bare between the long shirt and her knee socks. "I'm warm enough in this, anyway."

"Your knees are bare," he snapped.

She shrugged. "They're just knees." As she bent to put the lettuce in the refrigerator, the shirt rode up.

MacAlister noted the wide expanse of pale, slender thighs and swallowed hard. The long talk he'd had with himself while checking around outside evaporated in an instant.

"Is . . . was everything all right?"

She looked very small and vulnerable, all creamy skin, tumbled hair and wide eyes in her too-big shirt. Women in trouble had always been his downfall, the exception to his Don't Get Involved rule. "Yeah, everything's secure." He started unloading groceries to keep from making an idiot of himself.

"What's this?" she asked, touching a flat package.

"Microwave popcorn."

"I've seen the commercials, but I don't remember what it tastes like. Do you think I'll like it?"

He cast her a sidelong glance.

Roseanne saw the skepticism in his scowl. "I really don't remember who I am," she said quietly.

"Yeah." The crazy thing was, he was that close to believing her. While he was out, he'd called Stone and arranged a meeting for tomorrow to discuss that very thing.

She smiled up at him so sweetly he almost leaned down to kiss her. As though she'd read his mind, her eyes widened, and her lips parted. He thought about sliding his tongue between them, thought about kissing her deeply and thoroughly, until they were both breathless.

Roseanne's mouth went hot and tingly. He was going to kiss her, and she wanted him to. She'd read about it in novels, seen it on TV, but she'd never expected to feel desire herself. And certainly not for a man like MacAlister. She swayed, trying to resist the dark, sensual pull of MacAlister's gaze. The popcorn slipped from her fingers and hit the floor.

MacAlister blinked, bent to pick up the package.

She sighed shakily. "When do we eat the popcorn?"

"Er, maybe after dinner."

Roseanne nodded, regaining control with visible effort. "Speaking of dinner . . ."

"I bought some steaks." He couldn't decide whether or not to be grateful that she was fighting the attraction between them. It was wisest; he just wasn't sure he wanted to be wise—or that he *could* be with her.

"I've made something else," Roseanne told him.

"There isn't anything else here. We'll have steak."

She grimaced. "I don't like meat. We'll have what I made."

"What'd you make from the junk that was here?" He rested one hip against the counter, arms folded across his chest like some Barbary pirate issuing a challenge.

Despite her resolve to match his cool, her chin came out to meet that challenge. "You don't need much if you're a great chef like... Julia Child."

"Julia Child, huh?" He cocked his head as though weighing his words, and she tensed, expecting him to make a derogatory remark about her memory.

MacAlister took one look at her soulful expression and knew he'd lost, knew he couldn't hurt her again.

A few minutes later, Roseanne set a plate and a bowl down in front of MacAlister. "Looks like Caesar salad and fettuccine Alfredo," he exclaimed, mouth watering.

Roseanne brightened. "So they have names. I was afraid I had made them up."

"Well, I haven't tried your versions, yet. Maybe they don't *taste* like Caesar salad and fettuccine Alfredo."

MacAlister slowly tasted first the salad, then the pasta, watching her expectant little face out of the corner of his eye. She acted like his approval was the most important thing in her life. She acted nothing like the shallow bitch who'd been married to Deets.

"Well?" she finally demanded.

"Good. Damn good," he replied honestly. "The salad dressing could use some garlic."

"Garlic?" She frowned.

"Small white things... strong taste. Comes in a bunch."

"No. A... a head. I—I remember." She smiled, obviously pleased by the small accomplishment. "There weren't any."

"I'm surprised you got this far on what was here." He dug in. "It's not steak, but after years of eating out, I've learned to appreciate a home-cooked meal."

Which confirmed her belief that her wolf didn't have a mate. "I don't like meat. I wonder if I've always been like that," she mused as she stabbed a piece of lettuce.

MacAlister set down his beer. "Don't you remember anything from...before." He stared at her, eyes probing.

"I don't have any memories, not really. I just sense things,
like cooking or operating the washer." She sighed despon-
dently. "I'd give anything for even one memory."

He had a lot he'd like to forget, like the fact that she might
be a murderess. "What do the doctors say?"

"Give it time." She shrugged, but the shimmer of tears in her
eyes told him how close she was to losing it. Lowering her head,
she toyed with her pasta.

MacAlister stared at her shiny cinnamon crown, trying to
decide how to play this. If he came right out and asked her
about Deets's box, she'd wonder how he knew, then probably
turn tail and run. Gaining her confidence was the first priority. Once she trusted him, she'd tell him about the bank box and
ask for his help getting to the bank.

Roseanne felt MacAlister's gaze, but didn't look up. He'd
claimed he wasn't a kind man, but his actions said otherwise.
If only she could convince herself to trust him.

While Roseanne cleaned up in the kitchen, MacAlister found
a few logs and started a fire in the living room hearth. He
looked surprised when she set a tray down on the coffee table.
"I was expecting doughnuts for dessert." He eyed the tarts
she'd made from the canned peaches and vanilla wafers with
interest. Sitting cross-legged on the floor, he reached for one.
"Hey, pretty good," he mumbled around his first mouthful.

Hands wrapped around a mug of coffee, Roseanne snuggled contentedly into the corner of the high-backed sofa and
watched him demolish the tart. He picked up the last bits of the
crumb topping with his forefinger and licked it clean.

Groaning, he patted his lean stomach. "I'll have to work out
like a fiend if we're here very long."

Roseanne froze. What if he insisted on leaving before she
could get to the bank? "How long will we be here?"

"As long as it takes," he replied cryptically.

"Until your friend—Stone—finds the men who were after
us?" she asked in a small voice. When he nodded, she pressed
him again about how long that might be.

"Hard to say. Maybe a couple of days . . . a week."

Roseanne sat back. Surely in a week she could make up her mind about MacAlister. Surprisingly, the idea of spending a week in his company didn't seem as frightening as it had last night. He was staring into the fire, looking ruggedly handsome, a bronzed god gilded by the leaping flames. Like most wolves, MacAlister was nicer than he wanted people to think.

"What do you do, MacAlister?" she asked, impulsively.

He slanted her a quick, measuring glance. "I own an import/export business. Why?"

"Just curious," she said with a shrug. "About the kind of man I'll be spending the week with."

The kind that lies to stay alive and kills when the lies fail. "I'm just a businessman."

"But you carry a gun." *And handle yourself like Rambo.* "You don't work for this Bureau of Stone's?"

"No." *Not any more.* The half lie snagged at his conscience, and he wondered when he'd become sensitive about lying to her. Last night when they'd faced death together or tonight when she cooked his dinner? Hell, lying was part of his job. "The import/export business takes a man to a lot of . . . rough places."

For an instant he was kneeling in a dark, stinking Cairo alley trying to push the blood back into Jack Sabine's mutilated body, rage and frustration pouring through him. For reasons of their own, the Bureau Chiefs had prevented him from bringing in his partner's killer. That was part of why he'd resigned. That and a daughter he hadn't known he had, didn't want to be responsible for, but was because the same man who had killed Jack Sabine had killed his daughter's mother.

"MacAlister?" He turned at her call, in control again, his expression unreadable. But for a moment Roseanne had glimpsed something raw and primitive lurking beneath the thin veneer of civility he wore. Something that suggested Mac-Alister was very much at home in rough places.

"What?" His voice was dark, dangerous, warning that trying to get close to him would be like playing with fire.

Apprehension chilled her, stole her breath, but like the moth, she was drawn to his heat. "You aren't married, are you?"

"No. How about you . . . ever been married?"

"No." Her eyes met his easily, hiding nothing, or everything. MacAlister couldn't decide which.

"You're wondering how I know." Roseanne held out her left hand. "No rings, and no markings showing I'd worn any recently. The doctors at the clinic were thorough." *Very thorough.* She sought refuge in another subject. "Do you, ah, enjoy your work?"

"Yeah." MacAlister poked a log with the toe of his boot. Was she lying? He decided to press. "I spent a lot of years working for an import/export company overseas." *It was great cover.*

Roseanne leaned forward. *At last he was opening up.* "Now you own your own company?"

"A few months ago, I moved back to the States and bought a part interest in the Golden Circle Import/Export Company." His eyes held hers very intently.

Roseanne smiled. *He really was a businessman.* "It must be great to be your own boss." Wolves like independence.

"I wasn't the sole owner," MacAlister said slowly, weighing every word. *He'd get a reaction out of her now.* "Lucien Deets was my partner."

She didn't bat an eyelash. "Do you get along well with him?"

MacAlister scowled. "I did, but he's dead."

"Oh, I'm sorry to hear that. Were you close?" She'd be surprised if he said yes. Despite the thaw in their relationship, she doubted he welcomed closeness of any kind.

"No, we weren't. We hadn't known each other very long, but I feel a certain...loyalty to the man." His hooded gaze searched hers. "I feel an obligation to help find his killer."

"Killer?" Roseanne choked on the word. "Oh, my God," she whispered, eyes widening. "It was those men last night. At first I thought they were after me, but now I see they must want control of your business."

"Why the hell . . . ?"

"No, really. It happens all the time. Maybe . . . maybe they want to import drugs or something, and they need a front to..."

"You watch too much TV."

"Oh, my God," she breathed again, leaping up from the couch. "We have to find a way to protect you." Eyes glittering like green glass, hair wild and flaming in the firelight, she resembled a lioness defending her cub. One Gates MacAlister, ex-spy. The man sent to betray her.

He went hot with shame. "Sit down. Stone will take care of everything," he murmured, easing Roseanne's tense little body back onto the couch. Instinctively he hooked one arm around her shoulder and drew her into the shelter of his body. Again he was struck by how small and vulnerable she felt. She shuddered, and it seemed the most natural thing in the world to wrap the other arm around her and tuck her silky head under his chin.

Roseanne tangled her fingers in the front of his sweatshirt and gave herself over to his strong, warm embrace. It felt so good to be held, if only for a little while, that she sighed and burrowed closer. He smelled cleanly of soap and man. Beneath her ear, the hard wall of his chest reverberated with the steady, rhythmic beats of his heart. She wanted to stay here forever.

For a long minute, MacAlister held her, absently caressing the muscles bunched along her spine through her clothes. He was sure her skin would feel like hot satin in his hands, but resisted the urge to slip them under the shirt and find out. A little chaste hugging was the least he owed her. And the way he felt right now, if he did more than that, things wouldn't stay chaste long. When her breathing slowed, and she relaxed against him, he knew it was time to put some distance between them.

She blinked up at him like an owl just out of the nest as he released her. The naked yearning in her face twisted something deep inside him, and he had to know whether to believe in her or not. "What were you doing at the bank?" he asked gently.

Roseanne flinched. Her eyes widened and her mouth opened, but nothing came out.

"Easy," he murmured. "I just wondered why you'd gone there. Did you remember something about the bank?"

Reflected firelight shimmered in his eyes, mesmerizing her. She wanted to trust him, wanted to with all her heart. But something held her back. "I . . . I don't know."

"Another one of those things you sense," he grumbled, a hint of anger or impatience edging his tone.

Roseanne looked away, unable to face his unspoken censure.

"Can you explain it to me?"

A shudder shook her as she turned back to face him, her eyes filled with misery. "I want to," she whispered. "But I . . . I can't . . . not yet, anyway."

"You will," he said steadily, eyes locked on hers. "You'll trust me, then you'll tell me everything."

She didn't know whether it was a promise . . . or a warning.

At nine the next morning, MacAlister careened down the steep dirt driveway, signaled to agents Thatcher and Sanchez sitting in matching black sedans at the base of the hill. One of them would go up to keep an eye on the house while the other kept an eye on Roseanne. Confident that she'd be safe, he headed his Porsche into the Connecticut hills.

Stone had four agents assigned to the Deets case. Besides Sanchez and Thatcher, there as a freckle-faced kid named Andy Newcomber, and Greg Anderson, a veteran newly transferred from Chicago. Though MacAlister had met all four, he'd worked with Thatcher before, knew the man had a big mouth, and hoped Sanchez would be the one going up to keep an eye on Roseanne. Dream on, he thought. Thatcher had seniority and hated pulling stakeout duty.

The dark clouds overhead suited MacAlister's mood, and the challenge of navigating the narrow, twisting roads for which the state was famous should have kept his mind from the problem he'd left behind at the house.

When was the last time he'd lain awake thinking about a woman? Twenty years ago. No, eighteen. His mind ranged back to his sixteenth year and Sara Smythe. Sara of the soulful eyes and wealthy parents. Pursuing her had driven him mad for months until he'd finally gotten it through his thick head that her sights were set a lot higher than the son of the town drunk.

MacAlister tightened his grip on the wheel. Over the years, he'd insulated himself against that kind of hurt by never letting anyone get too close. Only Roseanne had the kind of soft, subtle weapons that snuck up on a man, striking when and where he least expected them, getting under his guard and ruining his concentration. Which was the last thing he could afford while working, even unofficially, on a case.

Swearing, he jerked his attention back to the road. Moments later, he pulled into a turnaround and parked behind an unmarked van. The back doors opened as he got out of the car.

"You're late," Michael Stone commented as MacAlister climbed inside the van.

"So dock my pay." MacAlister curled his six-foot frame onto one of a pair of thin, narrow benches facing each other in the back of the van.

Stone took the seat opposite him. "You don't work for me anymore." He was built like his name—average height, heavy body, square shoulders, face like hewn granite. They'd had their differences in the years since Stone had persuaded him to work for the Bureau, but MacAlister trusted his former boss.

From under the seat, Stone produced a thermos and two plastic cups. "How are things going?" he inquired casually as he poured the steaming liquid.

"Just peachy."

"You don't sound pleased."

"I haven't been pleased for the past six months."

Stone gave a long-suffering sigh and hunched forward, the cup cradled in both hands. "You know I did what I could to find Jack Sabine's murderer. But the Chief wouldn't stand still for ruffling any important foreign feathers."

"Damn, we both know Rousseau did it. And I could have taken him out without a fuss." MacAlister downed his coffee in one gulp. It burned all the way down; he welcomed it to counter the pain of Jack's death.

"We've been down this road before. Much as I hate to say it, Rousseau is a legitimate businessman, and you had no proof." He sighed. "I let you in on the Deets case."

"Yeah. I just happened to be handy when you needed someone to tail his widow," MacAlister retorted. He'd been pumping Stone for information on Deets's murder when the nurse had called from the clinic to say Roseanne had found the key.

Stone frowned. "You wanted in because Deets was your partner. I wanted to give you a crack at it because of Sabine."

MacAlister clenched his fist, crushing the plastic cup. "It's not the same, and you know it. Deets and I were partners for only a few months. But Jack and I lived in each other's hip pockets for years." His stomach knotted. He paused to get a grip on himself. Stone was right, in a way. Hashing over Jack's death was like picking at a sore . . . the pain continued and the damn thing never healed. He drew in a ragged breath. "You're right. I just hate seeing that filthy bastard, Rousseau, get away with murder." *Make that two murders, though no one but him cared that Lily had died, too.* Somehow, he'd see to it Rousseau paid. It was a vow he'd made over two fresh graves.

"Okay. So, do you want out of the case?"

Yes. "No, I said I'd stick with her and get the stuff from the bank box when she opened it. I finish what I start," MacAlister said grimly.

Stone smiled and nodded. "Made any progress with her?"

"She's been through a lot. It's made her wary. . . ." MacAlister knew that his face revealed nothing, but inside he felt that odd flickering of possessiveness just thinking about Roseanne. She'd been asleep when he went in to leave the note, her face serene, her hair spread across the pillows like a bright banner, begging a man to coil his fingers in the silken strands. His hand tightened reflexively. "I think she really does have amnesia."

Stone frowned his displeasure. "You read the doctors' reports. . .medically there's no proof Mrs. Deets has amnesia. We think it's just a ploy to avoid answering questions about her husband's murder."

"Yeah, then why did she show the nurse the key and ask her about the bank? Why didn't she just take off?"

"I don't know. Maybe to make her story seem more convincing in case she was caught," Stone said, brushing aside MacAlister's question. "I do know that we'd had Deets's house staked out for some time, so our guys were the first ones there when the shooting started. What do you think they saw…Mrs. Deets and a man running from the murder scene.''

MacAlister nodded. Stone had been over this before, but now there were details that bothered him. ''If Roseanne hired this guy to kill Deets, why did he shoot her?''

''Maybe he didn't. Deets had a gun in his hand, and he'd fired a shot. Maybe he hit her before he died, and she managed to run that far before she passed out. Hell, all I know is that she's a suspect in her husband's murder, and she has the key to a bank box that I need access to.'' He ran a hand through his hair. ''Look, I don't have a lot of time on this one. If you don't get results soon, I'll have to bring her down to HQ.''

MacAlister sensed Stone's anxiety and wondered at it. But his own mind buzzed with so many different questions he didn't know where to begin. ''Why the hurry?'' Stone had said Roseanne had her getaway money in that box and maybe proof she was involved in Deets's murder. But MacAlister had a strange feeling Stone hadn't told him everything.

As if he'd read MacAlister's mind, Stone shifted in his seat. ''Crenshaw wants this one solved ASAP,'' he said evasively.

MacAlister watched the sweat bead up on Stone's lip and got that same gut-wrenching feeling he used to get when a case was about to go sour on him.

''Maybe I'd better bring her in today,'' Stone said.

Every protective instinct MacAlister possessed screamed in silent protest. ''Not yet. She's beginning to trust me.'' He couldn't let Stone or anyone else question Roseanne. She'd been through so much already. The horror of having her life threatened, not once but twice in the past twenty-four hours, plus the trauma of losing her memory, had left her too vulnerable, too fragile emotionally to withstand any pressure at all. ''You have to give me more time,'' he told Stone flatly.

''I can wait until Monday. After that…''

''You trot out the rubber hoses.'' MacAlister swore under his breath as he got up to leave. Stone was playing this very close to his government-issue vest. Was it because MacAlister no longer worked for the Bureau? Or was there some other reason his former mentor didn't trust him?

Chapter 4

"'Course I know MacAlister. I was working the Mid-East Section out of Cairo when Stone hired him." Agent Thatcher gave the cards an expert ruffle, then laid them on the kitchen table.

Roseanne tapped the deck with her fingers to pass as he'd taught her. "How long ago was that?"

"Ten years." Thatcher smiled as he dealt, his gold-capped incisor gleaming exotically against his dark, leathery cheek. "MacAlister must have been about twenty-four or -five...hard to tell. He acted older, though. Tough, streetwise. Catch my drift? You going to play?"

"What? Oh." Roseanne picked up her cards, shifted through them absently. "How was he tougher? Why?"

Thatcher scowled at his cards, then looked up, shrugging. "Usual story. Mother died when he was a kid...father got lost in the bottom of a bottle. Guess MacAlister was on his own by the time he was fourteen."

Loneliness. Roseanne had sensed it in MacAlister from the first. Been drawn by it. "Surely someone must have taken him in...a relative, maybe. An uncle." Now, why had she said that?

"No family as far as I know." The agent drew a card, glowered at it and discarded. "MacAlister's never been one to let people get close, except maybe Stone and Sabine.... Of course, Sabine's dead."

"Who was Sabine?"

"MacAlister's partner...."

Roseanne frowned. "I thought Lucien Deets was his partner."

"How'd you know about Deets?" the agent asked sharply.

"MacAlister mentioned his name last night. Why, is something wrong?"

Thatcher looked at her strangely. "I just thought you might have remembered something."

Roseanne shook her head.

"Nothing? I mean, don't you remember anything?" he pressed, looking frankly skeptical.

"Believe me, no one wants my memory to return more than I do." She sighed. "I sense things, but I don't really remember anything about my life."

"What kind of things do you sense?"

"Ordinary things." Roseanne toyed with her empty coffee cup. "For instance, last night I cooked dinner...fettuccine Alfredo and Caesar salad...without a cookbook. I just...knew how they went together."

"Yeah?" Thatcher wasn't nearly as impressed as MacAlister had been. "What about people? Or names?"

Roseanne shifted uneasily in her chair. What had started out as a friendly chat was rapidly disintegrating into an interrogation. "No, nothing at all."

He went back to studying his cards, but Roseanne sensed he was tense.

Why? She ran quickly back over their conversation, but found no clue. "Who else was MacAlister close to?" she asked, returning to a topic that interested her.

Thatcher shrugged. "There was Lily.... You draw yet?"

Lily? Who was Lily? Her mind buzzing with questions, Roseanne snatched up a card, barely glancing at it before discarding it. "Is Lily MacAlister's wife?"

Thatcher was busy crowing over the card she'd thrown away. "That was a mistake," he warned, grinning.

"I can see I have to be more careful," she said thinly. And not just with the cards. "About his wife..."

"Doesn't have one, at least as far as I know. Lily left him for another guy a few years ago. Besides, she wasn't the kind of woman a man married. Catch my drift?"

She frowned. "Actually, I don't...."

"Morning, Thatcher... Roseanne."

She turned at the familiar husky baritone and found MacAlister lounging in the doorway, a thumb hooked in his jeans pocket, a shopping bag dangling incongruously from his thick wrist. He resembled that pirate again, dark and dangerous, returning home with the spoils of war.

"I'll take over here," he said to Thatcher, but his eyes held Roseanne's with a quiet intensity that made her forget all about Lily, made her remember instead the feel of his arms holding her close.

"We aren't finished," Thatcher grumbled, but he reached for Roseanne's cards. "Damn if you didn't have gin again."

"Beginner's luck," Roseanne said faintly, half dreading the moment when Thatcher left her alone with MacAlister. Was she strong enough to resist if he asked her about the bank again?

Shifting free of his spell, she stared at her hands until she heard the door close and the whisper of denim as MacAlister crossed the kitchen.

"You look rested this morning, but a little shy." He leaned one hip on the corner of the table. His fingers gently grazed her cheek, then cupped her chin, raised it so their gazes met and tangled.

Roseanne's heart skipped a beat and the air got stuck in her lungs again. "W-why would I be shy?"

"Embarrassed at being caught gossiping about me in the kitchen." He laughed at her flushed cheeks, then his expression turned grave. "Lily is a woman I knew... once."

Her skin burned, prickled where he touched her; her mind whirled with questions. Lily had left him for another man. *Why had she gone?* Was Lily's desertion responsible for the pain Roseanne had glimpsed in the hidden recesses of his eyes?

"If you're worried I'll run to Stone with anything you tell me, don't be. I retired from the Bureau six months ago," he said huskily, reclaiming her attention.

Why had he said that? "What exactly is the Bureau?"

"It's a government agency . . . like the CIA or FBI."

"Or the police?"

"Yeah. Are you afraid to speak with the police?"

"Not afraid," she said, sighing. "Just tired of being asked questions I can't answer."

As she gazed up at him, his fingers slid under her hair to excite the nerves at her nape. "Well, you can relax. I really don't work for Stone."

"Umm . . ." His touch muddled her senses. "But you went to see him this morning."

"To find out if he had any leads on our three friends. Any idea why they're after us. Nothing so far." His thumb slid around to lightly stroke her ear.

Roseanne's head fell to one side. "I-is it safe here?" she murmured, a warm haze spreading over her senses.

"At least until tomorrow."

"What happens then?" she managed to whisper.

"Well, I feel kind of responsible for you, so I asked Stone to let me stay with you until you get adjusted. But I don't work for the Bureau any longer, so on Monday, Stone will have to take you into protective custody. And I'm out of the picture."

Roseanne blinked, struggled to shake off the spell he'd woven around her. "No. I'm not ready to . . ." She swallowed the rest, looked away.

"Not ready for what, sweetheart?" When she didn't reply, he sighed. "You know what those goons were after last night, don't you, Rose?"

"No . . . I . . . I thought they were after you."

"You don't believe that. If you've lost your memory, you may not know what they want, but you . . . sense it, don't you?" His words were clipped, the muscle at his jaw jumped.

The key. Roseanne paled. "Please . . . don't push me."

He made a harsh sound in his throat and got up to pace, raking his hand through his hair. "I don't want to, honey," he said more gently when he stopped in front of her again. "But I want to help you, and I'll do whatever it takes to get you to trust me enough to accept that help."

Roseanne took a deep breath, but it did nothing to ease the tension building inside her. "I...can't...not yet. Please try to understand. I don't know who I am, or why any of this is happening. I thought maybe those men were after you because of your partner or your business, but if they aren't..." She couldn't get anything more past the lump of dread in her throat.

What did it all mean? Why would the men want the key? Why would this mysterious Bureau suddenly take an interest in her? Had she done something terrible in her past life? If only she could remember...

MacAlister's heart went out to her. She reminded him of a small, cornered animal. Hurting, needing help, but too frightened, too stubborn to accept it. Why did she have to be difficult? Why couldn't Stone give him more time?

Don't hate me for what I have to do, Rose, he thought. Hell, he already hated himself. Seducing information out of a woman whose emotional balance was so fragile was...criminal. Only a little better than threatening it out of her. But she refused to answer his questions, and he saw no other quick solution to the problem. *Once Stone has whatever is in the bank box, I'll make it up to you. I'll find the best doctors...*

"MacAlister, you groaned. Is something wrong?"

"What? No...." Heaving a sigh, MacAlister dug into the shopping bag, pulled out the slacks and sweater he'd gotten for himself, then handed her the bag. "Here...I bought you some clothes." *And so the game begins,* he thought cynically.

"You did? Why?"

"I thought you might be getting sick of those shirts."

She looked surprised, pleased. "They're beginning to remind me of hospital gowns," she admitted. "But I have no money, no way to repay you."

"How about I take those two tarts in the fridge and call us even." He smiled at her with a boyishness that reminded her of the youngster forced to fend for himself, and she didn't have the heart to turn him down.

"Deal," she tossed over her shoulder as she hurried to her bedroom.

Inside the bag there were two bundles wrapped in snowy tissue paper. Her fingers trembled in anticipation as she lifted out a soft green sweater. But her smile faded when she saw how small it was. Perhaps it would look better on.

It didn't, and neither did the matching slacks, Roseanne saw as she turned to study her reflection in the long mirror over the dresser. The pants and soft wool sweater clung to her body like a coat of paint. No way she could go to the bank dressed like this.

Draping the plaid shirt over her shoulders, Roseanne went in search of MacAlister. She found him in the kitchen washing down the last tart with a cup of his terrible instant coffee.

"Why are you still wearing that old shirt?"

"The things you bought are too... tight."

Too tight. MacAlister had seen pictures of Roseanne Deets in dresses so indecently tight you could count her ribs. The thought that that aspect of her personality had changed, too, pleased him...and alarmed him. He couldn't afford to like her any more than he already did. "I can't tell anything with that damn flannel covering you."

His eyes widened as she slid out of the shirt and turned in a small circle before him. The pictures had not done justice to her perfectly scaled figure...high, full breasts, wasp-thin waist, softly rounded hips and long slender legs. "H-o-l-y..." The rest of his words were smothered in a coughing fit.

Roseanne tried to pound him on the back, but he put both hands up to ward her off and stepped away.

"I—I'm fine," he croaked. "There's just..."

"A lot of me showing." Roseanne smiled ruefully, wrapping the shirt around her like a suit of armor. "I really appreciate your efforts, but I can't wear them."

God, she was beautiful. MacAlister wanted to kiss the protest from her softly parted lips, wanted to peel off the layers of clothing separating them and make love to her on the kitchen floor. The swift, raw hunger throbbing through his veins like liquid fire shocked him. He had not wanted anyone, not even Lily, as fiercely as this.

"Could I go with you while you take these back and maybe pick out something else?"

"Yeah, sure you can go," he said thickly.

She smiled and danced away toward the laundry room. "My jeans are torn, but they'll have to do." The shirt flew out behind her as she rushed by, giving him a tantalizing glimpse of her body in motion . . . all fluid grace and sizzling energy. The contrast was fascinating. As fascinating as the contrast between her bewitching beauty and her sharp, restless mind.

Dazed, MacAlister took a deep breath to clear his head of the erotic images that writhed there. If he wasn't careful, he'd forget who was supposed to be seducing whom.

"Ah . . . will we have to drive fast if no one is chasing us?" Roseanne asked as she buckled the seat belt.

"A Porsche was made for speed." MacAlister threw the shopping bag into the back seat and slid in behind the wheel. A shave and the change from his worn jeans and faded sweatshirt into the charcoal slacks and black sweater he'd purchased for himself made him look every inch the prosperous importer/exporter. The only reminder of the rough, ruthless man who'd come to her rescue on Friday night was the predatory gleam in his eyes as he backed from the garage and carefully scanned their surroundings.

"Rich people in books drive Porsches," she commented, looking at the leather upholstery and sophisticated instruments built into the dash with new appreciation.

"I am not rich," MacAlister snapped.

"Did you steal it, then?" a mischievous little imp made Roseanne say.

"No. I bought it. But it took me a hell of a long time to save enough to buy it . . . and I bought it because I liked the car. Not because it's a rich man's toy. Got it?"

"Got it," Roseanne echoed quickly.

He sighed. "Hey, sorry." Reaching across the console, he briefly squeezed her hand. "I grew up tough and poor, and I guess sometimes I'm . . ."

"Thatcher told me about your parents. Who took care of you after they were gone?"

MacAlister tensed. It wasn't something he liked to remember, much less discuss. "I got by," he said shortly.

Hearing the pain in his voice, she was silent as the car shot down the drive. She wanted to ask about Lily, but guessed that subject would also be off-limits. Apparently Thatcher was right about MacAlister not letting anyone get close. Yet he demanded *she* trust *him*.

Roseanne turned her attention to the passing countryside, trying to see if anything seemed familiar. "Oh, look," she said a few moments later, leaning forward as a trio of enormous buildings came into view between the trees. "Are those homes or...what?"

"Homes. Very rich people's homes," he said tightly.

"You don't approve of rich people, do you?"

MacAlister shrugged. "They think they're better than the rest of us."

"But you are just as good as they are. You own your own company. You have a beautiful apartment and you drive a—"

"Window dressing," he mocked savagely. "Underneath it all, I'm still a carpenter's son from the wrong side of the tracks. Oh, sure, the people who live in these houses would do business with me, but they wouldn't want me joining their clubs or dating their daughters."

And you're one of them, kid...born with a silver spoon and a father rich enough to buy me ten times over...whether you remember it or not. "Rich isn't a matter of how much money you have," he added, driving home his point. "It's a class by itself. It's being born with the right name and the right pedigree." He snorted, his eyes back on the road. "I don't have either. I'm a stray dog that got lucky and made a few bucks."

Roseanne studied MacAlister's rugged profile as he negotiated a sharp turn. Her glance skimmed his broad shoulders and corded muscles as he twisted slightly in the bucket seat. He drove the way he did so many other things...efficiently and confidently, the sleek, dynamic car almost an extension of his powerful body. Everything about him said he had no reason to feel inferior to anyone. Yet in some ways he was almost as vulnerable as she was.

As though sensing her eyes on him, MacAlister looked away from the road long enough to smile at her. "Sorry for the lecture, honey. Here I'm supposed to be showing you what a trustworthy guy I am." His lazy smile deepened enough to dazzle her.

And I'm afraid it's working. "I'm glad to get out," was all she said before glancing back at the modest homes and businesses they were now passing. She felt an affinity for the small cozy shops, their windows filled with colorful displays of merchandise. She wondered why she found them so appealing.

"Here we are." MacAlister turned in at the sign for the Stamford Town Centre.

"Is Danbury near here?" Roseanne asked as MacAlister cruised between the rows of parked cars.

His hands tightened on the steering wheel. *Danbury. Was that where the bank box was?* "My Connecticut geography is a bit rusty, but I think Danbury is forty miles north of here. Why do you ask?"

"No reason. I . . . er, heard the town mentioned." Roseanne sighed. It might as well be four thousand miles away. MacAlister would never loan her the Porsche...even supposing she remembered how to drive a car.

The mall was enormous. Seven stories of stores and boutiques jammed with bustling shoppers. More than a little intimidated by the noise and the crowds, Roseanne reached for MacAlister's hand.

As they touched, that strange tingling current moved from his body into hers again, jolting all her nerves to life. Tilting her head, she looked up. For one timeless minute amber eyes burned into forest green, then MacAlister laced his fingers with hers and lifted them to his mouth.

Though the brush of his lips across the back of her hand was soft, the tremor it sent cascading through Roseanne made her gasp. The people around them faded, but she was as vitally aware of MacAlister as if she'd crawled inside his skin. Every cell in her body quivered to attention, throbbing in time with the pulse that beat at the base of his throat.

"You're safe with me," he murmured against her hand.

Spellbound, Roseanne nodded. "I don't understand what's happening to me...."

"To us...." MacAlister gently corrected. "I feel it, too." His breath was warm on her skin, his lips seductive as they teased her fingers. "Chemistry, passion, desire," he whispered for her ears alone, his eyes locked on hers.

Her insides melted, slowly, deliciously. "I don't think I've ever felt this way before."

He wasn't sure he had either, and that's what worried him. "I'll take care of everything. Just trust me."

"I—I want to...." A shopper bumped into her, mumbled an excuse and hurried away. Roseanne shook free of the spell. "I, er, hadn't realized it would be so crowded today. I feel funny about shopping on the Sabbath."

MacAlister swore under his breath and schooled himself to patience. "Well, your jeans are shot, and you'll need a coat. They're forecasting flurries tomorrow."

Intimidated by the array of merchandise jammed onto the sea of racks on the department store's second floor, Roseanne felt like running. "It'll take hours just to look at all this stuff," she said frantically.

"Take your time," MacAlister replied. "I'll stand over here out of the way." Ignoring the flare of panic in her eyes, he assured her that he'd be nearby if she needed him and then he fled. Shopping with a woman, even Roseanne, was enough to give a strong man hives.

Roseanne suppressed the urge to run after him and forced herself to wander through the racks, touching the clothes randomly at first. Soon, she got caught up in the displays, admiring the colors, the textures, intrigued by the sensual slide of silk, the comforting weight of wool. On some level, she knew she'd shopped before, but today it seemed fresh, interesting.

"You don't have much here," MacAlister said, showing up suddenly at her elbow a few minutes later, making her heart beat too fast at the sight of him. He glanced at the pair of jeans and purple tweed sweater waiting to be rung up. "Are they packing up the rest of it in the back?"

"It was fun to look, but I really didn't need much," she replied simply.

"A frugal woman." He rolled his eyes skyward. "This is one for the record books."

Roseanne chuckled. "You, sir, must have been preyed upon by greedy women."

"A few." Because she asked for so little, MacAlister had a need to buy out the store for her. "What happened to that green outfit I bought you?"

The clerk who had been discreetly monitoring their banter swooped in. "We have that particular set in her size, sir," she chirped.

Roseanne protested that she didn't really need so much. But MacAlister was like a steamroller once he got started. After he'd paid for two pairs of jeans, the slacks set and two more sweaters, he insisted they look at coats.

"I'll be fine until we can get my fur coat back."

MacAlister gave her one of his probing looks. "Is that coat really important to you?" He hadn't asked Stone to have it picked up because of the risk of being followed.

"No. To tell you the truth, I felt very guilty about those poor little sables every time I looked at it," she added, fingering an electric-blue car coat.

"Good. We'll take one of these in black," he told the hovering clerk.

"The blue is prettier," Roseanne interjected, irritated by his habit of taking charge.

"Black is less noticeable, honey."

That subtle reminder of why they had met in the first place dampened Roseanne's spirits faster than a splash of ice water. "D-do you think they followed us to the mall?" she whispered as they left the coat department.

"No, I don't," MacAlister said calmly. "What about underwear?" He halted at the lingerie department.

"Underwear?" Heat crept up her neck as she thought about MacAlister picking out her panties and bras.

He shot her a wicked grin. "Yeah."

"MacAlister!" Her gasp of outrage had heads turning.

One dark brow rose. "Shy, aren't you?" he retorted, smiling roguishly. "Don't worry. I'll stand here with the packages. Buy something sexy." Pressing a fifty-dollar bill into her hand, he turned his back on the rows of dainty silk panties and matching camisoles. Arms crossed, legs braced like the captain of some ancient sailing vessel, he surveyed the passing shoppers.

Oh. Stifling the urge to stuff the money down his throat, Roseanne stomped over to the bins of sensible cotton underwear. It took her only a few minutes to decide on three bra-and-brief sets, a flannel nightgown and three pairs of socks. By the time the cashier had finished ringing them up, Roseanne's pique had vanished.

His high-handedness was annoying, but he had been more than generous in paying for her clothes. She hoped he'd be as generous with his car.

Thatcher had just repositioned his car in the trees at the end of the driveway and settled in for a boring afternoon when he got a call on his cellular phone.

"So how'd it go with the girl?" Stone asked.

"Well…" Thatcher ran a hand over his stubbled chin. "She seemed calm, real friendly and down-to-earth, considering who she is…. Rich, and all that."

Stone snorted. "You sound as bad as MacAlister. Find out anything we can use?"

"Not much. She says he doesn't remember a thing…just senses stuff…like cooking. If you catch my drift."

"Cooking? I send you in to see how your take of the situation compares with MacAlister's, and you discuss recipes with her?"

"You asked me what she remembered, and I told you," Thatcher grumbled into the receiver.

"Right." Stone sighed. "Where are they now?"

"MacAlister took her out to get some clothes. Sanchez followed them."

"How does MacAlister act around her?" Stone asked.

"Protective as hell. MacAlister was a good choice. He's stubborn enough to make sure she gets into the bank box…"

"And loyal enough to honor his word and turn the contents over to us," Stone said smugly.

"There's a video player at the house. How about we pick up a movie on the way home and watch it this afternoon?"

MacAlister asked as they drove away from the mall.

"Can we eat the popcorn?"

A smile lifted the corner of his mouth. "What's a movie without popcorn?"

He located a rental store in a small plaza a few miles from the house. Once inside, he headed directly for the Classic Movie section.

"I wouldn't have guessed you were an old-movie buff," Roseanne said, following close on his heels.

He quirked one dark brow at her. "Yeah, what, then?"

"Well..." Sweeping him with a teasing glance, she pretended to consider the matter. He had one hand on his hip; the other rested lightly on a rack of movies. A lazy, sexy smile lifted the corners of his mouth, exotic promises danced in his eyes. He looked big, solid and very desirable. "Rambo, maybe. Or James Bond," she murmured.

He snorted, shaking his head. "They shouldn't romanticize that stuff. Being an agent is hard, serious work, and having to watch a bunch of guys stalk and kill each other is not my idea of entertainment."

Too much like what he'd done for a living, Roseanne suspected. "What is your idea of entertainment?"

"Mmm." His hooded gaze swept her from head to toe, then back up, leaving a trail of fire in its wake. "Popcorn, a good movie and a beautiful woman to enjoy it with...for starters," he said low and huskily. The air in the narrow aisle suddenly sizzled with anticipation.

"Oh...."

"The sooner we pick out that movie, the sooner we can...get back to the house," he added, his eyes locked with hers in silent communication. This time, the message came in clearer. He wanted her.

Roseanne shivered. Was it possible to be afraid and excited at the same time? It must be, because she was, her chest tight with anticipation. What should she do? What should she say? Dazed, she dragged in a ragged breath and turned to stare blindly at the movie labels.

"Here it is," he informed her a few minutes later. "*To Have and Have Not.* Have you seen it?"

Roseanne frowned. "I don't think so. Is it good?"

"Yeah. Bogie and Bacall. You'll like it."

"You've already seen it."

"Not with you...."

"All right," she murmured, his smoldering gaze making her tremble again. And he knew it, too. His expression a mix of smugness and desire, he paid for the movie.

His lazy smile stayed in place, making her heart race as he laced his fingers with hers and led her outside to the car. They rode home in companionable silence. He watched the road; she watched him and wondered at the change that had come over him since last night.

Was it because he believed she really had lost her memory? She wanted to think so. It made trusting him seem easier and easier, she thought as they pulled into the driveway.

Roseanne changed into her new sweater and slacks while MacAlister got the movie ready to run. He had just put the popcorn into the microwave when she came out.

"It smells good." Bending down, Roseanne watched through the glass door as the bag twitched and swelled. "How long does it take to cook?"

"Another minute or so," MacAlister muttered, eyeing the soft curves revealed by her new clothes and the excitement glowing in her face. Her actions were so natural, so graceful and unpracticed, he sometimes had trouble believing she was real.

"It's done," she sang out when the timer sounded. Before he could stop her, she wrenched open the door and snatched out the bag. "Ouch..."

He caught the bag between a thumb and forefinger as she dropped it, tossed it on the counter, then stuck her hands under the cold water. "Better?" he asked a minute later.

Roseanne nodded. "Thank you. I was foolish not to realize I'd get burned."

"Yes. But then, you've never made popcorn before."

"I might have. I just don't remember." She looked up at him, and he realized the pain clouding her eyes had nothing to do with her singed fingers.

"I wish I could help."

"Maybe you can," she murmured.

MacAlister managed to smile down into her wistful face, but he didn't press the advantage he'd gained so far. Hell, he hated it. Hated the ease with which he'd gotten her to lower her guard and let him get close. *Run! I'll betray your trust,* he wanted to shout. But if he alienated her, Stone would send Thatcher or Sanchez, and he couldn't bear that.

They settled down on the couch, the bowl of popcorn between them. Roseanne quickly became immersed in the story. Everything about it fascinated her...the setting, the background music, the gritty dialogue. She had no difficulty casting MacAlister in Bogie's role of the tough skipper-for-hire. And herself...? She knew she'd never be half as beautiful, witty or clever as Bacall, but a girl could dream.

The first love scene caught her by surprise. Tension sizzled, electrifying the screen and her own recently awakened sensual receptors. Glancing over at MacAlister, she found him watching her instead of the movie, his eyes glittering beneath half-lowered lids.

"You're enjoying the movie." His voice was low, hushed.

She drew in a breath, whispered, "Yes."

He smiled, his gaze briefly touching her hair, then her mouth before coming back to her eyes. "I'm glad."

For an instant, she thought he might kiss her, and her pulse sped up. She knew his arms were strong, muscular, his chest rock-solid. What would his lips feel like?

Never taking his eyes from hers, MacAlister set the popcorn bowl aside and slid across the cushion separating them. Very slowly, he slipped one arm along the back of the couch, grazing her shoulders and nape. He let it rest there, close enough so she could feel its warmth.

His smile deepened slowly, too, as the fingers of his other hand brushed her cheek. "Don't miss any of the movie, honey," he said softly. "There'll be plenty of time for us...later."

Chapter 5

"Well, here goes," Roseanne muttered. Sucking in a deep breath to gather her courage, she lifted the tray and walked out of the kitchen. She had all but decided to trust MacAlister with her secret.

The afternoon had gone well—better than well. She'd relaxed and enjoyed herself in his company. He was smart, witty and as quick with a smile or a teasing comment as he was with his temper. They'd discussed what they liked and didn't like, argued about gun control and vigilante justice, debated the pros and cons of eating meat. He called her "honey" and found a dozen excuses to touch her arm, her face, her hair.

By the time they'd gotten around to dinner, Roseanne had lost whatever fear she'd had of MacAlister. The attention he paid her was exciting and very flattering to her fragile ego. Would he kiss her soon? Would she like it? A tingle of anticipation moved over her skin. She'd read about lovemaking in novels, seen couples kissing and more on television, but she had no memory of having done any of those things.

Please don't let me make a fool of myself, she murmured to herself as she entered the living room.

"I'm glad you bought a few more logs. I enjoy the fire," she said, trying to sound nonchalant as she set the coffee and store-bought cheesecake on the coffee table.

Hunkered down before the fireplace, MacAlister slanted her a glance, his eyes hooded, yet gleaming with reflected flames. "I enjoy the fire, too, honey." Though the words were ordinary, the endearment and the subtle emphasis in his velvety voice made them seem dark, intimate.

The warmth of his gaze sent shivers down her spine, heightened the tension crackling between them. A few hours ago, she wouldn't have recognized the subtle pull of sensuality, or measured the sexual undertones in his voice by the odd surge in her pulse.

With Bogie and Bacall's love scenes fresh in her mind, she knew where what she was feeling led. But was she ready to risk that kind of emotional and physical intimacy? All through dinner, MacAlister's nearness had played havoc with her senses. She'd watched his mouth as he ate, wondering what it would feel like on hers, watched his fingers as he lazily traced the pattern on the place mats, wondering what his hands would feel like sliding over her skin.

Roseanne shook herself, reached for a plate. "Dessert?"

"Yeah." MacAlister sprawled next to the coffee table, propped on one elbow. His eyes met hers, and a knowing smile spread across his face. Reaching up, he wrapped one large, warm hand around her calf. "Sit down here beside me."

His touch seemed to tighten something buried deep inside her, igniting a slow heat that spilled through her body, melting her bones, turning her muscles to jelly. Weak-kneed, she sank to the carpet.

"Careful." Still smiling, he took the plate from her in time to rescue the sliding cake. "Want some?"

Numbly, she nodded. He cut a small bite, held it out.

Operating strictly by rote, Roseanne opened her mouth. "It's very . . . rich," she murmured as the creamy concoction melted and slid down her throat.

"Mmm. You like?"

Helplessly, she stared into his darkening amber eyes, felt the tension escalate. "I . . . I don't know." He had another bite waiting, but she declined with a shake of her head. "It's too much on top of my meal."

"You didn't eat any of the steak."

My stomach was tied in knots. "I filled up on salad."

"Oh? Your face looks a little flushed. Do you feel warm?" he asked huskily.

"A—a little. . . . I think it's the fire."

"Yeah?" MacAlister set the plate aside and slipped the clip from her hair, ran his hands through the silky mass, then down her back, wordlessly urging her to lie down beside him.

She felt the heat radiating from him, and her heart did a cartwheel. Her breath caught as his finger stroked her throat, her collarbone, touched the diamond necklace nestled in the valley between her breasts.

"That's quite a necklace. Are the diamonds real?"

Roseanne swallowed. "I don't know, but I sense it is . . . was . . . important to me."

The flicker of pain in her eyes tugged at him. He fought to remember this was supposed to be business. "Have I told you how great you look in the slacks and sweater?"

"Not in so many words." To her surprise, Roseanne found her voice was as low and husky as his.

His smile was slow, intimate. "You caught me watching you. But it seemed only fair . . . you've been staring at me . . . wondering what it would be like to kiss me."

"It's because of the movie."

"Is it?" he asked, his head lowering until his breath fanned across her lips, making them part expectantly.

"I don't know. I don't remember anything. . . . I don't sense having done any of this before." She ducked her head, suddenly shy and a little afraid.

Logic tangled with fantasy. MacAlister knew all the wishing in the world wouldn't make her an innocent and him the first man to touch her sweetness. But he could treat her with as much tenderness as though he were. "I won't do anything to hurt you, or frighten you," he promised. Easing his fingers into her hair, he brought her face back up and brushed his lips over hers.

"You have to trust someone, sweetheart. Let it be me," he whispered, then his mouth touched hers again, stitched a string of tiny stinging kisses from one corner of her mouth to the other before closing over it in a caress so gentle it pulled a moan from her. In answer, he deepened the kiss, drugging her with the feel of his mouth molding hers until her very bones melted. "Tell me you want this," he said softly, his eyes locked on hers.

"I do." She sighed, the sound almost lost under his growl of masculine approval as his mouth slid across her cheek. She trembled at the first touch of his tongue on her ear. "Maybe I shouldn't . . . but I do."

"You're right to trust me, honey," he purred. "I want to take care of you." His tongue swirled wet patterns down the length of her throat, and her arms twined around his neck to pull him closer. "That's it, sweetheart. Come to me," he murmured. "Put yourself in my keeping."

"I don't know. . . . It's all happening so fast," she breathed, groaning as his mouth moved back to hers. His tongue slipped between her parted lips to delicately explore, to tangle and excite, dragging tiny pleading sounds from the back of her throat.

"What is it, sweetheart?" he asked softly. "Tell me what you want . . . what you need."

"I don't know. . . . I ache . . . so badly."

"Do you want me to stop?"

"No. . . ." She clutched his shoulders, moaning as his hand slid under her sweater. Her moan became a gasp, then a sigh of pleasure as he caressed her breast.

He rubbed his thumb across her nipple, felt it harden beneath the plain cotton and chuckled softly as she arched into his touch, pressing closer. "You like?"

"Yes. . . ." Her voice was thready, her pulse rocketing. "I never dreamed anything could feel so . . . *good.*"

"It's going to get better and better," he growled, unhooking her bra. He gently cupped her bare breast in his warm, rough palm, and she moaned. "So responsive," he murmured against her lips as she arched her back and pressed herself into his hand. "If I play with your nipples, will you go a little wild for me?"

She did, shivering as he caught the hardened tip between his thumb and fingers, crying out as he teased it to aching prominence. His mouth closed over hers, hot and urgent, and reality spun away. She had no breath but what he breathed into her, no will but the fire his touch spread through her veins. She was vaguely aware of a cool drift of air as he unzipped her slacks, but the warmth of his body kept it at bay.

Inside, she ached. Oh, how she ached. Deep, where his mouth and hands couldn't reach. She wanted more, but some ancient, inborn instinct warned her to be cautious.

"Don't be afraid," he murmured. "I won't betray your trust. I won't take anything from you. Say you trust me... give yourself over to me...."

"Yes... oh, yes," she whispered.

"You won't be sorry." His mouth closed over her breast, spreading hot, wet heat as he avidly drew down on her. His hands drifted lower, found the hungry pulse beating at the juncture of her thighs and caressed it with the same driving rhythm.

Inside her, a storm was building, wild, like the rushing of the wind, unstoppable, like the pounding of the surf. She cried out, suddenly afraid its fury would tear her in two.

"It's all right. I've got you," he whispered huskily. "Just let go. Ride it to the top." His touch shifted, the tempo deepening and quickening.

Roseanne caught back a small sob as the next wave took her, lifted her. A shudder raced through her, then another and another as the wave crested. Eyes closed, she threw her head back, cried out as the sweet tremors shook her in a pleasure so intense it brought tears to her eyes. Seconds later, she collapsed, gasping for breath.

MacAlister wrapped his arms around her and held her close, rocked her as the last of the convulsions fluttered through her. He'd never intended to take things this far. But then, he had never seen anything as beautiful, as compelling as Roseanne responding to him, her face shining with wonder as she reached the peak he'd brought her to. Once started, he was powerless to deny her pleasure. Now he was so hard it hurt to breathe.

Serves you right, you bastard, he thought. That he hadn't completely lost control was his only consolation. Groaning, he shifted to put a little space between her soft body and his own aching flesh.

Roseanne's lashes flickered up. "Oh, MacAlister..." She blushed, unable to meet his gaze, noted he was still dressed, and frowned. "I...you didn't..."

"No. You weren't ready.... It would have been too much, too soon. But you enjoyed what I gave you," he said with a flash of masculine triumph.

"Yes. I did," Roseanne said softly, feeling very feminine, safe and protected in his embrace. "But you...?"

"Enjoyed it, too. You're a passionate woman." MacAlister placed a small kiss on the satisfied curve of her mouth. "I took pleasure in watching you, listening to you." A blush spread over her whole body, and she squirmed delicately. "There's no need to be shy with me, honey." Smiling indulgently, he pulled her sweater back down and refastened her slacks.

His eyes turned serious as he pulled her into the crook of his arm. "You put yourself in my keeping...trusted me to do what was best for you, even though you weren't sure what that was."

Roseanne nodded sleepily, lulled by the warmth of his body and the steady beating of his heart beneath her ear.

"Now, tell me the rest," he urged.

"Rest?" Roseanne blinked herself awake.

"Tell me what you were doing at the bank," he pressed. "After opening yourself to me so...completely, surely you can trust me with that."

Roseanne felt a little fission of anger. "I don't think I care for your methods..."

"No matter how pleasurable?" he demanded.

"Right," she responded solely on principle.

"You are one stubborn lady," he growled. Then he surprised her by grinning and planting a kiss on her chin. "Blame yourself for forcing me to use desperate methods. I warned you I'd do whatever I had to to keep you safe. And remember, too...I could have taken things a hell of a lot further. If I weren't a trustworthy kind of guy."

Roseanne's anger might have withstood a dozen excuses, but his teasing and unrepentant grin melted it faster than ice in July. She wondered if all men were this hard to control.

"Come on, Rose.... Admit you trust me, and let me help."

Trust him? She was halfway in love with him. He'd become her anchor in an alien world.

Haltingly at first, then faster as the floodgates opened, she told him what she knew about the shooting that had landed her in the clinic, about finding the key in the pocket of the fur and going to the bank in New York City. "The nurse at the clinic said people keep family papers in their bank boxes, so I should find something in there that will help restore my memory. What I don't understand is how those men who broke into your apartment could possibly know about the key, or what they could want with my papers."

MacAlister hid his thoughts and doubts behind a smile. Gently lifting her chin, he kissed her slowly and thoroughly, his thumb tracing a lazy pattern over the angle of her jaw. "I don't know, either, honey," he lied smoothly. "But I'll take you to the bank tomorrow."

Roseanne nuzzled her face against his callused palm. "Thank you. You've been so good to me."

"Yeah." MacAlister ground his teeth on a wave of self-hatred. "I'm a real prince." He allowed himself the luxury of holding her for another minute, knowing this must be the last time. Thinking how incredibly good she felt in his arms, he drank in the scent of her hair, the silkiness of her skin, the warmth in her emerald eyes.

No one had ever looked at him the way she did, as though he were the most wonderful man in the world. Looks like that went to a man's head faster than raw whiskey. Unless that man's conscience was working overtime. "I think you'd better turn in," he said at last. "We'll have a busy day ahead of us tomorrow."

MacAlister waited until Roseanne had closed her bedroom door before he snuck out to the garage and his car phone.

He sagged back in the bucket seat and groaned. *It was for her own good,* he told himself. *Yeah, and you enjoyed every minute of it, you...*

"MacAlister? Did you get what we needed?" Stone asked.

"Yeah," MacAlister replied, but he wasn't really happy about it. After telling Stone they were going to the Danbury bank in the morning, MacAlister placed a second call. His fingers tapped impatiently on the steering wheel as his call was switched on with a series of muffled clicks to a second and a third station.

Finally, the phone was answered with a sharp "Yeah."

"Hey, Theo."

"Hey, yourself, Mac," Theo's deep bass rumbled over the airwaves. "Long time no hear."

"I've been pretty busy," MacAlister replied, slouching down in the leather seat. Theo was a comfortable kind of guy, an ex-Bureau man who'd opted for retirement a few years ago and returned to the States to open an investigative firm. "And I haven't got much time to talk right now. I need a favor."

"Anything. You know that. Jeez...after all you've done for me..."

"Thanks, Theo." MacAlister brushed aside his gratitude. "I need whatever you can get on Lucien Deets."

"Your dead partner?" Theo asked, clearly puzzled.

"Yeah. See if you can find out who might have had a reason to kill him." *Besides his wife.* "And why."

Theo grunted. "I'll start with his old pals."

"Old pals?" MacAlister straightened in the seat.

"Right. Deets started out in a pretty rough part of New York and clawed his way to the top of the heap. Word is that he bent a lot of rules before he struck it big and turned legit."

MacAlister's hand tightened on the phone. "Looks like I should have checked Deets out with you instead of his bankers before I bought into his business."

"I'm not saying he was crooked," Theo said hurriedly.

"Right." Inwardly, MacAlister cursed his own stupidity. He'd floundered those first few months after leaving the Bureau. All he'd been certain of was that he wanted to continue in the import/export business that had been his Bureau front, and that he needed to provide a more stable environment for his new-found daughter.

Deets had come across as a hard-nosed businessman looking to expand and needing someone to head up his East Coast operations while he handled things out west. At the time, it had seemed a good fit.

"See what you can turn up for me, Theo. I'll be in touch. Oh . . . and keep this strictly between us. Okay."

"Right. Ah, speaking of old *friends*, I heard something the other day I think you'd be interested in. A possible lead on where Rousseau may be hiding."

MacAlister snapped to attention. "He's surfaced?"

"Nothing definite," Theo said slowly. "Rumors, mostly. Like maybe Rousseau's moved his operation out of the Mid-East because the Bureau made things too uncomfortable for him there."

"See what you can dig up, will you?" MacAlister said tightly, every nerve reverberating with the need to avenge Jack and Lily.

"Sure," Theo shot back. "Where can I reach you?"

"You can't . . . right now. I'll call you."

Rousseau was just sitting down to a late dinner when the agent called.

"MacAlister's going to the Danbury bank tomorrow."

"Ah, at last we make progress." Settling back in his chair, he took a sip of the fine burgundy, admiring its ruby color through the delicate facets of the crystal glass. "Will the Bureau be sending men to back him up?"

"Of course. . . ."

"Make certain the back-up men don't reach the bank."

"How do you expect me to do that?" the agent sputtered. "I told you I wouldn't kill anyone."

"You will do as you are told," Rousseau countered coldly. "But in this instance, I agree with you. The death of some of their agents might cause the Bureau to pursue this case more . . . avidly. So you must think of something less . . . permanent. Disable their automobiles, send them to another location. Do what you must, but see to it the agents do not show up at the bank. I want MacAlister and the girl there . . . alone."

"What will your men do with them once they have Deets's book?" the agent asked hesitantly.

"Dispose of them," Rousseau said offhandedly. "MacAlister escaped me once—he will not be so lucky a second time. And if the girl should regain her memory, she would be a liability."

True to his word, MacAlister drove her to the bank early the next morning. Waiting for the bank clerk to finish with another customer, Roseanne studied the man who lounged against the marble-and-rosewood counter beside her.

Dressed in the gray slacks and black sweater, MacAlister looked very big and very solid. A pirate no longer, but a knight, ready to defend her. After what had happened between them last night, she was certain he cared for her, too.

On the drive up to Danbury, she'd often caught him staring at her speculatively. "It'll be all right, honey," he'd murmur, reaching across the console to touch her, his fingers lingering on her cheek or fiddling with the pins holding her hair in a tidy bun at her nape.

"Careful, you'll undo it," she'd cautioned.

"I like it better down."

"This makes me look more mature," she'd assured him.

"Honey, it's your signature they're interested in, not your age," he'd drawled. The warmth of his smile as their gazes tangled made her shiver with longing, made her feel protected and cared for.

"May I help you?" the bank clerk asked.

"Mrs. Deets would like access to her safe-deposit box," MacAlister said smoothly to the woman.

Roseanne smiled and tried to look calm. Last night, MacAlister's friend Stone had called with information about Roseanne Deets, who had recently disappeared. It was only a possibility that she was this Deets woman, but it fit with the name in the coat and matched the initials on the necklace she was wearing. She had heard the name somewhere else recently. But she wasn't sure where and shrugged the feeling aside.

Anticipation began to percolate through her as she filled the bank slip. Her pen faltered at the signature line. *Roseanne Deets.* She drew a deep breath, reached down inside herself for inspiration, then scrawled the name in the way that seemed most natural and pushed the form back under the Plexiglas barrier for the clerk to examine.

MacAlister winked at her, but didn't smile. He was nervous, too, she decided.

The clerk looked back at Roseanne, then down at the signature card again, her frown deepening.

"I-is there a problem?" Roseanne asked.

"Well . . ."

"If her signature looks shaky, it's probably because my sister's been very ill," MacAlister put in smoothly.

"Ah." The clerk's expression cleared somewhat. "There is a slight difference. . . ."

"I'm surprised it's only slight," MacAlister interjected, his voice lowering to a confidential tone. "She nearly died. This is her first day out since the . . . accident, and she's feeling pretty weak."

"Oh, I am sorry, Mrs. Deets." The clerk gave Roseanne a sympathetic look. "If you'll come this way."

Roseanne's eyes flew to MacAlister. *She must be Roseanne Deets.* Her heart soared; her pulse raced with the hope she'd soon regain the memories that went with the name. MacAlister's sigh tempered her excitement. "What is it?" she asked worriedly.

Damn, even though he didn't believe she had killed her husband, he almost wished she weren't Roseanne Deets. "It's okay, honey. I'll be waiting right here."

Despite his encouraging smile, Roseanne's hands shook as she opened the metal box the clerk had placed in the private cubicle. The first tingle of disappointment struck her as she stared at the pathetically few things inside.

"Damn," she said softly, tears blurring her vision as she touched the stack of money, the man's ring and the small black book. This was everything? She had expected . . . no . . . she'd counted on finding a whole life tucked inside this box, scores of documents just waiting to fill in the gaps in her mind.

Roseanne blinked back the tears that burned her eyes, and picked up the book. Maybe there was something in it, but a quick flip through the pages showed groups of letters with numbers after them. Despair washed through her a second time. There was nothing of her in here. Trembling, she tucked the contents of the box into her coat pockets and turned to leave.

Even though there was nothing in the box to prove it, she still might be this Roseanne Deets. The though was reassuring. Maybe Stone could find some more information for her.

Calmer now, Roseanne returned the box to the clerk and walked out into the main room. Her glance immediately sought out MacAlister.

As their eyes met, he frowned and started toward her.

"Oh, MacAlister." Despite her resolution to be strong, Roseanne longed to throw herself into the haven of his strong arms. "I . . ." Her bottom lip quivered.

"Wait until we're in the car," he murmured, wrapping his left arm around her. Nodding a brisk thanks to the clerk, he quickly surveyed the other bank patrons to make certain none exhibited undue interest in their departure. It was not cold outside, but Roseanne was shivering by the time he bundled her inside the Porsche.

"Okay. Tell me what happened," he said as the powerful engine growled to life. "Empty . . . right?"

Roseanne shook her head slowly. "There was money . . . and some jewelry . . . and a small black book." She dug the things from her pockets, held them out to him, unable to keep her hands from shaking. "There's nothing here about me."

MacAlister fanned through the money, surprised to see there wasn't more. Stone had theorized that Roseanne had her "getaway" funds in the bank box, but this sure wouldn't take her very far or last her very long.

"There's nothing about me," Roseanne repeated.

"Not even in this?" He flicked open the book. Inside, there were columns of letters and numbers . . . looked like some kind of code. He flipped through it quickly, wondering if there was something in here that would point to Deets's killer and hoping he wouldn't find Roseanne's name.

The name on the inside cover stopped him cold.

Gates MacAlister. His name, written in an unfamiliar scrawl. What the hell was it doing in Deets's book?

MacAlister's stomach rolled, and his mouth went dry from a good old-fashioned jolt of panic. It lasted for a second before training took over, the action as instinctive as breathing, and he was back in control.

Jaw clenched, he scanned the entries again. The code looked pretty basic, so he figured it would take no more than an hour for him to crack it. Which meant the Bureau's computer whizzes would take it apart in five minutes and hand Stone the evidence needed for a conviction. What if that evidence implicated Roseanne? Or himself? After all, his name was in the book.

"Find anything?" Roseanne asked.

MacAlister shook his head to clear it and snapped the book shut. "It's in code."

"Oh." Roseanne brightened instantly. "Could we decode it and see if there is anything in it about me?"

"I don't know. It could take a while." He'd stake his life that Roseanne hadn't had any part in killing Deets, and he couldn't bear to see her destroyed by whatever was in this book.

"Couldn't we at least try? The book is all I have to go on," she said, her voice small, weary, her eyes moist.

Hell. How could he say no? If need be, he could always lie to her about what he'd found and burn the book to keep Stone or anyone else from reading it. "Sure. We'll figure something out." MacAlister leaned across the console to cup her chin in his hand. "Just don't go to pieces on me now, brave lady."

Roseanne sniffed. "I don't feel very brave."

"You've been unbelievable," he said and meant it. "If this had happened to me, I'd be a basket case." His mouth closed over hers in a soft, healing kiss that gave more than it took. "It tears me apart to see you upset," he whispered against her mouth, "especially when I can't do a damn thing to help you."

"But you are helping me." The warmth of his touch seeped outward, chasing away some of the cold despair gripping her. "Oh, MacAlister, please don't leave me."

"Hey. You're stuck with me for a long time," he promised. "Let's go home." Later, he'd think of some reason to stall

Stone . . . at least until he'd decoded the book and figured out whose safety Deets's information compromised.

"I thought the name Deets sounded familiar, but I was too confused to make the connection earlier. MacAlister, didn't you say your partner's name was Lucien Deets?" Roseanne asked thoughtfully as he pulled out of the parking lot.

"Er, yeah," he said, feeling another lie coming on. Looking around for a way to avoid it, he saw a windowless black van leap away from the curb and fall in behind the Porsche.

He stiffened instantly. Hands tightening on the wheel, he squinted into the rearview mirror, trying to tell whether the driver was one of Stone's men. Stone hadn't said anything about sending backup, but then, Stone had been close-mouthed about this whole case.

Roseanne asked him something, but he tuned her out, his attention evenly divided between the traffic and the van. When the van stuck with them through Danbury's downtown section and followed them into a prosperous residential area, his vague uneasiness escalated to an icy shaft of dread.

"MacAlister," she said, her impatience breaking through his concentration. "Didn't you say your partner's name was Deets?"

He groaned silently. "Honey, I don't have time to talk right now. I think we're being followed." She started to turn in her seat, but he placed a restraining hand on her arm. "Hang on" was all he said before jerking the wheel left, sending the Porsche skidding around the corner onto a side street and slamming her against the door.

"MacAlister—what is going on?"

"Tighten your seat belt. This is likely to get rough." Behind them, tires squealed.

Despite his warning, Roseanne glanced over her shoulder at the dark shape careening around the corner. The van looked big, mean and determined. She swallowed. "M-maybe they just happen to be going the same way we are."

"Not a chance in hell." MacAlister was back to looking cold and ruthless, and the scenery was flying by faster and faster.

Roseanne buried her fingers in the soft leather side of the seat as the Porsche rocketed over the bumpy, curvy road. "I could use your car phone to call the police."

"No time." MacAlister's eyes were on the mirrors. The Porsche's engine barely complained as they pulled up a steep hill and away from the van.

Roseanne started to relax, but their pursuers gained speed on the downside. When the dark shape swooped alongside them, she recognized the face in the open window of the sprinting vehicle. "MacAlister. It's the man who chased me outside the bank in New York. H-he's got a gun."

"Figures," MacAlister spat as he downshifted. "I asked Stone to drop a set of mug books by the house. Tonight you'll have to try to put a name with that face."

"If we make it home," Roseanne muttered as the car whipped around the next bend in a controlled skid that took them into the left lane and forced the van to back off.

"Hah. Had a little trouble with that last curve, didn't you, bub?" But MacAlister's triumph was short-lived. In minutes the van pulled up beside them. "Damn. What kind of an engine do they have in that thing?"

There was a violent jolt and the loud crunch of metal striking metal as the van slammed the side of the car, followed swiftly by the thud of a bullet.

Roseanne screamed and grabbed the dash for support.

MacAlister floored the accelerator, swearing profusely over the sharp squeal of tires as the Porsche shot away like greased lightning. "Hang on . . . we'll lose them here." He negotiated a breathtaking series of hairpin turns with a steady hand and surprising calm.

At the base of the last turn, the road forked, offering a quick choice between Redding and Branchville. Dead ahead of them stood an enormous oak tree. In a split second Roseanne realized that they were traveling too fast for MacAlister to choose either town.

They were going to hit the tree.

Mouthing a prayer, Roseanne braced for the crash. In that instant, the Porsche plunged to the right, and her shoulder was rammed against the door. The sound of shrieking tires and the smell of burning rubber filled the cool country air as they fish-tailed down the narrow asphalt road towards Redding.

Behind them, she heard the heart-stopping squeal of tires as the van's brakes were frantically applied. The sound ended in a horrible, grinding crunch. Glancing back, Roseanne saw that the van's nose was wrapped around the tree. Smoke boiled from under the hood.

MacAlister brought the Porsche to a smooth stop and turned in his seat to survey the scene. "Ha," he exclaimed with obvious satisfaction. He didn't seem the least bit affected by their close brush with death, while her own heart was still jumping like an air hammer.

"Sh-shouldn't we check on them?"

"And give them the chance to take a shot at us if they're still in one piece?"

Roseanne swallowed. "Of course." She turned to face front, her arms wrapped around her trembling body.

"Take it easy," he said gently.

"I know it's silly... now that things are all over..."

MacAlister gave her a reassuring smile to let her think he also believed things were all over. "Let's get out of here before someone comes along."

"But we didn't do anything."

"I don't feel like answering any questions." *Not yours. And especially not the police's.* He checked the mirrors, then hustled his poor battered Porsche away from the crash scene. "What I feel like is a nice stiff drink to settle my nerves before I see how much damage that maniac did to my car," he said, mostly to divert the thoughts he knew were brewing in Roseanne's sharp mind.

She sighed raggedly. "I don't know how you learned to drive like that. But I'm grateful you did."

MacAlister reached over and gently squeezed the knot of white fingers that lay in her lap. "You were terrific. I think you only screamed once. Must be some kind of record." He uncoiled her left hand, laced his fingers through hers. "Try to relax. Let the adrenaline your body's been pumping fade away. You'll feel less jumpy."

"Thank you. For everything," she murmured before she snuggled into the curve of the bucket seat.

Yeah, I'm a real prince. MacAlister let her keep his hand until he needed to shift again. By then the tension had eased from her body. In the weary silence, he allowed his mind to search through the problems and possibilities. He didn't like the conclusions he came up with. *There had to be a leak in Stone's office.*

"I can't wait to get home," Roseanne said presently.

MacAlister shifted in his seat. "I don't think we'll go back to the house for a couple of days."

His tone warned her that this wasn't an idle suggestion, and she began to shake again. "Why? All of our things are at the house."

"Our *friends* in the van may have followed us from there to the bank," he replied, his eyes on the road. He knew they hadn't; no one had followed them this morning. The men had been waiting for them at the bank because, much as he hated to admit it, someone on Stone's end had told them he and Roseanne would be there this morning. Which meant, among other very nasty things, that the safehouse wasn't safe any longer.

Roseanne gnawed her lip. "But surely they were hurt too badly in the accident to..."

"For all we know, they're alive and able to track us. Lie back and get some sleep if you can," MacAlister added, mindful of the shadows under Roseanne's eyes. "I'll drive for a while, then get us a rental car and a hotel room."

"I'm sorry, MacAlister," Roseanne whispered. "If it weren't for me, you wouldn't be in this mess."

"Don't blame yourself, honey. I sure don't." Shame thinned his mouth into a grim line.

Chapter 6

Late in the afternoon, MacAlister spotted the sprawling white clapboard inn on one of Connecticut's windy back roads. Set well back among the trees, it looked like a peaceful haven. The desk clerk told him a large furniture company owned the place. Obviously, they were using the inn to showcase their wares. The two-room suite was crammed with chairs, lamps and tables. And in the bedroom, a giant four-poster bed gave him ideas he couldn't quite shake. Wasn't sure he wanted to.

Queen Anne furniture wasn't his thing, but women usually went for it. He'd hoped the tranquil prints and cozy wing chairs would counteract the day's violence. But Roseanne wasn't soothed; she was angry and suspicious as hell. It was his own damned fault for having arrogantly assumed he could prevent her from connecting Lucien's last name and her own.

She had, of course, and when he wouldn't explain things to her, she got absolutely furious. For over an hour, they didn't speak.

Cautiously shifting on the couch, he tried to tell if she was asleep or watching the situation comedy on the TV.

Now perched on the edge of the chair like a rocket about to launch, Roseanne caught his eye the moment he moved. "Have you decided to answer my questions?"

Damn. He was fast discovering his gentle Rose could be one stubborn lady. "I asked you to trust me on this...."

"I do...I did," she insisted. "But I want to know what's going on. Your name was on that book in my bank box. And if I'm Roseanne Deets, then I must be related to your dead partner, Lucien Deets. What aren't you telling me?" Accusation glittered in her green eyes. He might discount the anger, but the layers of emotion beneath it sliced him: Pain. Bewilderment. Fear.

MacAlister crossed the room before he thought twice about it. Hunkering down beside her, he gently sheltered her hands between his palms. "I've never seen that book before...can't explain how it got in the bank box," he said reasonably. "You're tying yourself in knots over this, honey, and there's no need. I'll take care of everything."

"You've decoded the book and you won't tell me what's in it. You have no right to keep things from me." She suddenly reared to her feet.

MacAlister rose with her, caught her around the waist before she could run and pulled her close. "Last night you gave me the right to decide what's best for you."

"No," she cried, too appalled to struggle.

"Yes," he insisted, gently but firmly holding her against the unyielding planes of his body. It was an unsubtle reminder of the intimacy she'd granted him. "You asked for my help. I agreed. I take my promises seriously."

"You know something...."

"I know you're tired...strung out." With one competent hand, he kneaded the tenseness from her shoulders; with the other, he pressed light circles into the small of her back, soothing and at the same time sensuous.

Roseanne shivered, desire colliding with reason. "Stop that," she whispered.

"I couldn't...even if you really wanted me to," he said huskily. "You feel so good." His arms tightened around her. "I can't explain it, even to myself. Maybe it's because you're so small and incredibly soft and you feel everything so deeply. I just know I would do anything to protect you.''

His speech moved her to tears, but not compliance, not yet, anyway. Though she felt herself slipping closer with every word, every touch, she resisted. ''There are things I have to know....''

''For a soft woman, you can be hardheaded,'' he murmured.

''Tell me,'' Roseanne demanded, her clenched fists trapped between them, her body stiff, her eyes growing wilder with rising desperation.

MacAlister sighed, disgusted with himself for letting things get out of hand. ''Lucien Deets had a wife....''

''Roseanne...?'' she whispered hoarsely. At his curt nod, she said, ''But I can't be her.''

MacAlister swallowed. ''You look like her pictures, but I never met the lady.''

''I can't be married....'' She looked trapped, terrified. He'd seen that look before in the faces of people pushed to their limit. ''It's impossible...at the clinic they said...''

''Let it rest, honey. You aren't in this alone.'' He ran his hands up her stiff back. ''I'm going to sort this out.''

''There's more, isn't there?'' she gasped, her fingers clutching at his shirt. ''Tell me....'' Her eyes locked on his, begging for answers, demanding the truth.

MacAlister exhaled a curse. ''You were in the house the night Lucien was killed.'' He hurt, felt the shock and pain rippling through her as though they were his own.

''Oh, God...I...you think I killed him....''

''No.'' He wrapped both arms around her, held on tight, aching for her, aching to protect her.

Roseanne tasted panic and fear, her blood ran cold with both, her breath came in desperate gasps. Dimly, she realized that if it hadn't been for MacAlister's embrace, she would have collapsed. If it hadn't been for the soft, sane words he whispered into her ear, she would have gone mad. Slowly, reason drew her back from the edge. Slowly, the hysteria faded, and the shuddering with it.

"Rose?" MacAlister murmured. He eased his grip enough to see her face was colorless, her eyes dark, haunted. "I'm putting you to bed, honey."

"I...I didn't do it...." Her voice cracked.

"I know you didn't, and I'm going to prove it." MacAlister swung her up and carried her into the bedroom, grateful that even though she still looked dazed, at least she wasn't fighting him on this. He stripped her of the blue warm-up suit he'd purchased earlier, left on the silky scraps of underwear that had made her blush when he'd picked them out, and bundled her under the covers.

"I can't have been his wife...." Roseanne protested.

"Close your eyes." MacAlister sat beside her on the bed, his wide hand stroking her head as he might a sick child's. "We'll talk it out in the morning."

Roseanne wanted to talk now, but she wasn't strong enough to fight him and the turmoil going on inside her mind. Though she wanted to stay awake and think things through, the emotional roller coaster she'd been on all day had drained her. Her eyelids were so heavy. His touch so soothing...so comforting...

MacAlister glanced down at Roseanne, her face serene in sleep, wiped clean of pain and fear, framed by a cloud of silky hair. She looked so beautiful, so innocent lying there. What might things have been like between them if they'd met under ordinary circumstances? he wondered. Would they have dated? Maybe lived together?

No. Take away the cloud of danger and suspicion hanging over them, and you'd still have two people from two very different worlds. A woman like her would expect things he couldn't give, like love and commitment.

Mouthing a curse, MacAlister turned away. He closed the door separating the sitting room from the bedroom and went to the phone.

"Stone. It's MacAlister," he said when the familiar gritty voice answered.

"Where the hell are you?" Stone demanded. "You were supposed to check in hours ago. The guys I sent to back you up

at the bank had a flat. By the time they got there, you and the
girl were gone."

"We got into Deets's box...."

"Great. What did you find?"

"Not much. A few thousand in cash...mostly hundreds.
And a man's diamond ring." Did Stone know about the book?
Nerves humming, MacAlister waited for Stone's reaction.

"That's it? Damn...I was so sure we'd find something."

"What kind of something?" MacAlister pressed. "You never
did say exactly what...."

"I can't tell you." Stone's voice crackled with frustration.
"So what else happened? They tell me you haven't been back
to the house."

"Things got a little rough on the way back from the bank,"
MacAlister said, feeling his way even more cautiously now,
partially because Stone was holding out on him, mostly because of what he'd found in Deets's book. "See what you can
find out about an accident on Route 53 north of Redding," he
added. "Black van...probably totalled."

"Who were they?" Stone asked sharply.

"They were the same guys who tried to break into my apartment last night."

Stone swore softly. "Either of you hurt?"

"The Porsche is in for repairs. You'll get the bill for my left
door, rear quarter panel and a new paint job."

"I take it you two are okay. When are you coming in?"

Not until I get some answers, MacAlister thought grimly.
He'd decoded most of Deets's book while Roseanne was in the
shower...enough to know the entries contained the addresses
of Golden Circle Import/Export Company warehouses, quan-
tities and dates...shipping dates, he'd assumed. The dates
stretched back a year and had been confined to the East Coast
until six months ago, when they had shifted to San Francisco.
One shipment every other week. Deets had definitely been up
to something.

"Why can't you tell me what Deets was involved in?"
MacAlister asked in a carefully controlled voice.

"I told you it was classified," Stone growled. "I'd like to see the stuff from the box. I can't believe Deets was killed for a few thousand bucks and a ring. Blows my theory."

What theory? And how do you think I fit into it? MacAlister frowned down at his bare toes curled into the thick beige carpeting. Damn. He'd known Stone for ten years, trusted him instinctively from their first meeting, and the big man had never let him down. But now something was wrong.

MacAlister felt it in his bones, heard it in the dark current beneath Stone's words. This case was going bad, fast, and somehow he had to keep Roseanne and himself from getting sucked down with it.

"Well?" Stone sounded impatient.

MacAlister stalled for time. "I figure the money and the ring are hers...unless you have enough on her to arrest her. And as for coming in...I think we'll wait until things die down. A few days should give you enough time to plug the leak in your office." Providing Stone wasn't the leak.

"Leak? What the hell are you talking about?"

"Those guys in the van didn't follow me to the bank ... but they were waiting for us outside," MacAlister said tightly. "Which means they knew where I was going. And you were the only one *I* told."

"Only eight people at this end even know about the case," Stone protested. "People I trust."

"Either your trust is misplaced, or your phone is bugged. I'm not taking any chances. We'll stay put."

Stone swore under his breath, then sighed. "Okay. But leave me a number where I can reach you, just in case...."

"My reflexes may be slower, Stone, but my mind is still sharp," MacAlister snapped. "I'll be in touch."

"MacAlister..."

MacAlister slid the receiver back into the cradle and stared off into space, plotting his next move. He'd wait a couple of hours, then slip back to the safehouse and get the mug books. If Roseanne could ID the guy in the van, it might give him a starting point.

Meantime ... He drew the black book from his hip pocket and slumped down on the couch. Tomorrow he'd go down to the Manhattan office of the Golden Circle and look through the manifests. Maybe he could find a pattern, common points of origin and destinations for shipments made on the dates noted in Deets's book.

Given Roseanne's stubbornness, she'd probably protest being left behind, but it wasn't negotiable. He'd buy her a book to keep her occupied after she'd finished with the mug files.

MacAlister frowned. It felt strange having someone to worry about . . . unfamiliar. For years he'd steered clear of things like that. Lily hadn't needed looking after. Born in Saigon, she'd grown up tougher than most agents he knew, but in the end, her reflexes hadn't saved her.

His daughter had Lily's aunt and uncle to look after her, and MacAlister preferred that arrangement, too. He didn't want Amber counting on him, didn't want her to be disappointed when her father wasn't there for her, as his own father hadn't been there for him.

MacAlister dragged a hand through his hair and shut down his dark thoughts. Jamming the book back into his pocket, he opened the bedroom door to check on Roseanne. She was still sleeping soundly. Backing out of the room, he left the door open so that if she woke up, it wouldn't be to darkness. Then he went out to pick up the mug books.

Just about that same time, a call went out to Rousseau.

"Something has gone wrong," Rousseau said as soon as he recognized the caller. "My men haven't reported in."

"MacAlister took them out of the picture," the agent said. He was using his car phone and could speak more freely.

"And the merchandise?"

"MacAlister has it."

The Frenchman swore. "Where is he?"

"I don't know. But he said the only things he found in the box were money and jewelry."

"Impossible," Rousseau hissed. "Roseanne herself assured me Deets's book was in there."

A woman who would betray her husband was not a reliable source, the agent thought. But knowing how obsessed Rousseau was with a woman when the affair was fresh, he kept quiet. Roseanne wouldn't be around for very long in any case. Rousseau's women never were. "MacAlister wouldn't hold out on the Bureau."

"He would if he had learned I was involved in this," Rousseau pointed out. "He and I are old enemies."

"Christ, I know that. I was in Cairo five years ago when it started. But Deets and I were the only ones who knew you're part of this. Deets is dead, and I sure as hell haven't told—"

"No one is accusing you," Rousseau snapped. "And I do not really care why our friend MacAlister has chosen to keep the book. I want you to get it for me . . . immediately."

"I'm doing my best, but the situation is delicate," the agent argued. "With the search for Crenshaw's replacement going on, I have a lot of people looking over my shoulder."

"Perhaps if I explain the seriousness of the situation, you can persuade yourself to try harder," Rousseau said with soft savagery. "You have heard of the Iceman?"

"Deets's supplier?"

"Indeed. The mystery man who manufacturers the ice. Deets stubbornly refused to divulge his name to me, nor does the Iceman know mine. I was content to let Deets keep his little secrets . . . until he became greedy," Rousseau said silkily. "He thought himself untouchable, but when Roseanne confided to me that Deets had boasted about this little black book of his and told her the Iceman's name was in it . . ."

"Deets became expendable."

"Exactly. MacAlister has delayed my getting the book. This must be corrected before our window of opportunity closes."

The agent understood the urgency he heard in Rousseau's voice. The designer drug trade was volatile. A seller had to strike quickly, making as large a profit as possible before his rivals could duplicate his formula and flood the market with goods, driving down the price.

"There is only enough product in the pipeline for one more shipment—San Francisco, at week's end," Rousseau added.

"And if you don't get more stuff by then, you'll have nothing for your dealers to sell."

"This must not happen. Disgruntled dealers find other sources. As I can hardly seek the Iceman by taking out a per-

sonal advertisement in one of your newspapers, it is impera-
tive I have the book. You will get it for me.'' Rousseau's voice
turned silky again. ''If you manage to eliminate MacAlister in
the process . . .''

''No. I couldn't do it.''

''If you don't, I will make public those documents and pho-
tographs I have,'' Rousseau continued smoothly.

The agent swallowed. Hell, he wanted to draw the line at
killing an old friend, but knew he couldn't afford to. An investigation would flush his aspirations, and twenty years of service, down the tubes. ''I can't afford to be linked to his death,
either.''

''But that is easy. MacAlister still has many contacts, does he
not? I would imagine you know who they are and could arrange to lay a trap for our friend.''

Roseanne came awake with a start, uncertain what had
jerked her from a restless sleep. Senses alert for the slightest
sound, she sat up. The room was dark except for a narrow
wedge of light filtering in from the partially open door.
Through it, she heard a distinct click from the other room. At
the subtle whoosh of a door opening, she panicked, instinctively diving off the bed and onto the floor.

Sobbing silently, she clawed her way under the bed, trying to
squeeze into a space nearly too narrow for dust. The rough
carpet scraped her breasts and belly, the prickly underside of
the mattress scuffed her back. Over the pounding of her heart,
she thought she heard footsteps.

Where was MacAlister? Through a veil of chenille spread,
she saw the light grow stronger, knew someone had opened the
door and come into the room. Panic replaced fear.

''Roseanne,'' hissed a wonderfully familiar voice.

''MacAlister?'' Roseanne cracked her head on a wooden slat
as she raised her head.

''Where the hell are you?''

''U-under the bed.''

''What?'' Something heavy crashed to the floor, then the
spread was jerked aside, replaced by MacAlister's flushed face
peering at her sideways. ''Jesus Christ . . . this is a hell of a time

to play hide and seek,'' he snapped, reaching for her hands. "You scared ten years off my—''

"Ouch," she cried as the top of her head struck the bed frame. "Wait..."

"Of all the stupid—"

"It wasn't stupid. I heard someone come in, and I hid."

"That was me. Duck your head."

"Okay." He pulled, but something else snagged her.

"Wait... I'm caught."

MacAlister bit out an oath, crawled around to the side of the bed and looked under. "Damn, I can't see a thing." He reached under, found the back of her calf and started working his way up her leg.

The feel of his warm hand on her skin sent Roseanne's thoughts spinning backward to last night and the wellspring of sensations he'd coaxed from her body. She had felt so close to him then, closer than she had imagined it was possible to be with another human being. Yet she knew little more about him than she did about herself. "MacAlister... do you have a first name?" she asked.

"You want to know that now?" he grumbled, his hand sliding over her thigh, leaving a trail of fire in its wake.

"It seems like as good a time as any, since you've got your hand on my..." His fingers slid under the elastic edge of her briefs, and Roseanne moaned softly, her legs moving restlessly as the small shock waves he'd set off coalesced in one throbbing pulse point at the juncture of her thighs. The situation—being intimately caressed by the man she was half in love with, yet unable to respond fully or touch him—was strangely, incredibly stimulating. If only he'd move his hand down and to the right...

"Stop wiggling," MacAlister growled. "Your damned panties are hooked on a piece of wire, and I can't get them loose."

"Sorry..." she managed, trying not to moan again. Her whole body ached with need now, despite her pressing circumstances. Unfortunately, she wasn't being pressed in any of the right places, she thought, stifling a giggle.

MacAlister heard her and stopped. "Am I hurting you?"

"No. Frankly, I'm . . ." Now, what was the expression? Ah. "I'm feeling very frustrated."

"Me, too. I'll have you out of there in a sec. . . ." His fingers were moving again, coaxing the silk from the wire and a groan from her throat.

"Roseanne?"

"I groaned."

"Ah, honey, I know you're scared. What the hell—I'll buy you another pair tomorrow." He ripped the silk free and tugged her out from under the bed before she could utter another sound.

Still on the floor, he cradled her across his thighs, holding her against his chest and rocking her like a child. "It's all right. There's nothing to be afraid of," he crooned.

"I'm not afraid...not any more. I'm...Lord, I don't know how to say this." Trembling, she buried her face in the curve of his neck. He held her tighter, trying to absorb her fear.

When she raised her head, he saw her eyes were dark and heavy-lidded, but not from fear. "Are you still mad at me?" he asked, trying to understand her strange mood.

"A little, I guess," she replied, thinking back to the argument they'd had that evening. "I need you to help me, not keep more secrets from me. And I couldn't possibly have been married to—"

"We'll work it out," MacAlister said firmly. He wasn't crazy about her having been Deets's wife, either, but that didn't change things. "What you don't need is anything more to worry about. I'll help you all I can, but we'll do it my way."

"Did anyone ever tell you you're stubborn and arrogant?"

"Yeah. All the time." His grin was a pale slash in the dark, quiet room.

She wasn't smiling, and a small tremor racked her. "I—I . . . You said I look like Roseanne Deets, and my signature matched at the bank, but . . . I don't think I could have killed . . ."

"Shh. Don't think about that now," MacAlister said gruffly, shaken by how vividly he felt her pain and confusion. "It'll be all right," he added, more to convince himself, he supposed.

She drew in a ragged breath. "Will you stay with me?" she asked in a small voice.

"Until I know you're going to be okay," he promised.

"I mean now." She snuggled closer, one arm reaching around his neck. Her breasts pressed against his chest, and through his shirt he felt her nipples harden.

Desire ripped through MacAlister, making him achingly aware of her warm body sprawled across his lap, naked but for the two scraps of silk that begged to be removed. *Easy, she's scared and looking for comfort,* he told himself. "Let me help you back into bed, then I'll sit with you until you fall—"

"No." Her arm tightened around his neck; her gaze met his evenly. "I want you to hold me . . . like you did last night."

MacAlister swallowed hard. *Hell.* It was late. His resistance to her was low, his hunger for her running fever-hot. "I don't think that's such a good idea."

"MacAlister . . ." She stopped, smiled slowly. "I can't keep calling you that . . . especially after last night. What is your first name?"

The siren song in her voice had him trembling. "Gates . . ."

"Hold me, Gates," she whispered against his mouth. Her fingers framed his face; her lips parted beneath his. "I need you to hold me. I need to feel close to you . . . like I did last night. I need that so much. . . ."

He surrendered without a whimper, even knowing where this was leading and that he'd probably hate himself in the morning.

Magic. Their first kisses had been heaven; this one was magic. Roseanne clung to his muscled shoulders as the quivers spread from their open, eager mouths and raced through the rest of her body like wildfire. The kiss deepened; the intimacy built until she was breathless. Dizzy with anticipation.

MacAlister raised his head, groaning with the effort it took to release her lips. "We shouldn't be doing this. . . ."

"Why?" Even in the dim light, he could see the hurt on her face. "Is it because you don't believe me? Do you think I might have . . ." She shuddered, unable to say the rest of the words.

"No," MacAlister said so sharply she jumped. He drew in a slow, careful breath, wanting to tell her the truth, but unable to stand the thought of the trust in her eyes turning to revulsion when she found out who he was. "You may not think so, honey, but you're a little too strung out right now to know what's best for you...."

"You're what I need," she insisted, her voice low and urgent. "Don't you want me?"

His arms tightened around her. "I'm half out of my mind with wanting you," he said grittily. "But..." Yesterday, the day before, he might have taken what she so willingly offered. Now... He scanned her upturned face, pale and fragile, in the muted light, her eyes impossibly dark.

Her beauty had drawn him originally, still did, but now he saw so much more when he looked at her. Sweetness, gentleness, strength and passion. Passion slowly awakening. And innocence. A fresh, beguiling innocence that moved him almost beyond reason.

"Please, stay with me. I'm frightened and I need you. I...I couldn't stand it if you turned me away."

"Rose," MacAlister breathed, fighting for control. Maybe if he hadn't touched her last night, maybe if he didn't remember the tiny sounds she'd made when she'd surrendered to her pleasure, maybe if she hadn't chosen that moment to draw his head back down, he would have won.

Her lips were sweet, hot, opening under his like the petals of an exotic flower, drowning his senses in a flavor, scent and texture uniquely her own, luring him to savor and explore.

MacAlister surrendered with a deep, ragged groan, his mouth devouring hers from a new angle as he lifted her onto the bed and stripped off his clothes. He felt the change in her as he lay down beside her. Felt the heat and wildness building inside her as she cried his name, running her hands over his neck, his shoulders, his chest.

He'd expected softness and sweetness, not passion and fire. "God, you're beautiful...so beautiful." She was elemental, she was woman, she was a soaring, dizzying flight into every fantasy he'd ever had, and he told her so with sultry touches and dark, erotic whispers.

"Yes...oh, yes. Touch me...teach me." Roseanne quivered as he pushed aside the ivory silk covering her breasts, arched off the bed as he took the hardening peaks into his mouth, first one, then the other. The sensation was so intense, she cried out, teetering on the brink of delirium.

His fingers drifted down, slid under the remaining triangle of silk that guarded her femininity. The delicate muscles deep inside her clenched in anticipation as he lightly teased and tormented her layered softness. Of their own accord, her legs parted and her hips lifted in counterpoint to the rhythm he set, her body tense, straining as she sought to reach the elusive peak. She called his name, shuddering as the crest caught her, swept her up on a wave of pleasure.

Even as she spiraled down, she felt MacAlister's hands on her hips, felt the remnants of her panties snap and the roughness of his legs on the insides of her thighs as he parted them. His weight pinned her to the bed; but she didn't feel trapped, she felt safe, cherished.

"Gates," she whispered in awe.

"Here, baby. Here where I belong." He grasped her hips and plunged into her waiting warmth.

Pain.

It exploded through Roseanne when she'd least expected it. Stunned, she gasped and dug her nails into MacAlister's skin.

"Rose?" Breathing hard, MacAlister stared down into her pain-filled eyes, his mind refusing to accept what his body told him. She'd been a virgin. Impossible.... But now sure wasn't the time to sort it out. "I'm sorry, honey," he said thickly. "I—I— Are you okay?"

Roseanne nodded. The pain was fading, replaced by a sense of being stretched, invaded. She gazed up at the face of the man she loved, taut with the strain of control, traced by lines of concern. "I—I just didn't expect it to hurt...." she murmured with a faint smile.

"Hell. Neither did I." He didn't return her smile. Sighing raggedly, he brushed his mouth across hers. "I'm sorry...."

Roseanne felt his sigh all the way to her soul. "I-it hurts less now." Deliberately, she relaxed the muscles that were bunching and clenching to repel him.

"That's it, honey. Try to relax, and I'll make it up to you. I'll make it good for you again."

"Just hold me." *Just love me.* Roseanne encircled his neck with her arms.

"Rose. Sweetheart." Her acceptance went to his head like strong wine. He wooed her with sensitive caresses and hot kisses. His hands moved between their bodies, stroking the pleasure points his mouth couldn't reach. She responded with eager abandon.

This was the way it was supposed to be, Roseanne thought. Both of them giving, both of them taking until it was impossible to tell where one left off and the other began. "Oh, Gates. I feel like you're part of me," she whispered. "I love you." She wrapped herself around him.

When she arched up to meet him, MacAlister thought he would go mad. Gathering her close, he led them deeper, faster, and instead of surrender found strength, instead of leading found himself following her lead. Then the floodgates burst within her, sending wave after wave of ecstasy shuddering through her body and into his.

He caught her hips and buried himself in the heart of the explosions, groaning as her delicate muscles convulsed around him. Crying her name, he reached the crest of his own shattering release.

Chapter 7

The gray half-light of early morning was filtering through the curtains when Roseanne opened her eyes. It took a moment for her to realize where she was and what was different about today.

She was not alone.

Gates stood beside the bed, zipping up his jeans. Covertly, her gaze swept up his lean hips and muscular torso to his rugged face and arrogantly set jaw. She didn't delude herself that he was an inherently gentle man. The rough life he'd alluded to had shaped him along harsher lines, tempered him until any softness he might have had had become hard as steel. But he could be gentle . . . for her. She'd felt it in his touch, seen it in his eyes when he'd made love to her. Loving him, she wanted to bring those tender emotions back into his life.

As though sensing her thoughts, Gates glanced over, his amber eyes locked with hers, gentled for a heartbeat, then slid away. "Sorry I woke you."

"It's all right." *No it wasn't. Something was wrong.*

He exhaled harshly and raked one hand through his disordered hair. "See if you can go back to sleep.... You, ah, didn't get much last night."

Roseanne's face grew warm, the pleasure her memories brought dulled by his refusal to meet her eyes. "I don't regret it . . . but you seem to."

He was beside her before her aching whisper died away. "I don't. . . . God knows I should, but. . ." The mattress dipped as he sat down, and all her senses came alive.

Her skin tingled where the calluses on his palm creased her cheek as he lifted a wayward strand of hair and tucked it behind her ear. It was a man's hand, warm, solid, wonderfully familiar. Hard to believe that only four days ago that hand had felt rough clamped across her mouth.

"There's no reason for you to feel guilty because I was. . ." She swallowed the word. "I wanted it to happen. I wanted it to be you." She turned her head to nuzzle his hand where it now rested on the pillow.

He frowned. "How did you know you were a virgin?"

"I told you the doctors at the clinic were thorough. And I couldn't resist reading my chart."

"You should have said something . . . before. I never would have . . ." He made a disgusted sound in his throat.

Roseanne smiled, touched by his gallantry. "I wish you wouldn't say that. It was wonderful. I'm glad I lost my memory *before* I met you instead of after, because I'll never feel more special than I did last night."

MacAlister growled something fierce under his breath and leapt up, looking ready to chew nails.

"You don't feel the same," Roseanne said shakily. "It . . . wasn't special for you?"

"Ah, hell," he groaned. "You know better than that." Bowing his head, he massaged the back of his neck with one hand, then sighed deeply. "Let's just say things have gotten pretty complicated. And until I can sort them out. . ." He sighed again. "Look, my lousy mood doesn't have anything to do with what happened between us. I've got a few calls to make." He started for the door. "If you can't sleep, why don't you get started on those mug books I picked up last night?"

Roseanne frowned at the pile of books he'd dropped on the floor beside the bed. "I really don't want to."

"The sooner you identify the guy, the sooner we can find out who's behind this." His expression implacable, MacAlister set the books on the bed and went out into the sitting room, closing the door behind him.

Roseanne reluctantly opened the first one. Dark, soulless eyes stared back at her from a heavily bearded face. A shiver of apprehension arrowed down her back. The man looked capable of... anything. She moved on quickly, turning the pages, scanning the photos. Black man. White man. Thin man. Fat man. She was just wondering how long this would take, when she saw *him*.

The heavyset blond man seemed poised to leap out and grab her. He was not the man from the bank, but she had run from him before. In her nightmare.

And before that....

The night was cold and wet and... dangerous. But not as dangerous as what she had left behind.

She remembered thinking that, remembered the night and the fog and the man, chasing her....

Panic moved through her, and a scream rose in her throat. She tried to choke it back, but it bubbled out as an agonized moan. Low and raw. With it came the memories....

Blood. So much blood. Lucien sprawled in the crimson river that pumped from his chest. A man with a gun bent over him. The big, heavyset blond man. He saw her... came after her. They ran through the fog. A shot. Pain. Darkness.

Heart pounding wildly, she sagged back against the pillow.

She knew who she was.

Not Roseanne. Rebecca.

Rebecca Elizabeth Danforth. Age twenty-seven. Only child of Stephen and Elizabeth. Orphaned at twelve. Raised by her Aunt Margaret and Uncle Charles, Roseanne's parents. Her fingers closed around the diamond necklace they'd given her for her twelfth birthday.

She lived by herself now, in the house that had been her parents' first home. The house she was remodeling when she wasn't at Le Petit Gourmet, her bakery. And...

And she had to tell Gates....

Quickly, Rebecca slipped out of bed, pulling the thin bed-spread around her to cover her nakedness.

Out in the sitting room, MacAlister felt his temper slip the leash. "Never mind how I found out she isn't Roseanne Deets," he was snarling into the telephone receiver. "I know she isn't. And you knew it when you asked me to follow her."

Stone sighed, not bothering to deny the charge.

"Who is she?" MacAlister demanded.

"Rebecca Danforth," he said, reluctantly. "Roseanne's cousin. They look enough alike to be twins, and..."

"So you asked her to play a role?" MacAlister's eyes narrowed to angry slits. *She'd taken him in.*

"No, I didn't," Stone shot back. "There was an accident.... Rebecca claimed she had lost her memory, but she was there the night Deets was killed, and she had the key to his safe-deposit box, so..."

MacAlister's feelings for her veered wildly from enraged to protective. "You mean you let an amnesia victim out of the hospital? Exposed her to—"

"That's what I needed you for, MacAlister, to guard the girl and get the stuff out of the bank."

"The hell you did," MacAlister lashed back. "You've got a dozen men on your roster. You roped me into this by playing on my sympathies for both Sabine and Deets. You let me think that unless we got into that safe-deposit box, Deets's murderer would go free like Sabine's did. What I want to know, dammit, is why?"

"It was necessary." There was an edge on Stone's voice that hadn't been there before. "I think you and the Danforth girl had better come down to the office."

"Right," MacAlister snarled back. "As soon as you find out which one of your people is being paid by the other side." He needed time to find out who "the other side" was and what Deets had been involved in that had gotten him killed and attracted the interest of the Bureau.

"I'm working on it," Stone said tightly.

"Well, I'm not coming in until you do." MacAlister was hot and getting hotter. "In case I haven't gotten through to you...these guys are playing for keeps. This whole damn setup stinks, Stone. As of right now, I'm off this assignment."

Assignment? What did he mean? One hand still clutching the handle of the partially opened door, Rebecca stared at Gates. Little of his conversation had made sense, but the implications of the word "assignment" made her feel queasy.

He stood with his back to her, naked but for the dark jeans, his head hunched forward, the muscles of his shoulders bunched with a tension that was nearly palpable.

"I agreed to get you the stuff from Deets's box, but you haven't been straight with me. As of now, Rebecca and I are out of this."

Rebecca. He knew her name. She swayed where she stood. *He'd known who she was.* How he must have laughed at her pitiful efforts at self-discovery. Unconsciously, she drew the spread closer, but it didn't alter the bitter coldness settling around her heart.

"God, how could I have been so stupid?" Rebecca moaned. MacAlister had used her to get the things from Roseanne's bank box. It had all been an act. Only an act. Stunned by the shattering force of his betrayal, she stumbled back toward the bed, a wounded creature intent on escape.

MacAlister caught up with her before she reached it.

"Put me down," Rebecca cried, trying to twist away.

"Rose, what's the matter?" He laid her on the bed and followed her down, pinning her milling limbs with his superior strength. A strength she had welcomed last night. Now the feel of his heavy body sickened her.

"Get off me. And stop calling me Rose when you know I'm really Rebecca."

His eyes widened. "You know...?"

"Yes." Rebecca lay still, panting. "Someone I saw in your mug books jogged my memory. How long were *you* going to keep up the pretense?"

"Hey, wait. Stone just told me—"

"Right," she scoffed.

"Rebecca, you have to listen to me." He sounded on the verge of hysteria himself.

"Why are you upset? Afraid you'll lose your...your bounty?" She pushed futilely at his chest.

MacAlister slanted her an impatient glare. "There is no bounty," he grated. "I was doing a favor for a friend..."

"Hah, so you admit you used me...."

"My partner had been killed, and I—"

"Used me to get into the bank box," she taunted. "What did you expect to find?"

MacAlister groaned, a muscle in his cheek twitching as he clenched his jaw. "Information that would lead us...Stone...to Deets's murderer."

Rebecca's chin came up. She was back in control now, her pain buried as deeply as it had been two years ago when Randy had broken their engagement upon learning their marriage would not assure him a vice presidency at Danforth Pharmaceuticals. "Let me up," she said disdainfully. "I have no wish to continue this discussion."

His anger drained away, and pain flickered briefly in his eyes. *Pain? Hah, more likely disappointment as his fat reward money flew out the window.*

With a sigh, and the hint of a caress on her upper arms, he released her and sat up. "You're upset right now.... We'll talk this out when you're...calmer."

Rebecca steeled herself to ignore the tug of the rough gentleness in his voice. "What more do you hope to get from me? You already have what you came after. And then some."

He winced as her barb struck. "I want you to understand why I agreed to help Stone."

"I fail to see why you need my understanding," Rebecca snapped, angry with herself for wanting to soothe away his stricken expression. Their brief, tempestuous relationship had been one-sided, she reminded herself. He hadn't loved her the way she had loved him. To him, she had been an assignment. "The only thing I want is for you to leave me alone."

MacAlister's fists balled at his sides. "I'll take a quick shower. We'll talk it through over breakfast."

Rebecca didn't respond. With a fierce effort of will, she lay perfectly still until she heard the bathroom door close. As though the click of the latch had released her, she buried her face in the pillow that bore his scent, and cried for what might have been.

The tears had barely begun to fall when she realized what a fool she was. Instead of crying, she should be leaving. Thoughts of facing MacAlister over a cup of coffee sent her scrambling off the bed. In minutes, she was dressed in the blue sweatsuit.

A quick search of the sitting room failed to turn up the contents of Roseanne's safe-deposit box. He must have them with him. Well, she'd worry about explaining their loss to Roseanne when she was safely away.

The pulsing beat of the shower ceased.

God. She had only minutes. Grabbing up the few crumpled dollar bills and the keys to the Mazda MacAlister had rented yesterday, Rebecca unbolted the door and ran.

"It was cruel of you not to tell us that you would be away visiting a friend." Margaret Danforth's whine came from the depths of a white velvet wing chair drawn up before the fireplace. Her hand trembled as she raised her cup of "tea" and drained it. "You have no idea how terrified I was when that policeman came here, hinting that Roseanne had something to do with Lucien's death. And there you were off on some undeclared holiday...."

"How inconsiderate of me," Rebecca said through gritted teeth, nerves vibrating with the urge to leave.

Her aunt's puffy, waxen face crumpled like that of a hurt child, and she shakily rang for more tea.

Rebecca felt an instant jolt of remorse. Poor Aunt Margaret was not responsible for MacAlister's betrayal, and although Margaret had never been there when she needed her, Rebecca couldn't turn her back on the frightened woman any more than she had been able to refuse Roseanne's unprecedented call for help ten days ago.

Idiot. If you had said no to Roseanne, you would not have landed in this mess. Rebecca shoved the idea aside. What was done, was done. As she had so often in the years since she had come to live with her aunt and uncle, she set herself to soothe her frail aunt.

"Sorry, Aunt Margaret . . . I've had a trying few days, and I had only just walked in the door when you phoned and asked—" *begged* "—me to come over."

"I'm sorry that you've had a trying day." The older woman's hand shook as she grabbed the bell and rang a second, nearly desperate peal for the maid. "Please stop pacing, dear, you're making my head throb."

"Sorry." Rebecca clenched her fists and turned away from the French doors that opened onto a sweeping stone patio. Her eyes burned with the tears she had yet to shed, and a lump filled her throat. She was frightened and needed someone to confide in, but there had been no one since her mother had died when she was eight. Her father had immersed himself in his job as chief chemist for the pharmaceutical firm he and his brother, Charles, were starting. When she was twelve, her father had been killed in a lab explosion, and she'd come to live with her aunt and uncle. Then she'd found out what loneliness really was.

With great strength of will, Rebecca crossed the austere sitting room and took the chair opposite her aunt's. *Cold*. Despite the fire blazing in the hearth, the house was as cold as ever . . . as cold as the block of ice in her chest where her heart had once beat. "What did the police want?" she asked in a tone designed to soothe.

"It was dreadful," her aunt whimpered, twisting a square of lace-trimmed linen in her smooth white hands. "They've been here twice looking for Roseanne." Her voice dropped to a conspiratorial whisper. "I suspect Lucien was in some kind of trouble. I never could understand what Roseanne saw in him." She shuddered delicately and dabbed at her bleary eyes.

Rebecca sighed. "He was wealthy and powerful," she absently replied. Her shoulders ached with the strain of holding herself together. For an instant, she was tempted to share her problems with her aunt, but one look at the vague, fragile woman reminded Rebecca of the night her fiancé had demanded his ring back. Rebecca had come to her aunt for solace and ended up consoling the woman because one of her prize orchids was fading.

No, Aunt Margaret wasn't strong enough to handle her own problems, much less someone else's. Rebecca closed her eyes for a moment and prayed for strength. The darkness behind her eyelids was soothing, and she longed to stay there, but she had immediate problems to settle before allowing herself that luxury. Opening her eyes, she asked, "Have you seen Roseanne lately? Or heard from her?"

"N-not since she went sailing in the Caribbean a month ago. Though...yes, she called once, looking for you. She was most put out that you weren't here."

Rebecca nodded. At home, she had spared a moment to play back her messages and found several from Roseanne. Her cousin's irritation had turned to anger and, finally, veiled threats. Typically, Roseanne hadn't asked how Rebecca had survived the fix she'd gotten her into, nor had Roseanne left a number where she could be reached.

There was little hope Roseanne had contacted her father, either. For as long as Rebecca could remember, her uncle had disapproved of his daughter...even going so far as to cut her from his will when she'd married Lucien. "The man is filth," Charles had shouted, refusing to relent when Rebecca had tried to plead her cousin's cause.

"Rebecca, dear, it's been too long since you came to visit us, anyway." Aunt Margaret's mild blue eyes glazed over as her train of thought wandered. "You shouldn't lock yourself away in the musty old house.... You'll never find a husband that way. Not that having one guarantees happiness. Charles wasn't so disapproving before we married...."

"I've no interest in a husband," Rebecca said, bracing for an argument, but her aunt's mind had veered off onto another topic.

"I was so pleased that Charles agreed with your decision to leave Danforth Pharmaceuticals. You've no need to work. Not with your father's trust to draw on.... And he was right to be angry when you insisted on moving out of our home.... How will you meet suitable men? You don't do charity work...or attend any social events.... You should join my garden club—there is a nice young man from a good family who is interested in raising orchids...."

"I have a business of my own to run, Aunt. And that keeps me far too busy for gardening," Rebecca said stiffly. In their own way, she supposed her aunt and uncle loved her, but they didn't understand her need for independence. Uncle Charles called her fledgling bakery business a passing fancy. Aunt Margaret claimed her obsession with refurbishing her parents' old house was a substitute for the husband and family she so badly wanted.

Maybe they were right, but after her disastrous experience with Randy, Rebecca had decided a business and a house were more satisfying, and lots easier on the heart, than a man who wanted you for your money, not yourself. After what had happened between her and MacAlister, she was swearing off men for...

Wait a minute, Rebecca thought, something her aunt had said finally sinking in. Roseanne hadn't been away sailing for the whole month. Ten days ago, Roseanne had called from her house in New York and begged Rebecca to help her out of a jam.

"Rebecca," Charles Danforth called from the doorway. "My dear. Where have you been?" A hint of reprimand tangled with the warmth in his voice as he entered.

His wife's eyes lit up, but her avid gaze was for the maid who followed Charles through the double doors carrying a small porcelain pot.

Without breaking stride, Charles correctly interpreted his wife's glance and her mental state. "Take the whiskey back to the kitchen, Anna," he said over his shoulder.

"My tea . . ." Margaret whimpered. Too well bred to countermand her husband in front of a servant, she twisted her hands together as the maid bobbed a curtsy and fled.

Rebecca doubted her aunt had stood up to her husband in thirty years . . . publicly or privately. But then, Charles Danforth's aggressive bearing and aura of power discouraged disagreement of any kind. Briefly, she wondered how her gentle, studious father had fared as his brother's partner. Then her uncle was upon her, and the moment for self-examination had passed. She'd need to be on her toes, or her uncle would divine more of what had happened to her these past few days than she wanted him to.

Smelling faintly of leather and expensive cologne, he towered over her, forcing her to rise to grasp the two hands he extended. Charles Danforth wasn't the sort of man who inspired love, but she respected him. Like her father, he was a workaholic. All her life she had found herself competing with the family-owned business for a measure of a man's time . . . first her father's, then her uncle's.

As her uncle's sharp green eyes appraised her, she was glad she'd taken a moment after her aunt's call to change into a periwinkle-blue cashmere sweater set and coordinated plaid skirt, holdovers from her two unhappy years in the finance department of Danforth Pharmaceuticals.

"We've been quite worried about you, Rebecca," he said formally. The soft, wide palms encasing her hands tightened briefly before letting her go.

"I was visiting a friend." Rebecca toyed with the idea of telling him everything . . . or nearly everything.

"A man?" he demanded so sharply she flinched. His piercing gaze made her feel like some minion in the testing lab whose oversight had drawn the wrath of the FDA down on the company.

God, what would he say if he knew that she'd spent a week in a psychiatric clinic, and the past few days dodging thugs and cavorting with an ex-agent?

Perhaps because her uncle had never been able to control Roseanne, he'd tried to rule Rebecca's life . . . especially when it came to men. He'd never liked the few men who'd shown an interest in her and had been pleased when her engagement ended.

The urge to unburden herself to her uncle withered. "No...I wasn't with a man," she told him. "I was the guest of a woman who owns a small inn and restaurant in . . . Vermont."

Charles frowned. "Still investigating the possibilities of expanding your business, despite my objections, I see," he grumbled. "Margaret," he growled, rounding on his wife so suddenly the timid woman squeaked. "You have been calling all over town for me. You know how I dislike that sort of thing.'' His green eyes had turned glacial. "I have stopped here on my way to the airport to discover what the problem is this time.''

Poor Aunt Margaret blanched. "That...that policeman was here again this morning,'' she moaned.

"What did he want?'' her spouse demanded.

"H-he asked about Roseanne...and about Rebecca, too....'' Margaret blinked. "What in the world could he want with you, Rebecca?''

Oh, Lord. "I—I have no idea.''

"It's that man, Stone,'' her uncle muttered.

"S-Stone?'' Rebecca whispered.

Charles scowled. "Michael Stone. He is with the government . . . Special Bureau. He insists on questioning all the family members about Deets's murder, even though I have already assured him the three of us had had little contact with the man.'' Eyes flashing with the light of battle, he walked to the door. "I will call and remind him of that on my way to the airport.''

So, there really was a Stone and a Bureau, Rebecca thought. MacAlister had told the truth about that part, at least. She didn't know whether to be relieved or not. But she did know she couldn't answer Stone's questions . . . yet.

"Y-you will take care of things?'' Margaret stammered.

"Don't I always?'' he said sharply. "Rebecca,'' he added, his voice and features softening, "please see if you can settle your aunt's nerves. I will be at the research facility in Arizona for the next few days, and I don't want to be bothered by her foolish calls while I'm gone.''

"I can stay a little while,'' Rebecca mumbled, though after ten days' absence, she was anxious to see how things had fared at her bakery without her.

Somehow Rebecca managed to hold herself together and get through a dismal lunch. She even turned a blind eye to the two cups of "tea'' her aunt consumed while she talked about the garden club festival where she would be exhibiting her orchids. After lunch, Rebecca suggested they look at the family photos.

While her aunt commented on the pictures, Rebecca's mind wandered over the past few days, trying to convince herself that it was all a bad dream. But the sensual aches in the secret places of her body were proof enough it had been all too real. And then there were the memories of Lucien's broken body... and the man who had killed him....

"Here's a picture of you and Roseanne," Aunt Margaret said, her voice soft with whiskey and memories.

Rebecca blinked and refocused her eyes from the near past to the distant. The picture had been taken a month after her father's death, capturing two young girls, one gangling and shy, the other beautiful and defiant. Roseanne looked petulant because her domain had been invaded by the small, thin, sad-faced girl standing slightly behind, in her shadow. Always in her shadow.

How was she going to explain to her self-assured, cruelly arrogant cousin that a man had seduced her and stolen the very property that Roseanne had entrusted her to retrieve? Rebecca wondered, her spirits sinking further.

It was early afternoon when Rebecca pulled her car into the tiny lot behind Le Petit Gourmet. During the forty-minute drive, she had convinced herself to forget the past ten days. It was probably unrealistic, but she didn't much care. After ten days of fear, uncertainty and emotional pain, she craved peace, quiet and normalcy. She refused to let any of it, even Mac-Alister's betrayal, shadow the rest of her life. She had plans, and, if anything, she was more determined than ever to get on with them.

"Rebecca!" Her assistant manager, Susan Fielding, practically vaulted the counter getting to her employer. "Where have you been? I've been worried sick."

Rebecca hugged Susan's plump body, fragrant with soap and the reassuringly familiar scent of the bakery. "I told you I would be away...."

"You've been gone ten days," Susan accused, her face flushed, her brown eyes grave. "Without calling once."

"I'm sorry, Suz. There was something I had to do for Roseanne... there wasn't time to call."

Susan nodded, smiling. "I know how that goes. Last year when I went down to Atlanta to baby-sit for my sister's tribe while she had her fifth baby, I didn't have time to turn around, much less make phone calls."

She gave Rebecca a final squeeze and stood back. "It's great to have you back . . . but you look like you've missed out on a little sleep and a few meals." Her chubby hand closed assessingly on Rebecca's waist. "You've lost at least six pounds. Why couldn't it have been me?"

"I wish it could have been anyone but me," Rebecca mumbled, but her caustic remark was drowned out by the phone.

By the time Susan had finished taking down the order, Rebecca had tied on the long white eyelet apron with her name stitched in green script, and regained her composure. "Anything happen while I was gone?"

"Mmm." Susan stuck the order into the folder marked Thanksgiving and picked up another pad. "Business has been brisk . . . we're up to our 'you know whats' in holiday orders already. The classes went well . . . though the kids missed you." She grinned wryly. "I don't have your patience."

"Sorry to leave you in the lurch. I didn't think I'd be gone that long." *That long. A few days that had torn her carefully ordered life to shreds.* It would have to be put back together again piece by piece, but she could do it.

"Oh, you had some calls. A woman called several times. She was angry, but she wouldn't leave her name or number."

Roseanne. Her plans to forget the whole incident went up in smoke.

"And a little while ago a guy called. Deep, sexy voice . . . Didn't leave his name, either."

MacAlister? No, he had what he'd wanted from her. It must have been Stone. She hoped her uncle could keep the agent at bay until after she'd talked to Roseanne.

"Oops, looks like the reprieve is over," Susan observed as the bell over the door tinkled to life and the Mott sisters tottered in arm in arm. "They've been hinting around to have your recipe for pumpkin bread again."

Pasting on a smile, Rebecca came out from behind the counter to greet the two elderly spinsters who'd been her first customers when she'd opened the bakery and cooking school eighteen months ago. By the time she had them seated at one of the dozen round tables in the little café, Gracie, the baker, was waving from the kitchen doorway.

"Do you have a minute?" Gracie called excitedly.

"Excuse me," Rebecca said with a smile for the Motts, grateful for an excuse to duck their request for her famous bread recipe. It wasn't that she feared they'd open a rival bakery, but exclusive culinary creations were all the rage these days. And she planned to use hers as a stepping stone to a full-fledged gourmet restaurant.

The twin bake ovens were going full-blast, and Gracie's two helpers were up to their dimpled elbows in dough. Rebecca smiled and waved as she followed Gracie back to taste the "unbelievably fantastic carmel cheesecake" the woman claimed to have finally perfected.

Rebecca's gaze moved lovingly over the vast, spotless room with its white walls and large windows. The stone floors had been swept clean, and the large glass jars that lined the shelves above the oaken work surfaces were filled with the staples of her trade—flours, sugars, dried fruits, berries and nuts. Her smile broadened. How wonderfully reassuring to find things here unchanged when the rest of her world had been set on its ear.

In the midafternoon, her students started arriving. Their hugs and kisses put a spring in her step that hadn't been there when she'd walked in this morning. Maybe, just maybe she'd survive after all, she thought as she led the six children of upwardly mobile, well-heeled parents into the section of the kitchen known as "the school."

They'd been dropped off by nannies and baby-sitters who were only too happy to be relieved of their charges for a time. It reminded Rebecca of her own childhood. Filled with activities, but devoid of love. The Danforth's cook had been her cooking instructor, and at times, her only friend.

From the moment she'd conceived the idea of opening Le Petit Gourmet, Rebecca had known she was going to hold classes for children. She didn't have any children of her own, might never have any of her own, but because kids were very important to her, she was determined to at least have them in her life.

In fact, once she had gotten over the initial hurt of Randy's defection, Rebecca had realized she hadn't been so much in love with him, but in love with the idea of having a husband and children.

Perched on six high-backed stools arranged around a semi-circular counter that allowed Rebecca to stand in the middle and demonstrate, her children hung on her every word. Ranging in age from six to eight, four girls and two boys, they had one thing in common . . . exuberance.

"Cindy. Mark off six tablespoons on the stick of margarine, and cut it with your knife." The little redhead picked up the table knife as Rebecca turned to the next girl. "Mary. You can measure out one cup of sugar and put it in the bowl. Then pass the canister and cup to George. George, I want you to put in one cup, also." Both children beamed. She let them do everything except cut with sharp knives. No matter that it slowed things down and often resulted in ingredients having to be thrown out. People learned from their mistakes.

Most people, Rebecca thought with a twinge of pain as she recalled her most recent mistake. She obviously hadn't learned that men weren't to be trusted. But it wouldn't happen again. She was determined to improve. She *was* improving. It had been all of twenty minutes since she'd thought of Gates MacAlister.

"Now we'll beat the batter," she told the children, locking the beaters in place with a vicious snap she'd like to have applied to MacAlister's neck.

"Me first," Teddy yelled, grabbing the handle.

"Turn them off now and give Jean a chance," Rebecca said after a minute. Batter flew from the bowl as Teddy lifted the beaters out of the bowl. Suppressing a gasp, she took the mixer in hand. "Now you see why we never bring the beater up like that," she gently remonstrated. Five grave, wide-eyed children nodded. Teddy was busy scooping up the scattered dough and licking off his fingers.

Rebecca was pulling the first tin of muffins from the oven when the skin at the back of her neck tingled. Someone was

watching her. She looked at the six pairs of eyes glued to her
every move and wondered if she was being foolish. Her eyes
warily skipped to the window behind her as she set the pan
down to cool. It was dusk, and she couldn't see anyone in the
gathering gloom, yet the feeling persisted while she and the
children cleaned up.

"Whew. What a day," Rebecca exclaimed when the children had gone. Both hands massaged the small of her back as
she arched her spine.

Susan turned from tallying up the day's receipts and smiled.
"It's so good to have you back."

"It's good to be back," Rebecca said with feeling.

"You'd better get out of here or you'll be late for your home-
remodeling class."

"True...and I've missed the last two weeks as it is." Rebecca glanced from the clock to the glass display cases with
their crumb-littered trays. One lone blueberry muffin and a few
oatmeal cookies were all that remained of the day's offerings.
"But we aren't done...."

"Don't worry about it. Gracie and I will clean up. We're
eating out together tonight, anyway."

Rebecca wavered, feeling guilty as sin about leaving after
she'd been away so much. Even though cleaning up was part of
Susan's responsibility, she often stayed to help, enjoying the
easy after-hours chatter and cozy camaraderie.

"Go on with you," Susan urged. "If you miss something
vital in the wiring demonstration, you're likely to fry yourself
when you try to replace the wires in that old house of yours."

Rebecca chuckled as she slipped off her apron. "We're still
into basic carpentry...very basic. And I'm flunking that, so
your point is well taken. I really do enjoy working with
wood...if only I wasn't such a complete klutz." Susan chuckled, and Rebecca added, "I hope I catch on soon, because I
can't afford to hire a carpenter to undo all the mistakes I've already made on the house."

"But Le Petit Gourmet is turning a nice profit."

Rebecca sighed. "Yes, that's part of the problem. Now is the
time to expand the business, but I can't do that and continue to

remodel the house, even if I do most of the work myself. I guess I just want too much, too fast.''

''Would your Uncle Charles let you dip into your trust?''

''Even if he did believe in investing in fledgling businesses and ramshackle houses, which he doesn't, I'm doing this on my own,'' she said with grim determination. *She utterly refused to take another dime from the business that had been responsible for her father's death.*

Rebecca lost no time in changing into a clean pair of jeans and a sweatshirt she kept in the back bathroom. Waving gaily to her faithful crew, she hurried out into the cold night air, her sweater and skirt folded over her arm.

The wind rattled branches against the side of the building, sending a chill down Rebecca's back. Uneasy, she glanced around to make certain it was only the wind, then quickened her pace, feeling not at all foolish to be running from night sounds and her own imagination. She'd run from much worse only a day ago.

Her fingers trembled as she unlocked the car and jerked the door open. The interior lights didn't go on.

''Damn.'' Rebecca slid inside and felt blindly for the ignition. When the engine growled to life and the dash lights came on with the headlights, she let out a sigh of relief and reached for the gearshift.

Suddenly, a hand snaked around the seat and clamped over her mouth. Before she could make a sound, she was dragged backward, her head pinned against the headrest.

Chapter 8

Rebecca's heart beat wildly against her ribs, visions of the cold-eyed man she'd seen bending over Lucien's bloody body exploding into her mind.

"Slide over into the passenger seat, princess."

MacAlister. Terror fled in an instant flood of outrage. She mumbled a few heated words into his wide, muffling hand. When he didn't remove it, she bit the fingers that imprisoned her.

"Ouch! Heathen woman." Releasing her mouth, he grabbed her under the arms and lifted her bodily over the console.

"Don't you dare—" Her bottom hit the passenger seat with a resounding thump.

Her groan made him chuckle. "Serves you right for biting me," he added.

Rebecca tried to lever herself back into the driver's seat, but MacAlister had shoved the seat forward, blocking her path. While she wrestled with the seat, he calmly opened the door and climbed out. "Stop, dammit..."

"Watch the language, princess." He pushed the seat back, dumped her legs over into her side of the console and slid behind the wheel.

Rebecca scrambled upright, pushing the hair from her eyes. "What the hell do you think you are doing?"

"Rescuing you . . . again." Throwing the car into reverse, he spun out of the parking space.

"I am not going anyplace with you." When he merely shrugged and started to move the lever into drive, she made a grab for the door handle.

"Whoa." He reached out, captured her arm and pulled her back from the door.

"Let me go," she grated, her heart galloping with anger and a dozen other emotions she didn't want to feel.

MacAlister grinned crookedly, charmingly in the dim light from the dash. "Thinking of biting me again?"

"Definitely."

"Mmm. Kinky." Before she guessed what he intended, his hand was on the back of her neck, and his lips were closing over hers.

Rebecca opened her mouth to bite him. She would have, too, if his tongue hadn't slipped in so sweetly and stolen her reason. A languorous haze enveloped her as his kiss worked its magic on her. She couldn't trust him . . . mustn't . . . But she was sinking in a whirlpool of confusion and rapidly building desire. Her hands stopped pushing and tangled in his Windbreaker.

"That's it, Becky. Don't fight me," he whispered against her moist mouth. "Come with me, and I'll keep you safe." His lips brushed over hers to seal the bargain.

His words pierced her languor quicker than a pin deflating a balloon. Sitting back quickly, she studied him in the shadowy car. Why was he here? And why was he acting so . . . so strange, so unlike the angry Gates MacAlister she had left behind this morning? "What are you doing?" she asked again.

"Taking you to San Francisco."

"San Francisco?" She blinked and collected her scattered thoughts enough to ask him, "Why?"

His teasing grin vanished. "Because I have business there, and you'll be safer with me than kicking around here until Stone catches those guys who are looking for you."

Rebecca's eyes narrowed. "What happened? Did you think of some other way to use me?"

"I did not use you," he said tightly.

"Decided you needed a convenient bed warmer on your next business trip?"

"There's nothing convenient about you, Becky."

Her teeth met, grated. "Good. Then leave me here."

For an instant, his expression turned grave. "Can't do that, Becky, honey."

"Oh, yes, you can. And stop calling me Becky."

"Why?"

"M-my father is the only one who called me that."

"Good choice. It suits you better than Rebecca. Buckle your seat belt like a good girl. We have to get going." He shifted into drive as though the matter were settled.

Rebecca grabbed the door handle.

"Don't try it." The icy sting of command replaced his light, bantering tone. "I'll tie you up with my shoelaces and carry you through the airport like a bag of laundry if you force me to."

She hesitated. Did he mean it? "Boots don't have laces."

"Your sensible cotton bra strap then. Or are you wearing one of those expensive little silky numbers now that you know who you are?" he teased.

If he was trying to confuse her with this flip routine, he was doing a fine job of it. Rebecca raised her chin. Maintaining control around MacAlister was very important. "Give me one good reason why I should go with you."

He sighed. "Damn, you're stubborn. Why can't you just do as you're told?"

"Would you?" she snapped.

MacAlister swore softly under his breath. "Okay. Here's the story. Stone wants to question you about Deets's murder, and Harvey Shaw is waiting for you to show up at your house."

"Oh…" The breath left Rebecca's lungs with a whoosh, and she sat back in the seat.

"Yeah. Good thing you went to the bakery instead of going home." He eased the car forward. "By the way, where have you been between the time you ran out on me and the time you got here?'' The harsh streetlight glinted off the grim mask he'd slipped on.

Rebecca briefly considered telling him it was none of his business, but the dangerous gleam in his eye discouraged games. "I was home for a few minutes, just long enough to change my clothes. Then I went to my aunt's and uncle's in Greenwich."

"Lucky break." Some of the tension eased from his shoulders. "Shaw showed up there a couple of hours ago...just about the time I found out you owned this bakery and decided you must be here." He maneuvered her car out onto the street.

"Why the sudden interest in my safety?" she demanded. Ignoring the tiny glow of pleasure kindled by his concern, she sternly reminded herself he'd undoubtedly kidnapped her because he wanted something.

"You know why," he said grittily. Brief flashes from the streetlights played over his rough-hewn features, emphasizing his strength and arrogance. He was more buccaneer than gentleman, really. Yet even after what he'd done, the sight of him had the power to make her feel weak.

Rebecca fought to stay strong. "If this is about my asking for your help... Well, you took me to the bank, and...and that's the end of it. Now, please take me home."

"This is about last night." The intensity of his glance frightened her, made her wonder if he was remembering her hasty declaration of love. "And this isn't the end of it...not by a long shot," he said so fiercely she shuddered.

He broke eye contact first, thankfully, because she hadn't the strength to move. His attention returning to the road, he took the next corner, going too fast, as usual.

"My house is the other way," Rebecca cried, grabbing hold of the armrest.

"I know...I spent a few cold hours waiting in the woods behind it for you to come home. You could use a new roof, by the way," he offered conversationally, as though he hadn't just kidnapped her. As though he hadn't just reminded her of how they'd spent last night making love, of how somehow in the process she'd lost control and opened her heart to him.

NO RISK, NO OBLIGATION TO BUY...NOW OR EVER!

GUARANTEED

PLAY "ROLL A DOUBLE" AND GET AS MANY AS FIVE GIFTS!

HERE'S HOW TO PLAY:

1. Peel off label from front cover. Place it in space provided at right. With a coin, carefully scratch off the silver dice. This makes you eligible to receive two or more free books, and possibly another gift, depending on what is revealed beneath the scratch-off area.

2. You'll receive brand-new Silhouette Intimate Moments® novels. When you return this card, we'll rush you the books and gift you qualify for ABSOLUTELY FREE!

3. Then, if we don't hear from you, every month we'll send you 6 additional novels to read and enjoy months before they are available in stores. You can return them and owe nothing, but if you decide to keep them, you'll pay only $2.71* each plus 25¢ delivery and applicable sales tax, if any*. That's the complete price, and—compared to cover prices of $3.39 each in stores—quite a bargain!

4. When you subscribe to the Silhouette Reader Service™, you'll also get our newsletter, as well as additional free gifts from time to time.

5. You must be completely satisfied. You may cancel at any time simply by sending us a note or a shipping statement marked "cancel" or by returning any shipment to us at our expense.

"That house needs a lot of work," he continued as they raced down the road. "The porches are a total loss, and the windows aren't thermopane...which probably means the plumbing and wiring are subcode. A woman like you has no business living in a handyman's special. When we get back from San Francisco, you should sell it...buy a condo...much less upkeep."

Rebecca bristled, a common reaction when someone criticized her house. "My house is my business. And I'm not going to San Francisco. Haven't you been listening to me?"

He was listening all right, heard the change in her voice when she defended the house. Wondered at it, but decided now was not the time to press. "You aren't safe here."

"Why should anyone be interested in me now that you've turned the contents of Roseanne's bank box over to your friend Stone. I gather that was what you and Shaw were after."

"I haven't given the things to Stone...yet."

Rebecca straightened. "Will you give them back to me?"

"I'm not sure."

"Oh, MacAlister, you have to. I promised Roseanne I'd go to her box and get the money and the book for her."

"Did you?" His voice was sharp, angry. "I wondered how you got mixed up in this. You can tell me on the plane."

Rebecca looked ahead, saw the bright banks of airport landing lights. "I can't just pick up and go with you," she exclaimed. "I have responsibilities. My business to run, my house to renovate. And my aunt isn't strong, she needs me...."

"Stay behind and you miss the chance to talk me out of turning your cousin's things over to Stone."

Rebecca glared at him, but found no give in his hard-edged profile. "You were right. MacAlister, you really are a genuine bastard." Her voice vibrated with impotent anger.

In contrast, his was almost cheerful now that he had what he wanted. "All's fair, princess. I warned you I'd do whatever I had to to protect you."

"In the morning, I'll need to call my business and my aunt," she said frigidly. "My cousin, too. She's frantic with worry." *And angry.... I never could please Roseanne.*

"Fine, as long as it doesn't jeopardize your safety." The urge to touch her, to assure her he'd take care of everything if she'd just trust him, was almost overwhelming. Knowing it was too soon, he offered what solace he could. "I brought our things from the inn and the safehouse."

"I thought you said the place was being watched."

He shrugged. "You need clothes...."

"You could have been shot," she cried. "Why did you risk your life for my jeans?"

"And your sensible cotton underwear." His teasing grin faded, and he shifted in the seat. "I figured you'd be more comfortable with familiar things. And I didn't want to make you any more unhappy than I already have," he added gently.

Oh, MacAlister. What am I going to do about you? Rebecca tried to swallow and found a lump in her throat. With him, her usually placid emotions ran too close to the surface. His betrayal had cut her deeply, his arrogance made her want to scream, and his tenderness... Ah, when this tough, ungentle man turned gentle, he brought her close to tears.

"He's not here," Peck said when the man at the Bureau called for Rousseau that same evening.

"When will he be back?"

"Maybe not till morning. He and Roseanne are out sailing. Wanted to show her the Caribbean by moonlight. Bet they don't do much stargazing." Peck snickered. "What's up? Did you find MacAlister?"

The agent hunched over the steering wheel, cradling the cellular phone against his shoulder. "He's on his way to San Francisco."

"Why would he go there?"

The agent sighed. Easy to see why Peck was in charge of Rousseau's security, not his strategy. "Do you think maybe MacAlister's found out about the shipment?" he asked dryly.

"Damn. The boss isn't going to like that. Any idea when MacAlister's getting there or where he's staying?" Peck asked in a rush.

"Tomorrow morning is all we know. And we wouldn't have that much but we've been monitoring his credit-card use and turned up a car rental for tomorrow morning...San Francisco airport. He must have paid for his plane ticket in cash, but luckily for us the leasing companies won't rent a car without a credit card.''

"Okay...I'll get someone on it. Is the woman with him?''

"We don't know where she is,'' he lied. It was all the protection he could give Rebecca. If he mentioned that Charles Danforth had called earlier to say Rebecca had shown up at his house with some story about having been away visiting friends in Vermont, Rousseau would send someone over to kill her.

The agent wasn't sure why Rebecca hadn't leveled with her family. Maybe she'd only regained part of her memory and didn't remember what had happened at Deets's house the night he was murdered. For her sake, he hoped that was true. It might save her life.

"We had Shaw watching her place just in case the two of them showed up there...guess I'll pull him in and send him to the Coast,'' Peck muttered.

"One more thing...the Bureau is sending a team out to track down MacAlister.''

"Oh, the boss'll love that. You goin'?''

"Of course,'' he snapped.

"Yeah, I keep forgettin' what an important man you are,'' Peck sneered. "I'll tell the boss. Stay in touch,'' he ordered arrogantly. "Meanwhile, we'll see if we can't cook up a warm California welcome for my old friend.''

"Aren't you going to eat your snack?''

Rebecca turned from the airplane's tiny window and stared across the empty seat that separated her from intimate contact with Gates MacAlister. Mercifully, the night flight to the West Coast wasn't crowded.

He sighed. She'd been quiet since they'd reached the airport. Her silence and the misery shadowing her eyes were more upsetting than the accusations she'd hurled at him this morning. "Not speaking to me?''

"I hate being lied to and manipulated.'' Her hands curled into fists in her lap.

"If you're thinking about punching me, go ahead.''

Her lower lip trembled, but her gaze never wavered from his. "You deserve it."

"That and more," he agreed, hurting for them both. Damn. Her pain and vulnerability were almost more than he could bear. "All I'm asking is that you hear me out...give me a chance to explain." When she said nothing, just stared at him with her broken heart in her eyes, his control snapped. He reached for her, breaking his vow to let her make the first move.

Her knotted fists were ice-cold, so small he could encircle both with one palm. She flinched, but didn't shake him off. It was a start, he supposed.

Looking deeply into her eyes and willing her to understand, he said, "The only thing I won't apologize for is last night. You told me you didn't regret making love with me, and I hope you haven't changed your mind, because being with you meant more to me than anything that's ever happened to me."

Tears welled up in her eyes; still, she said nothing.

"You don't believe me?"

"I...I don't know what to believe anymore. It's all been...too much...happened too fast..."

MacAlister swore under his breath, damning the lack of privacy. If ever someone needed to be held, Rebecca did. Almost as much as he needed to hold her. "Ah, Becky," he said softly. "You're right. Things happened so fast this morning I didn't have a chance to tell you how glad I am you've regained your memory. I know how hard it was for you."

"It was terrible," she agreed with a sigh that seemed to release some of the tension in her body.

He echoed it. "Everything I told you was the truth...except our meeting wasn't accidental, and I did know who you were." At her quick gasp, he hurried on. "At least, I thought I knew who you were." He took a sip of his Scotch to steady his nerves.

"Yesterday Thatcher told you I used to work for the Bureau. I left six months ago because Jack Sabine, my partner and friend, was murdered. Politics scotched the investigation into his death. I got fed up and quit. Pure and simple." *The daughter I didn't know I had made matters a little more complicated, but that's another story.* "When Deets was murdered, the situations were similar enough so that I fell in with Stone when he asked for my help. Easy little job, he said."

"What did Stone want you to do?" Rebecca asked, curious despite her reservations.

"Help Deets's wife, who was the prime suspect in her husband's murder, get into her bank box. And once she had, turn the contents over to the Bureau."

"Why?"

"Stone told me there might be proof of her guilt in it," MacAlister said blandly, keeping his own theories to himself.

Rebecca digested the news for a moment. "If there was, it must have been in that black book."

"Smart girl," he said, smiling faintly.

"Elementary, my dear MacAlister," she said with a trace of her usual wit. "It couldn't be the money or the ring. But," she added, frowning thoughtfully, "the entries were written in some kind of code."

MacAlister's smile widened. "Right again."

"You've decoded the book." It wasn't a question. "Was my cousin involved in Lucien's death?"

"I don't know," he said after a minute. "Her name doesn't appear in it, but I haven't followed up all the leads yet."

"I don't think she did it. What reason could she have for wanting him dead?"

MacAlister shrugged. "Money. Another man."

"Roseanne has money of her own," Rebecca said defensively. "And with her, there is always another man waiting in the wings. But she hasn't killed anyone over it."

His gaze sharpened. "Did she have a lover?"

"Probably." She sighed, looked down at her hands, then up again. "She and I weren't . . . close."

"Yet you were at her house the night of the murder. That's how you came to be shot and lost your memory, isn't it?"

Rebecca nodded and sidestepped, not wanting to discuss what had happened that night. "Were you hostile toward me at first because you thought I was Roseanne?"

"Yeah." MacAlister read reluctance, decided not to press. They'd get back to Deets's murder eventually. "You gave me some pretty rough moments, honey. You didn't act at all like the rich, shallow bitch I'd been expecting. Worse, I found myself falling hard and fast for the woman who might have murdered my business partner.''

Rebecca smiled at the quiet desperation in his voice, wondering what he meant by "falling hard and fast." Did he love her, or was it only desire? "That explains why you were a bit . . . inconsistent . . . kind and gentle one minute, lashing out at me the next.''

"Inconsistent, hell." He raked his hand through his tousled hair. "I thought I was losing what little moral sense I have left. There I was just getting my life patched back together, and the next thing I knew, I was blown out of the water by a beautiful woman and lying through my teeth to my old boss to buy myself enough time to prove she didn't kill her husband." He shook his head in disgust.

A small glow of hope kindled in Rebecca's chest. "Did you really lie to Stone to protect me?''

"Yeah, honey, I did." MacAlister sighed deeply. "And last night, when I found out you were a..." His hand tightened briefly around hers. "When I knew you couldn't possibly have remained a virgin married to an old lecher like Deets, I knew something was rotten. I took Stone apart this morning. Told him what he could do with his case. . . .''

"Yes, I heard," she said quietly, eyes glowing like banked coals. "Why did he lie to you?''

"That's one of the things I need to figure out," MacAlister said tersely. "And I'm not letting you out of my sight until I come up with a satisfactory answer.''

His fierceness made her smile, turned the glow inside her into a tiny fire, blossoming out to melt the ice around her heart. "I guess Stone used us both.''

"Stone doesn't think of it as using. To him, the end justifies whatever means it takes.''

"No matter who gets hurt?''

"He's never lied to me before?'' The rawness in his voice made her tremble.

"You're angry with him . . . and you don't trust him.''

Damn. She wasn't supposed to see that; people usually couldn't read him. "I'm mad as hell at Stone. But I'm also

certain he's got his reasons for handling things this way."
MacAlister glanced out the tiny window at the velvety blue
night sky, wishing everything could be as clear as the heavens
were tonight. "I was part of the organization for so long, I
guess I'm having trouble adjusting to the fact that Stone can't
level with me like he could when I worked for him." At least,
he hoped that was why Stone was acting so strangely.

One of the first things he'd learned when he'd been forced
out on his own at fourteen was to trust his instincts to pick up
on the things his other senses couldn't tell him. It wasn't something he could explain or teach—you either had it or you didn't.
Over the years, his survival instincts had kept the scars on his
body to a minimum, and his neck out of more than one ambush. They were the reason he was alive and Jack Sabine
wasn't. His gut instinct on this one said, "Run like hell." But
he knew he wouldn't, not while Rebecca's safety and his neck
hung in the balance.

"Things certainly are mixed up," Rebecca said slowly.
"There's so much I don't understand...."

MacAlister snorted. "You and me both, honey. But you look
like you're feeling a little better since we've talked," he added
hopefully. "Still mad at me?"

"I should be...." Rebecca met MacAlister's watchful golden
eyes head-on. They were more shadowed than when they'd met.
How many of those shadows had come from the pain of be-
traying her trust? He felt things more keenly than he let on, to
others or to himself. She'd learned about loneliness when her
father had died and she'd found herself living with three people who were incapable of giving love. Needing love in her life,
she'd found other outlets: making friends, starting her business, restoring her parents' home and teaching children—the
most satisfying of all. But MacAlister's lessons had cut him
more deeply, scarred him so completely he'd closed himself off
from people. She wondered if a woman had hurt him. The
mysterious Lily, perhaps?

She wanted to give him another chance, but suddenly she felt
afraid. What if he was incapable of loving? What if he broke
her heart again?

As though sensing her indecision, he touched her cheek. "Don't be afraid. I won't let anyone hurt you."

Not even yourself? She drew in a deep, steadying breath. "The last few days hardly seem real to me.... It's almost as though you lied to my cousin, not me."

MacAlister closed his eyes for an instant to hide his vulnerability; when he opened them, his smile dazzled. "You won't be sorry you've forgiven me...."

"I haven't exactly forgiven you," she said quickly.

His smile never faltered. "You do, your pride just won't let you admit it yet. That's okay, honey. I don't want your pride, just your trust."

While Rebecca sputtered, MacAlister asked the flight attendant for another Scotch and a white wine.

"Speaking of trust," MacAlister said when the woman stopped fussing with their drinks and left. "Tell me what happened the night Deets was killed."

"What does that have to do with our trip?" Rebecca asked, but her hand shook as she sipped her wine.

"I know you were at Deets's the night he was murdered, and I'm guessing that whatever's got you shaking like a leaf has to do with what happened then." He reached out and stroked her hair. "I can't keep you safe unless I know what we're up against. Trust me, honey, I won't let you down."

"I'm not afraid of that. I'm afraid you're going to be angry," she said quietly.

MacAlister's eyes narrowed. "Tell me."

"Roseanne called me that afternoon...said she needed help and asked if I could visit her for a few days."

"I thought you said you two weren't close."

"We aren't. I'm younger than she is by two years, yet she's always seemed much older." He snorted, but she ignored him. "When I first went to live with Uncle Charles and Aunt Margaret, Roseanne resented me, saw me as a rival for her parents' attention, which was ridiculous. My uncle doesn't know anything exists outside Danforth Pharmaceuticals, and Aunt Margaret has her orchids and her...tea."

"Tea?" MacAlister's eyebrows rose.

"Whiskey, really.... She, ah, drinks."

"Every family has one," he said darkly. "Go on."

Rebecca sighed and reluctantly continued. "I couldn't refuse Roseanne—she sounded so desperate. It was late when I reached her house, and she hustled me up the back stairs and into her room like an . . . an illicit lover. She wasted no time in getting to the point. She planned to divorce Lucien because he was involved in something illegal." Rebecca remembered back to that night. . . .

"He won't like it," Roseanne had told her. "But if I can get hold of some business papers he has in our bank safe-deposit box, he'll have no choice but to let me go."

Suddenly they heard the sound of shots downstairs.

"Oh, my God . . . what's that," Rebecca asked.

Roseanne paled. "There . . . there wasn't supposed to be any shooting. . . ." She looked confused, then frightened. "Something's gone wrong. . . . We have to get out of here."

"Leave? Where will we go?" Rebecca wanted to know. "Shouldn't we just call the police?"

"No. No police. We have to get out of here before they come up here and find us." Wild-eyed, Roseanne rushed to the bed and grabbed up her sable coat. "You go down the front stairs— you should be able to find a cab on the avenue. Go straight home."

"Oh, no. I—I can't leave you here."

"You must," Roseanne urged. "Our best chance is to split up. I'll go out the back way."

"Roseanne, no . . ."

"Do it, you foolish child," Roseanne snapped. "We don't have all night." She stooped to pick up the sable coat that had fallen to the floor. "Wear this . . . the key to my safe-deposit box in Danbury is pinned into the pocket. Tomorrow, go to the bank and get the things out of the box. You still remember how to fake my signature, don't you?"

Numb, Rebecca nodded. She'd written most of Roseanne's high school papers and could sign her cousin's name as easily as she could her own.

"Good girl," Roseanne purred, smiling. "Take everything out of the box, go home and wait for my call."

Rebecca felt like a whirlwind had invaded her life. "But...why do you want me to go?"

"Because Lucien has men watching me. Please, Rebecca, I need to hire a lawyer and divorce Lucien as soon as possible, but I can't do that without the papers, can I." Her eyes were suddenly as hard and as bright as emeralds.

"No, of course not."

"You'll do it?"

Returning to the present, Rebecca looked at MacAlister. "Naturally, I agreed. But as I crept past the study on the first floor..." She drew in a shuddery breath as she remembered what she'd seen through the open doorway. "Lucien was lying on the floor in a river of blood. I—I've never seen so much blood," she whispered.

"Shh. I understand," MacAlister muttered, stroking her hand as he recalled his own horror at witnessing his first shooting. "You managed to get out of the house?"

Rebecca nodded. "There was a man leaning over Lucien, going through his pockets. Behind him, I could see that the study was a mess, drawers pulled open, papers thrown on the floor. I... The man saw me and shouted at me to stop." She shuddered. "I—I was terrified, and I ran...but he came after me."

"Can you identify him?" MacAlister asked tightly.

Rebecca nodded. "His picture in Stone's mug book triggered my memory."

MacAlister glanced quickly at the man dozing across the aisle, then lowered his voice. "Who else knows about this?"

"No one," she whispered. "I wanted to tell Uncle Charles, but he was leaving for Arizona."

"Ah, Becky..." MacAlister had both armrests up and was beside her before she'd finished speaking. He set her drink aside and took her in his arms despite the close quarters, hugging her so tightly he took her breath away. Against her heart, she felt his hammering to the same frantic beat. "Do you have any idea what this means?" he growled in her ear.

"I knew you'd be angry." She pressed her forehead into the reassuring strength of MacAlister's shoulder.

"Angry doesn't begin to cover it." He loosened his grip and set her back so he could see her face, his features harsh in the dimly lit cabin. "I take it Harvey Shaw wasn't the man you saw that night."

Rebecca shook her head.

"Damn." His eyes narrowed furiously. "Suppose I hadn't come for you?" He felt her tremble, knew he'd pressed too hard. "Never mind. Do you remember the man's Bureau ID number?"

"No. My memory came back, and I ran out to tell you..." She ground to a halt.

"And heard me talking to Stone." MacAlister sighed, his guilt-ridden gaze locked on hers. "I'm sorry, sweetheart. Jeez, what a mess...."

"What are we going to do?"

"I've got a few leads to follow up."

"You *did* learn something when you decoded the book," she guessed, surprising him again.

"Yeah. There are dates and the addresses of a couple Golden Circle warehouses. I went to the New York office this morning after you...left." His expression hardened. "From now on I'm not letting you out of my sight for even five minutes." His hand tightened almost painfully around hers. "Got it?"

Rebecca nodded, but MacAlister still couldn't let go of his anger or his fear. "You could have been killed." Hell, she still could be, and he didn't even know who had sent Shaw after her. "What the hell were you planning to do? Just bury your head in the sand and hope this guy wouldn't find you?" Though quiet, his voice vibrated with fury.

"Sort of," she sheepishly admitted. "I guess I hoped he wouldn't know where to find me."

"He would if your cousin is mixed up in Deets's murder."

Rebecca's eyes widened, and the air hissed out between her teeth. "No...I know you don't approve of my cousin, but she'd never do such a thing."

"Money makes people do strange things."

"Roseanne doesn't need money," she protested. "Our fathers set up trust funds for each of us when we were born." True, Uncle Charles had threatened to disinherit Rose for marrying Lucien, but now that he was dead, Charles would relent. "I think she just wanted out of a bad marriage, and...and I think Lucien was killed because of whatever scheme he was mixed up in."

"Right," MacAlister growled. He could see he wasn't going to change Rebecca's mind about her cousin, and his mood was black enough without hearing how filthy rich the Danforth family was, without having spelled out for him exactly how far above him Rebecca really was. Besides, it was a safe bet Deets had been killed for the book. "Promise you won't run off again."

"I won't," Rebecca promised, equally glad to end the discussion. Roseanne was spoiled and willful and inclined to wildness, but murder...? Impossible.

"Where were we?" His arm was still around her. His fingers had relaxed their grip, and his thumb whisked gently over her knuckles. To the flight attendant who came by to see if they needed refills, they probably looked a couple of lovers stealing away for a romantic weekend in the City by the Bay.

Rebecca refused more wine, half wishing that were true. Which showed how hopelessly in love with him she was, if she could so easily forget he'd seduced her to gain the book. "You were looking for proof that Lucien had been using the Golden Circle to ship some kind of contraband goods."

MacAlister smiled at her. "That isn't what I told you. You figured that out on your own. Unfortunately, I didn't find proof. The manifests indicated shipments had moved on the dates in question, but they appear to be in order. Still, something is going on. Something illegal, otherwise Stone wouldn't have been watching Deets, and Deets wouldn't have gone to the trouble of making up that book and hiding it in his bank box." Sighing, he dragged his free hand through his hair. "In a way I feel responsible. If I hadn't been so busy with...other things...if I'd been paying closer attention, maybe Deets wouldn't have felt free to compromise our company like this."

Other things...like Lily? Rebecca stifled the urge to ask him about the mysterious woman Thatcher had mentioned. "You've come out here to investigate the San Francisco operation?"

MacAlister nodded, looking even grimmer. "According to the book, something's happening there in two days. I plan to take apart every crate that moves in or out of the Golden Circle warehouse that day," he said fiercely.

"That could take hours...days, even. Why not leave it for Stone's organization?"

He squeezed his eyes shut briefly. "There's the leak in Stone's office, for one thing. And for another...has it occurred to you that I might be involved in Deets's scheme?"

Rebecca snorted inelegantly. "No. If you were, you're far too clever to get caught."

"Thanks, I think," MacAlister said dryly. "But Stone may not be as trusting if he gets a look at the book before I find a way to clear myself."

"Oh, Lord..." Rebecca said softly. "There's something in it about you?"

"Well, my name *is* on the inside front cover, and I *am* part-owner of the Golden Circle." She groaned again, and he nodded. "Yeah. Which means I've got to get to the bottom of this, prove I wasn't involved."

"Oh, MacAlister...what if you can't find anything?"

"If there's something there to find, you can bet I'll find it. I have to." He polished off his drink in one gulp and nested the glass with her empty. "Enough talk." Setting the glasses on the floor, he reclined first her seat, then his own, settling back with a sigh.

"What are you doing?"

"Trying to make us a little more comfortable. Lean up against me and shut your eyes. We've got four hours before we land, and neither of us got much sleep last night."

For a moment out of time, their eyes met, and awareness arched across the small space separating them like heat lightning, heightening all his senses to a throbbing roar.

Her startling green eyes widened, and he knew she was remembering last night at the inn. Remembering the taste and feel of each other and reliving the passion they had shared. The memory had been there all evening, lurking under the surface of the bantering and the bickering and the anger and the fear. A bed of hot, fiery coals aching to burst into flames at the slightest provocation. "We'd better get some sleep," he repeated hoarsely.

Rebecca blinked and nodded, her skin still tingling from the sensual caress of her memories. Folding her arms over her raggedly beating heart, she closed her eyes.

But sleep proved as elusive as forgetfulness.

MacAlister felt her fight sleep, then eventually relax and surrender, burrowing her head into his shoulder. She was so precious, he thought, looking down at her serene profile in the dimly lit cabin, filling in the shadowed hollows from memory.

Rebecca's brand of magic went beyond the classically arranged features, sparkling green eyes and sensational figure that had originally drawn him. She was gutsy, sassy, savvy and tender. From outside the bakery window, he'd marveled at her gentle patience as she'd worked with the children. She'd make a great mother, he'd found himself thinking, picturing her doing the things with Amber, his daughter, that still seemed impossibly foreign to him.

MacAlister sighed. Even though he knew deep inside she could never be his, a man could dream. Hell, when a man had led the kind of life he had, dreams were as close as you got to a classy woman like Rebecca.

As though she'd read his mind, Rebecca sighed sleepily and snuggled closer, her hip nudging the half arousal he'd been battling to subdue ever since he'd picked her up. "Ah, Becky. If only I'd met you years ago," MacAlister murmured into her hair, shifting to put a little space between himself and instant insanity.

Suddenly, MacAlister wished Jack Sabine could have met Rebecca. Jack had been a perceptive kind of guy, sensitive where MacAlister was hard-edged. His old friend would have kidded him about how easily she had reached deep inside MacAlister, past a lifetime of carefully constructed barriers, to stir something no one else had even touched.

MacAlister realized, with something akin to shock, that if...when...he got things straightened out and they parted, he'd be the one left with a huge, aching hole somewhere in the vicinity of where his heart should have been. And a lot of "If onlys."

But it couldn't end any other way. He was flawed, and the flaws in him had already cost one woman her life. He wouldn't . . . couldn't . . . sacrifice Rebecca.

Chapter 9

There was only one room waiting for them at the elegant Fairmont Hotel, perched high atop Nob Hill.

The suite, containing a sitting room, a bath and a single bedroom with one large bed, was reminiscent of the inn in Connecticut. Too reminiscent. Though she loved him, Rebecca found she had too much pride to tumble right back into bed with MacAlister so soon after his betrayal.

She turned at the sound of his soft footfalls crossing the carpeted room. "MacAlister..."

"Problem?" MacAlister asked calmly, slinging his duffel bag onto the foot of the king-size bed. He cocked a dark eyebrow, divided a glance between her face and the bed, then smiled crookedly. "Don't worry, honey, I asked for this room because the couch in the sitting room converts into a bed."

"Oh." She didn't know whether she was relieved or disappointed. Talk about being mixed up.

"Keep looking at me like that, and I'll think you're still interested." He touched her lightly on the shoulder. When she didn't pull away, he sighed deeply and drew her gently into the circle of his arms.

"When I'm with you, I don't know what I want." Rebecca's arms slid around his waist, and she lifted her mouth.

Groaning, he bent to meet her, found she tasted even sweeter than he remembered. He savored her unique flavor, so achingly familiar, spiced by the hint of mint from the toothpaste they'd used on the plane. The kiss started out leisurely, rich with memories of last night, then deeped suddenly, grew hungry in anticipation of the memories yet to be made.

MacAlister dragged himself away, buried his mouth in her hair as he pulled her tight against him. "Oh, lady, you turn me inside out, too," he growled roughly. "I'm usually a controlled kind of guy, but with you... Fantasizing about being with you was bad enough. But after last night, knowing how damn good it is between us, I want inside you so badly I'm nearly out of my head with it."

"Oh, Gates," she whispered, her fingers sinking into his shirt, pulling him closer. "I want you too, but..."

"I know...I know, and it's killing me not to give us what we're both aching for," he muttered grittily. Drawing in a ragged breath, he eased back and looked down at her, his eyes glittering through lowered lids. "I brought you with me to keep you safe, not because of...this. I can't deny that I want you, or that I'm glad you still want me, but you have to be sure."

"This has all happened pretty fast. We're good together, so damn good it takes my breath away. But just so there aren't any more lies between us, I want you to understand what you're getting into. I can't make you any promises. No strings attached. If you decide to come to me, it has to be with your eyes open." His own locked on hers, dark with sensual promise, ripe with unspoken words.

No commitment. He was offering her an affair of uncertain length, not marriage, maybe not even love. A cold lump of misery congealed in her stomach. Could she be with him, loving him, yet knowing the relationship had no future?

"If the answer is no..." His arms tightened briefly around her; a shadow flickered in his eyes. "I won't touch you, but you have my word I'll still protect you until this thing is done."

He had the inner strength to maintain that distance, too, she thought, searching his eyes, trying to see past the shadows to the vulnerability he had walled off. But she saw only what he wanted her to see. Desire. Determination.

"I . . . don't know what to say," she said unhappily.

MacAlister let out the breath he'd been holding, his hands stroking down her back one last time before releasing her. "Take your time," he forced himself to say. Whatever her decision, he'd already prepared himself to accept it, because for once in his life he was determined to do the right thing, the unselfish thing. "I've got a few phone calls to make. Why don't you take a shower and grab a nap. You still look tired."

Rebecca nodded numbly, watched through a veil of unshed tears as he walked from the room and closed the door behind him quietly, but with dread finality. If she couldn't take him on his terms, he would shut her out as effectively.

Was half a loaf better than no loaf at all?

Out in the sitting room, MacAlister waited until he heard the water running in the shower before he picked up the phone and ordered a pot of coffee from room service. He paced to the window, stood staring out at the fog-shrouded park across the street without really seeing it. He regretted he'd given up cigarettes a few years ago, because he could sure use one now.

He'd sounded pretty sure of himself in there when he'd laid out the rules for Becky. A hell of a lot surer than he really felt deep inside. If she turned him down cold, did he have the strength to hold up his end of the bargain and leave her alone?

The water stopped running; he tried not to think about Rebecca, climbing out of the tub, her skin rosy, water sliding down her . . .

"Snap out of it, man," he muttered. He had a job to do, and thinking about her at the wrong time could cost them both their lives. Damn, he never should have offered her a choice. It would have been better for both of them if he could have ended it cleanly this morning, kept their relationship strictly business.

Fat chance. He could do that about as easily as he could stop breathing.

A knock at the door announced room service.

Instinctively, MacAlister slid the gun from the small of his back and checked the guy out before letting him in. He paid for the coffee as he had for the room, with the cash from Deets's bank vault. Using the money wasn't strictly ethical, but he didn't dare use his credit card again on the chance that Stone was monitoring its activity. Using it to reserve the rental car had been unavoidable.

Feet propped up on the coffee table, MacAlister dialed Theo's number in New York.

"Hey, man, about time you called back." Theo sounded tense.

MacAlister sat up. "You've got something for me?"

"Yeah. You're not going to believe what happened. Last night I got a call from a guy I used to know. He was looking for a place to lie low and some fake ID. Seems he was Deets's driver, and after the big man died, this guy had a couple of close calls himself. Like he loaned his car to his girlfriend, and the thing blew up when she tried to start it. Like he came home from her funeral and nearly got gunned down in front of his apartment."

"Any idea who did it?"

"Sure, he knew the guy... It was Peck."

The gnawing in MacAlister's stomach turned violent. "The same Peck who used to work for Rousseau?"

"The same Peck who still *does* work for Rousseau. And that's not all. The reason they want my informant out of the way is because he can link Rousseau to Deets."

The breath hissed out between MacAlister's teeth. "Are you telling me Deets and Rousseau were partners?"

"Yeah," Theo said in disgust. "This guy said it started about a year ago. He used to pick Rousseau up at a private airport in Jersey and drive him to a secret meeting site. Turns your stomach, doesn't it?"

"Damn." MacAlister felt tainted, as though Deets's handshake when they'd cemented their own partnership had transferred to him the filth from Rousseau's hands. His lip curled, and he wiped his palms on his jeans. "What were they involved in?"

"One of those new synthetic drugs. Something they called ice. Ever hear of it?"

"Yeah," MacAlister ground out, shocked by what he was hearing. "Highly addictive and unpredictable as hell. It turns people into paranoid basket cases."

Theo grunted. "Right. That's what tipped off the feds—there was a sudden rash of murders and suicides among the teens and college kids Rousseau's guys were dealing to at some fashionable East Coast schools."

"Jeez...Rousseau was selling that stuff to school kids?"

"Sure...it's cheap. My guy said they were making money hand over fist and getting ready to go national with the stuff when the Bureau became interested in what was going on and started watching Deets's Golden Circle warehouses."

"So Deets shut things down for a week or so and moved the operation to the West Coast," MacAlister muttered, remembering the notations in the black book. "And I bet the reason he took me on as a partner was because I'd once worked for the Bureau."

"You do have a reputation for being clean."

MacAlister spit out a ragged oath. "I hate being used." Deets was beyond his reach, but maybe he could somehow use the information in the book to get Rousseau. "Did your source have any idea whether Rousseau is still dealing the ice?"

"He doubted it, since Deets was the only one who knew who the Iceman was—"

"The Iceman?"

"That was their code name for the guy who supplied the ice."

MacAlister's gaze narrowed thoughtfully as he drew the black book from his hip pocket and thumbed quickly to the last page. "Iceman...seadot" was what he had decoded, but it didn't make any sense. Was it some kind of code within a code?

"I hope Deets took the secret with him," Theo muttered savagely. "It would serve Rousseau right after what he did to Jack Sabine...and poor Lily."

MacAlister flashed back briefly to the moment six months ago when he'd opened the door of his Cairo office and nearly stumbled over the trunk someone had left there. The trunk containing Lily's mutilated body and the note.

"You can have her back...I've finished with her." The note had been unsigned, but he'd known it was from Rousseau.

MacAlister had reread it and suffered through a jolt of guilt for what had happened. It was his fault Lily was dead.

"I figure Rousseau had Deets killed, but he could have told them who the Iceman is before he died," Theo said.

"Don't think so." Given the ferocity with which Rousseau's goons had tried to get the things from Deets's safe-deposit box, MacAlister guessed Deets hadn't talked. At least now he knew why they wanted the book...and how important it could be to the Bureau if they could identify the Iceman and shut down Rousseau's drug operation. Maybe even put Rousseau behind bars.

"Good. If Rousseau can't locate the Iceman, he'll be out of business," Theo observed, chuckling. "Man, I'd love to see that scum brought down."

MacAlister grunted in agreement. "Could be this will force him to surface." Rousseau had dropped out of sight right after Jack's and Lily's deaths. Not even MacAlister's extensive network of informants had been able to uncover the Frenchman.

"My informant had a tip on that, too. Deets bragged that profits were so good, Rousseau had recently bought an island in the Caribbean . . . planning to set up his own dictatorship there, I guess. Pretty smart, huh?"

"Especially if he's outside U.S. jurisdiction, where even the Bureau wouldn't be able to touch him," MacAlister growled. "Did the guy know which island?"

"He hinted that he might," Theo said slowly. "But I think he wants to trade the information. He asked if I could set up a meeting between you and him...."

"Why me?" MacAlister shot back, warning bells going off in his head. This whole thing suddenly struck him as too pat.

"Because you were Deets's partner, I guess."

"Oh, yeah? Why doesn't this guy go to the Bureau?"

"I asked him that," Theo said quickly. "He said it was because Rousseau had someone at the Bureau on his payroll...someone pretty high up who's working on the Deets case. My guy was afraid Rousseau would find out he'd talked."

MacAlister's stomach clenched. "Did the guy say which agent is Rousseau's man?"

"If he had, I'd have been on the phone to Stone last night," Theo assured him. "As it happens, I did call the Bureau, first thing this morning...'cause I hadn't heard from you." Theo paused, as though weighing his words. "Would you believe none of the agents assigned to the case was available to take my call? So I spoke to a hacker in the computer section who's worked with me before. He said Stone and his guys had gone to San Fran." Theo snorted. "'Strange thing to do in the middle of a big drug case,' I told the hacker. 'They're following up on a credit-card usage lead I uncovered for them,' the guy shot right back."

MacAlister groaned. "You're just full of good news."

"Glad I could help," Theo said cheerfully. "Anything else I can do for you? Want me to see if I can track Stone down and tell him about the informer?"

"Find out where he's staying, if you can, but don't talk to anybody until we know for sure which man is Rousseau's. And for God's sake, be careful."

"You too, man. Rousseau'd like nothing better than to retire you permanently."

"I mean it, Theo. This informant of yours sounds fishy."

"He's trustworthy."

"Yeah? Seems awfully convenient, him showing up right now with this story linking Rousseau and Deets and drugs."

"He gave us a lot of good information," Theo protested.

"That he did. Just enough to whet my curiosity and make me hungry for more." And maybe lure him into a trap. If he hadn't been three thousand miles away, if he hadn't had Rebecca's safety to worry about, he might have fallen for it.

"I told you, he's looking for help.... I offered to trade mine for what he knew about Deets."

"Okay. Just be careful," MacAlister said grimly. He hung up and walked to the window. One hand propped against the frame, he stared morosely down at the street.

Theo was right, Rousseau would stop at nothing to get the book...and kill him in the process. And Rebecca...

MacAlister shivered as he glanced over at the closed bedroom door. He had no trouble picturing her curled up in the big bed, her hair still damp, her face rosy. No matter what else happened, Rousseau couldn't get his hands on Rebecca.

To Rousseau, women were expendable commodities. That, in fact, was how MacAlister had first met Rousseau, and through him, Lily. Six years ago, MacAlister had been investigating the disappearance of a fifteen-year-old American girl who had been visiting Egypt with her family. A week of greasing palms and knocking on doors had finally brought them to a sleazy bar cum house of prostitution.

Posing as a customer, MacAlister had picked up Lily, a young Eurasian, from the throng of bar girls. Poor, beautiful Lily, who'd gone on to become the mother of his daughter. He'd chosen her because she looked cleaner, more intelligent and more desperate than her weary, haggard sisters. Once upstairs behind locked doors, she'd proven a wise choice. He'd made it clear he was there on business, not pleasure, and Lily had agreed to cooperate...providing MacAlister would take her with him when he left the bar.

The vile living conditions and abuse from customers she'd described to him made him determined to close the place down. Unfortunately, he'd been too late to save the young girl whose kidnapping had sparked the investigation. Acting on Lily's tip, he and Jack had found the girl in a bag in the alley with the garbage. Remnants of the ropes that had bound her to one of the beds still clung to her bruised wrists and ankles. She had been drugged, but the coroner had cited loss of blood from repeated rapes and beatings as the cause of death.

The owner of the bar, and dozens like it in Cairo, was Jean-Claude Rousseau. According to Lily, in addition to prostitution, he also dealt in white slavery and drugs while posing as a financier.

When Jack and MacAlister had confronted him in the posh office in the luxury high-rise building he also owned, Rousseau had shrugged off their accusations, claiming the bars were merely investments managed by others.

"Naturally, I will make inquiries into the death of the unfortunate young tourist," he had blandly assured them. "But

I expect little will come of it as the manager of that particular bar committed suicide this morning.''

Suicide, my... foot. There goes our case, MacAlister had thought, glumly. With his expensively tailored suit, darkly handsome features and cool, reserved manner, Rousseau appeared every inch the legitimate businessman. Not at all the sort of guy a government agency operating in a foreign country could push around without substantial proof... even if he did have hard eyes and a smug smile and you didn't believe him for a second.

Jeez, the guy probably gave money to all the right charities and most of the city's politicians, MacAlister had thought at the time. He could just picture himself explaining to Stone that they'd embroiled the Bureau in an international incident by arresting a prominent businessman on the strength of his ruthless expression and a bar girl's accusations.

He and Jack had left, but they hadn't given up. Calling in favors owed them by the Cairo police, they'd managed to get some of Rousseau's bars closed down and a few of his drug dealers run out of town. It wasn't much, but it was a start.

Rousseau had taken it as a declaration of war. And Jack and Lily had been the costliest casualties.

MacAlister had vowed they'd be the last.

Rebecca awoke to the sound of the shower. A quick glance at the bedside clock showed it was only 11 a.m. She'd slept for four hours and felt a little better. Had MacAlister gotten any sleep? she wondered. Her heart gave a quick little thump at the thought of him in the shower, only a call away. She'd lived alone for two years now and wasn't used to sharing her space. Oddly, it felt good knowing he was nearby. Was it because he represented security and protection? Or because he could come to mean so much more?

Her mind and her heart both shied away from the question.

Groggily, she sat up, trying to calculate what time it would be in Connecticut. Two, she thought. The bakery had been open for hours, and Susan was probably worried sick about her.

"Rebecca! Where on earth are you?" Susan demanded when she answered the phone. "I was about to drive over to your house and check things out."

"I..." Belatedly, it occurred to Rebecca that she hadn't prepared a story. "Er...it's Roseanne.... She—"

"Called here this morning looking for you," Susan interjected. "She said you were helping her with a very important project and you two keep missing each other on the phone. She left her number this time."

Rebecca copied it down, half relieved, half dreading the fact that she could now call her cousin. "I, er, may be away for another few days," she explained finally.

"Is everything all right?" Susan asked sharply.

"Yes...yes," Rebecca insisted. "Now that I have Roseanne's number, I'm certain everything will be fine. I'll call you again in a day or so."

"I, ah, hope you won't be mad," Susan said hesitantly, "but I called your aunt's house when you didn't show up this morning. I gather your uncle's away, and I tried to low-key things when I found out you hadn't spent the night there, but maybe you'd better give her a call."

After assuring Susan that she wasn't angry, Rebecca hung up and dialed her aunt's number.

"Mrs. Danforth is sleeping," the maid informed Rebecca. "But I'll tell her you called. She'll be very relieved ... your bakery manager's call upset her."

Rebecca sighed gloomily. At the first hint of trouble, her aunt had undoubtedly panicked, drunk too much "tea" and passed out. "Did she call Uncle Charles?"

"Unfortunately, yes."

Sighing again, Rebecca bowed to the inevitable. She'd have to call him, but she earned a slight reprieve ... her uncle was busy with an experiment in the lab and couldn't be disturbed. She left her name and the number of the hotel. Then, anxious to get all her unpleasant calls out of the way, she dialed the number Roseanne had given Susan.

The call didn't ring through as it should have. Instead, a series of high-pitched clicks and strange whirrings sounded in her ear. They went on for so long she was about to hang up and ask the operator for assistance when things straightened out and proceeded normally.

"Yeah?" a rough male voice demanded on the third ring.

"I—I'm looking for Roseanne Deets."

"Who's calling? How'd you get this number?" the man snarled. The sense that she'd heard this voice before startled Rebecca more than his rude questions.

"Sh-she asked me to call. . . . I'm her cousin, Rebecca."

"It's about goddamned time," he growled. "Hold on."

Rebecca shivered, fighting the urge to hang up. For as long as she could remember, even before she'd gone to live with her aunt and uncle, she'd dreaded confrontations with her cousin. Roseanne was poised, beautiful, confident, everything Rebecca was not. Time, maturity and some modest success in her own right hadn't changed her feelings. The run-in with the strangely familiar-sounding man who'd answered the phone hadn't exactly boosted her self-confidence.

"Rebecca. Where have you been?" Roseanne demanded, her voice tight and high.

Rebecca swallowed. "I—I was shot and . . ."

"What about the things you took from my bank box? Do you still have them?"

"Yes, I do. . . . But . . ."

"Oh, good. I was afraid you'd screwed things up. You don't know how important those things are to me."

"Yes, well . . ." What now? She needed a few days' delay so MacAlister could clear his name. Rebecca took a deep breath. "Roseanne. Did you know that the police are already convinced that Lucien was involved in something illegal? You may not need the things from his box."

"Yes, I do. When can I get them?" Roseanne snapped out faster than an army drill instructor.

"I don't know. . . ."

"I'll come to you. Where are you?"

Rebecca swallowed. "I . . ."

"You sound very strange, Rebecca. Are you certain you haven't lost my things and you're afraid to tell me?"

"No...I—I haven't lost them...." The question, coming so close to the truth, rocked her, left her scrambling for a way out. "N-no, I have everything—the money and the ring..."

"And the book?" Roseanne cried. "Do you have the book?"

Rebecca wished she were better and quicker at making up lies. *MacAlister, where are you when I need you?* she thought, glancing at the bathroom door.

A deep, imperious male voice broke into the background at Roseanne's end of the conversation. Rebecca couldn't make out his words, but when Roseanne came back on the line, she sounded even more worried. "Rebecca, I'm sorry to cut this short, but my...my host has to make an important call. Give me your number, and I'll phone you back when he's finished."

"Oh, all right," Rebecca replied distractedly. Hoping Roseanne wouldn't call until after she'd had a chance to discuss this with MacAlister, she located the number on the hotel phone and read it off.

Just as she finished, a wide male hand, the back liberally sprinkled with dark hair, clamped down on the disconnect button, severing the connection.

"What the hell do you think you're doing?"

Rebecca jerked her gaze up from MacAlister's hand to his face. His hair streamed water, his eyes blazed fire. The rest of him blocked out the room, a solid chunk of wet, bronzed muscle. Her eyes skimmed across the dark whirls of hair covering his muscular chest, to the damp towel slung precariously around his lean hips. From this angle, or almost any other, Gates MacAlister was a lot of man.

"I...er..." Her mouth went dry, and she struggled to remember his question.

"Who were you talking to?" he demanded.

"Roseanne...she'd left word at the bakery, and I returned her call, but someone needed to use the phone, so I had to give her my num—"

"Pack," he growled.

"Pack? But why? We just got here."

He had the duffel bag on the bed and was tossing the things she'd worn on the plane into it.

"MacAlister?" Keeping the sheet wrapped around her naked body, she scrambled to the edge of the bed, put her hand on his arm. "What is it?"

The look he gave her was hard and brutally honest. "She could use the phone number to trace us to this hotel."

Rebecca blinked once. "You still think Roseanne is a threat to me? To us?"

"I'm not taking any chances." He went back to packing.

"I think you're wrong. But I am sorry I've upset you." She sat back on her heels, her teeth sinking into her lower lip. "Roseanne asked, and I . . . I didn't think."

MacAlister reached out, stroked his hand over her hair, then cupped her chin, lifted it so she could see he wasn't angry any longer. "My fault, honey. I keep forgetting you haven't been at this very long . . . you still trust people."

"And you don't trust anyone." *Not even me.* The realization shook her.

"Conditioned response," he said flatly. "Better get dressed, we're leaving in a few minutes."

"Where are we going?"

He shrugged. "Not too far." He had to be in San Francisco to tear a warehouse apart on Friday.

"Is the Napa Valley a possibility? I've been wanting to expand my bakery into a full-scale gourmet restaurant, and they have some of the best—"

"This isn't a pleasure trip," MacAlister growled. He regretted it the instant the light went out of her eyes and they turned dull with fear again. "Yeah, sure. Why not," he said quickly, but she didn't smile, just tugged the sheet off the bed and ran into the bathroom holding it up with one hand and the green slacks and sweater in the other.

Rebecca maintained a tense silence until after they'd crossed the Golden Gate Bridge, then she sat back in the bucket seat of the Toyota he'd rented and began to watch the scenery slide by.

"Amazing how quickly you leave the city behind," Mac-Alister observed, looking for a way to distract her from their situation as they climbed into the unspoiled hills.

"Do you think Thatcher is the one?" she asked, her mind clearly on more serious matters than the tasteful roadside signs advertising the vineyards, restaurants and bed-and-breakfast places in the Valley up ahead.

"Honey, don't get yourself all worked up. . . ."

"I may have endangered us because I was too trusting. I think it would help me not to repeat the mistake if I knew exactly who you trusted and who you didn't. You said there was a . . . a leak in Stone's office. Who do you suspect?"

Glancing over, he met her implacable gaze and sighed. "At this point . . . I don't trust any of them." *Including Stone.*

"I see," she said firmly, but she couldn't hide the tremor that shook her. "Maybe you should tell me about the other agents assigned to this case."

He wanted to change the subject, but maybe Becky had a point. Maybe she had a right to know some of what he knew. "You've met Ron Sanchez. Stone hired him a couple of years ago. Sanchez is a good agent, married, with a couple of kids. Andy Newcomber's only been with the Bureau for two years. Got a face like Howdy Dowdy, but he's sharp as a tack . . . kid'll go far. Greg Anderson's the only one I don't know personally. On paper he looks good. Ex-football player, expert marksman, served two years in the Middle East . . . Saudi Arabia . . . I think, then Chicago before he came to New York."

"I see," Rebecca said thoughtfully. "Do any of them have any vices?"

"Vices?"

"Yes. It's always the cop with the secret gambling habit or the expensive mistress who goes bad," she told him in all seriousness.

MacAlister started to laugh, then remembered with a chill Thatcher grumbling about the Deets case. "Wouldn't you know, we get a case that's going to be a bastard to break, and everybody on the team's got an ax to grind," the veteran had complained. "Stone's sweating bullets over making Chief, Sanchez is working a second job on the side to pay his kid's medical bills, Anderson's on the phone every day tryin' to square things with his bookie over his sports bets, and Newcomber would sell his soul to step over all of us and into Stone's job."

"I mean, Thatcher *seems* nice...." Rebecca said slowly.

"Thatcher talks too damn much," MacAlister grumbled. So much for honesty. "Are you getting hungry?"

Rebecca gazed at his closed profile. "Don't shut me out. I'm involved in this, too."

"Don't remind me," he said tersely. "Is this okay?" The sign promised gourmet dining in a restored house complete with antiques for sale. When she only shrugged half-heartedly, he pressed. "Is this the kind of thing you dragged me up here to see? If not, we'll keep going until we find it."

"I dragged?" Rebecca bristled, turned on him and saw a teasing smile lifting one corner of his mouth. He was trying to lighten her mood. His compassion made her heart skip a beat. *Oh, Gates. What am I going to do when you leave me?*

A few minutes later, MacAlister pulled into the restaurant's parking lot. "This is amazing," Rebecca said as he helped her out of the car. "Here it is mid-November, and it's as warm as summer." She turned her face up to the sun, letting the heat melt away her worries.

He didn't need the sun to warm him. The sight of her impossibly long legs and the curve of her hips beneath the green wool pants, the thrust of her breasts against the soft sweater as she arched her back like a cat, were more than enough. "You look like a sunflower," he said huskily.

The rough edge on his voice sent her temperature soaring. Rebecca slanted him a provocative glance. "And you look like a man bent on picking a bouquet."

He'd never seen her like this. It captivated him. "Not a bouquet...just one flower." She blushed, unsure what to say next, and he wondered at her inexperience. "Why aren't you married?" he blurted out.

"I was engaged once, two years ago."

"And?"

Rebecca shrugged. "Randy wasn't really interested in me. He was looking for an easy way to become a vice president at

Danforth Pharmaceuticals.'' Surprising how easily, how pain-
lessly the words came now.

"I should say I'm sorry," he muttered.

Rebecca looked up at him, smiling faintly. "Don't be, on my
account. Oh, at first, I was hurt. When I recovered, I realized
I had been more in love with the idea of being loved than I was
with Randy. And I want children," she added quietly.

"I saw you working with the kids at your store. . . ."

"So. . ." She scowled at him. "I had a feeling someone was
watching me that night."

"Guilty," he said without a blush. He'd told himself he
needed to keep tabs on her until he could figure a way to get her
to the airport, but he had enjoyed watching her. That she cared
about her business was evident in every gesture, everything she
did. The warmth of her smile as she greeted a pair of elderly
customers had reached him as he stood outside her window and
chased away the cold. But the way her eyes had danced when
the children arrived had surprised him. "You were very patient with the kids. You'd make a good mother."

"Yes, I would," Rebecca said simply. "And someday, I intend to be one."

Her words hung awkwardly between them.

MacAlister stared down at her for a moment, his eyes bleak,
his mouth set in a stubborn line, then he shook himself. "Let's
go in and get something to eat."

"Sure." She let out a sigh as she preceded him into the cool,
dark interior of the restaurant. When this was over, he'd walk
out of her life and leave a gaping hole in it. She knew she should
maintain her distance from him and spare herself the pain, but
it was becoming more and more difficult.

Harvey Shaw wedged himself into a phone booth around the
corner from the Fairmont Hotel and dialed from memory. Peck
answered on the second ring. "Mr. and Mrs. Johnson checked
out of room 414 an hour ago," he growled.

Peck swore. "How the hell did MacAlister find out we were
onto him so quick?"

"You said he was good."

"What about the beeper?"

"All set. Our guy out here planted it in MacAlister's car before he picked it up from the rental company." Shaw smiled wolfishly. Thanks to the electronic tracking device, MacAlister wasn't going to get away this time. "He headed north, but he's got a lead on me, so the signal's not too strong. I'd better get a move on.... Just wanted to check in before I left."

"Don't screw this up," Peck warned. "The boss wants the book, and he wants MacAlister out of commission before that ice shipment comes in on Friday."

Shaw's expression hardened as he touched his broken nose. "Don't worry about a thing. I have a little score to settle with him myself. Still want the girl done for, too?"

"Yeah. She may not remember what she saw at Deets's house the night he was killed, but I ain't takin' any chances."

Chapter 10

The restaurant was spacious, with large windows through which they could enjoy the lush green gardens just outside or the panoramic sweep of the distant hills and the vineyards shimmering in the warm sun. At the same time, it was cozy. Subdued tones of rose and pewter blue accented the pecan paneling, and mellowed antiques gleamed softly in the diffused light.

From the minute they'd walked in, Rebecca had been captivated, imagined owning a place like this herself one day. The colors, the textures, the mingled scents of herbs and fresh baked bread drew on her senses. Briefly she forgot her weariness, her bittersweet relationship with MacAlister, even the danger hanging over their heads.

Like a bee on the wing, she lightly touched here and there as they wended their way through the tables. Running her fingers over the smooth pewter candlesticks, she thought how pleasantly they contrasted with the rough, handwoven place mats.

As the owner handed MacAlister a pair of menus, Rebecca paused to sniff a bowl of field flowers on the beautiful hutch placed between the bay windows.

"We'd prefer another table," MacAlister said quietly.

"But..." Rebecca looked up, startled. This table, directly in front of one window, yet somewhat shielded from the rest of the room by an oaken sideboard, was clearly the best table in the house. "This one is—"

"I like to be able to see the door," he explained. His low, intense tone shattered Rebecca's good mood.

The owner, a friendly woman in her early thirties, shrugged and led them to the center of the room. "Is this all right?"

MacAlister nodded. "This will be fine. Becky, would you mind sitting on my left?"

Rebecca shivered, knowing it wasn't an idle request. *I shoot best with my right hand,* he'd once told her.

Sensing her disquiet, MacAlister tried to divert her with a story. "Have you ever been to Cairo?" he asked as the waiter finished pouring their water and retreated to get the wine MacAlister had ordered.

"Planning to take me there next?" she quipped.

He laughed, a genuine, mirthful sound, and she felt a jolt of longing to bring more laughter into his life.

"No. Seeing the olive trees outside reminded me of my house in Cairo," he went on. "There were olive trees in the back courtyard, and my houseboy had a pet monkey..."

By the time the waiter returned with Rebecca's pasta salad and MacAlister's steak sandwich, they were both laughing over the monkey's attempts to evade his master and steal the olives.

"You should do that more often," MacAlister said quietly, his eyes bright and unshadowed.

"Order pasta salad?"

"No, laugh."

"Funny, I was just thinking the same thing about you."

MacAlister sighed. "I guess neither one of us has had much to laugh about recently."

Rebecca shrugged, taking great pains to spear a piece of pasta and avoid his questing gaze. "I was feeling almost carefree...then I remembered, we aren't." She reached for her water to wet her mouth. "Do you think we're safe?"

"Safe is a relative term, honey," he said carefully, wishing he could say what she wanted to hear. "But there's a lot of country up here...we'll be damned hard to find."

"San Francisco is a big city...we'd have been harder to find there if it hadn't been for my...mistake."

MacAlister didn't say anything, but he cut into his meat with unwarranted savagery.

"I still don't think Roseanne has done anything...."

"How did she sound?" he asked, taking a sip of wine.

"Impatient with me, as usual."

"Hmmm. Hostile cousin, alcoholic aunt, workaholic uncle—doesn't sound like you had a very happy childhood, either, honey," MacAlister said slowly.

"But at least I had money," she added for him.

"I didn't say that."

"No. You implied it." Rebecca set her fork down, her expression thoughtful. "We were both orphaned young...or I guess you were...you never mention your father."

"He died when I was fourteen, but he hadn't been any kind of father to me since my mother died when I was ten." His expression darkened. "Pa drank. A lot. It took him a year to drink his way through my mother's insurance money. We wouldn't have had a roof over our heads after that if the rich guy he did carpentry work for hadn't let us stay in the room behind the garage. When my old man got so he couldn't get up most mornings, and shook too badly to hit a nail when he did, I took over. I was strong for my age, and I'd inherited Pa's way with wood."

"Oh, MacAlister," Rebecca whispered. "Wasn't there anyone else to care for you?"

"Nope." His tone was flat, expressionless; his eyes were anything but, and she hurt for him. "When Pa died, the guy I'd been working for turned me over to the juvenile authorities. I didn't want any part of a foster home. I begged him to let me stay. That's the last time I ever begged anyone for anything." He drew in a ragged breath. "I ran away from the first home they put me in and never looked back."

"Where did you live? How did you eat?"

"I worked odd jobs, ate what I could find and slept with one eye open." He shook his head, smiling slightly. "It was a hell of an education. And I got into some pretty bad scrapes. By the time I was big enough to lie my way into the service, I knew more about survival and self-defense than they did. But they taught me how to put what I'd learned to *good* use, and they sent me to school. When I got out, I knew I wanted to make something of myself.''

"And you have," Rebecca said, reaching across the table to lay her hand on his clenched fist. Beneath her gentle touch, his fingers relaxed and turned, lacing with hers. She smiled into his eyes, understanding what had put some of the ghosts there. "You're made of strong stuff, Gates MacAlister, or you wouldn't be where you are today," she said proudly.

"Not strong enough to resist you," he teased. Lifting her hand, he began nibbling her fingers.

"Stop that," Rebecca whispered, blushing and looking around at the other diners. "I'm trying to be serious."

"So am I."

"MacAlister. Not here."

He wiggled his eyebrows. "In the car, maybe? I've never made love in a car."

If only it were love, she thought glumly, tugging on her hand. She got it back only because he let it go, grinning all the while at her red cheeks.

"The car would probably be too . . . cramped." His husky growl and the sensuous promise in his eyes had her squirming in her seat. "Better drink some water, honey. You look a little warm."

Rebecca glowered at him. "You're pressing."

"I'm not pressing. I'm tempting."

Very. But could she settle for desire when she wanted love? Clearing her throat, she sat up straighter in her chair and changed the subject. "This is the sort of restaurant I'd like to have someday. Not too large," she said looking around. "Pleasant ambience, good food . . . and the antiques are a nice touch. Maybe I should take a class in restoring furniture after I complete my home-remodeling course and get the house done."

"You mean you're actually thinking of doing the work on that tumbled-down house yourself?" He looked shocked.

"I am doing it. Er, that is, I'm trying to." She smiled ruefully. "Just between you and me, MacAlister, I'm not doing very well. And I don't understand it. I've taken lessons since I was five...."

"You started woodworking lessons that early?"

"No. Tap and ballet when I was five. Piano when I was nine.... That didn't work out too well, either," she confided. "I'm a little tone-deaf. But I've always done well at manual things...sewing, any kind of crafts, flower arranging, boot making, bookbinding, cooking..."

"Why did you want to learn how to do all those things?"

"I didn't, but lessons filled up time after school and on weekends. And even if I didn't know anyone at first, by the time the session was over, I'd usually made a friend. What is it?" she asked, seeing his scowl.

"You must have been lonely."

Rebecca shrugged. "Money doesn't buy happiness. I know you don't see it that way, but I'd gladly have traded my trust fund for a little of my father's time. He worked night and day getting Danforth Pharmaceuticals off the ground, but he died before it became really prosperous. My uncle ruined his marriage, and maybe my aunt's and cousin's lives, trying to make the business bigger. I have never taken a dime from my trust fund," she said hotly. "And I don't intend to."

"Okay," he said, holding his hands up in mock surrender. "But why remodel the house? Why not sell it and buy a condo?"

"My parents bought that house when they were first married. It was my home...I was very happy there," she said softly. He had seen her hold back tears of fear and pain these past few days, so the single tear sliding down her cheek touched him all the more deeply.

"Honey..."

Rebecca dashed the errant tear away with the back of her hand and laughed shakily. "Enough gloomy talk. I need to go outside and stand in the sunshine."

Harvey Shaw slunk down behind the dash of his sunbaked rental car and watched from a few cars away as MacAlister helped the woman into a black Toyota and drove off.

"Gotcha now," he muttered, wiping the sweat from his upper lip. Damn, it was hot, but he hadn't wanted to call attention to himself by sitting in the busy parking lot with the motor idling and the air-conditioning running.

As MacAlister's sporty car turned out onto the highway, Shaw glanced at the tracking device on the seat beside him. Its steady beep made him smile. With its help, he could afford to let MacAlister get out in front of him, maybe even wait until they'd settled in for the night so he could make his move without causing a scene that might alert the police.

"'Calistoga Soaring Center,'" MacAlister read from the billboard. "There's something I've always wanted to try."

Rebecca tried to focus on the sign as it whizzed by.

"Are you game?"

"As long as it isn't another winery." She'd lost track of the times they'd stopped to sample the fruit of the vine. One tasting room had begun to look like another, cool and dim and sharply redolent of wet oak and fermenting grapes. "I think I've been overserved."

MacAlister chuckled. "No, I've kept careful track of what you've had, honey... you're just feeling mellow. I like seeing you like this... all soft and relaxed."

"Being with you makes me feel comfortable," she replied, smiling over at him.

Comfortable? He'd been called cold, dangerous and mean before. Never comfortable. But a warm feeling wrapped itself around him as he remembered their drive up the valley. In between wineries, she'd detailed her plans for the house and her hopes for the bakery. How she'd sparkled, her cheeks rosy, her hands flying, building castles in the air, and he'd found himself thinking his own plans to make as much money as he could sounded cold by comparison.

And then there was Amber. He hadn't told anyone he had a daughter. He would have told Jack, of course, but Jack had died the day before MacAlister had found out about Amber. Rebecca needed to know about Amber... and Lily. Only he didn't have the heart to spoil things by telling her now.

"Here it is." MacAlister turned into an unpaved parking lot and stopped the car next to a wide, brown field. A low hut with a tin roof stood off to one side, and the field itself was rimmed with small planes. One Rebecca recognized as an old biplane. The Soaring Center must be some type of museum, she thought as she got out and stretched.

MacAlister paid their entry fee in the hut, then strode out onto the sunbaked field. Shielding her eyes from the glare, Rebecca followed more slowly. He stopped beside one of the small planes to talk with a wiry guy in shorts and a T-shirt emblazoned with "Kelly" in crimson skywriting.

The plane sat so low to the ground that it came only up to her hip. "It's hard to imagine anyone flying in something this little, isn't it?" she asked shakily.

Kelly chuckled. "You don't fly it...you soar in it. Hop in," he offered, lifting the glass canopy to reveal two narrow seats set one in front of the other.

"Oh, no...I don't think so," Rebecca said uneasily.

"In you go, honey," MacAlister said cheerfully, scooping her into the plane. Before she could protest, he slid in behind her. Butting her back up to the hard wall of his chest, he cradled her hips in the V of his slightly bent legs. His lips brushed her neck as his arms came up to enfold her. "Ah, perfect fit."

"MacAlister. I don't want to go up in this thing," she said, her heart racing.

"It's perfectly safe...and I'm here with you."

The plane dipped as Kelly climbed into the rear seat, and the glass cover closed with a faint whoosh.

Rebecca swallowed. "MacAlister. I don't want to make a scene, but...I'm definitely getting out of here." She struggled to get her feet under her, but the close quarters made leverage impossible.

"Stop wiggling, honey. You'll be fine. Believe me, I won't let anything happen to you." He kissed the back of her neck and gave Kelly the thumbs-up signal.

The line between their small plane and the larger one pulled taut, but not as tight as Rebecca's screaming nerves. "I hate heights," she cried.

"So do I," he said forcefully.

Rebecca glanced around at him as the plane bounced down the field. "Then . . . why . . . ?"

"Because I heard soaring was terrific . . . a not-to-be-missed experience. And I refuse to miss it because I'm afraid of heights. Especially since this plane is perfectly safe."

"Okay, so I'm being illogical. Now turn this thing around before it leaves the . . ."

Too late. The planes were already airborne and climbing steadily.

With a moan, Rebecca closed her eyes and curled into MacAlister's traitorous, but strong arms like a babe returning to the womb.

"Becky. Open your eyes . . . it's not scary," MacAlister said, his hands soothing her hair.

"Pull the cord," Kelly called above the roaring noise of the tow plane.

Rebecca felt MacAlister's muscles bunch as he leaned forward. There was a slight jolt, and then the plane was rising. Nothing but air stood between them and the ground.

Rebecca whimpered and dug her nails into his arm.

"Open your eyes," MacAlister whispered against her ear. "There's nothing to be afraid of, and you're missing the most magnificent sight in the world. Don't run from your fear, don't let it steal your pleasure," he urged, his voice low. "Come on, brave lady, open your eyes."

Drawing in a ragged breath, Rebecca slitted her eyes and peeked out.

The sun was just setting beyond the distant foothills, a fiery ball bathing them in pink and gold. Against the tropical sky, palm trees stood out like black silhouettes. The Napa Valley stretched between the ridges, a patchwork of brown fields and green vineyards. It was so peaceful, the only sound the soft rush of the thermal drafts that held them aloft.

Her stomach dropped as Kelly banked the plane, but just then the woods below parted to reveal a storybook castle, and she forgot her fear. "It's magnificent," Rebecca breathed.

"You're magnificent." MacAlister tightened his arms around her and rested his chin on her hair.

* * *

It was seven-thirty and dark by the time Harvey Shaw drove past the nearly deserted Calistoga public parking lot. Instantly, the beeper on his tracking device went from a pulsing beat to a steady scream.

"Gotcha." Shaw slanted a glance at the black Toyota sitting alone in the lot and turned his rental car into the lot of the restaurant next door. Keeping low, he snuck up to one of the windows and scanned the faces of the patrons. MacAlister and the Danforth girl were not among them.

"Damn." He stomped back to his car and kicked the tire that had gone flat earlier in the day. "Damn rental companies." He wondered if he could sue them for leasing out a car without a spare. He'd lost two hours hitching a ride to a gas station and persuading them to fix it.

Grumbling under his breath, Shaw slid into the car and settled down to wait for MacAlister and the woman. If they didn't come back for the car in a couple of hours, he'd assume they were spending the night at one of the local hotels and start cruising. It was a small town... shouldn't be too hard to find them since most of the hotels were only a few doors away.

"Had enough?" MacAlister asked.

Rebecca sighed and pushed the half-finished dish of raspberry sorbet aside. "Yes. I don't think I could eat another bite. Everything was delicious. The salad, the hot rolls, the mesquite grilled chicken with peach chutney... It made a nice contrast... the tangy fruit with the meat... I'll have to remember that. I even liked their Calistoga mineral water. I've gotten some really wonderful ideas to use when I have a restaurant of my own."

MacAlister grinned and signaled for the waiter to bring the check. "Kelly gets points for negotiating a smooth landing and picking a great dinner spot. The Mount View Hotel is everything he said it would be."

Rebecca nodded and glanced around the airy, open room. Candlelight cast a rich, mellow glow on the oak furniture and peach table linens. Even MacAlister's features looked gentler, less rugged, bathed in their soft light. If she could save one day out of her life, preserve it like a flower pressed between the pages of a scrapbook, today would be that day.

Today, she had truly fallen in love with him.

Today, she'd learned so much about him, learned he had many good qualities. And he had brought out the best in her. Why couldn't he see that they belonged together forever, not just for a few days or weeks?

Was the mysterious Lily the problem? Did he still love her? Or had her desertion soured him on all women?

"What is it, honey?"

"Nothing," Rebecca said quickly, unwilling to ruin the rest of her perfect day.

MacAlister saw the unease flicker in Rebecca's eyes and wondered what she was thinking. She'd looked at him like that when she'd come out of the bathroom of their room upstairs after cleaning up before dinner. But she'd refused to answer his question then, too.

"Still mad at me for taking you up in the glider?"

"How could I be? It was beautiful . . . worth every scary minute," she said, smiling easily.

Okay, then she must be worried about the mess they were in, MacAlister decided. Not that he blamed her; it had been on his mind all day, too, lurking just below the surface of his teasing and banter. "Ready to go?"

She nodded, the candlelight picking out the red glints in her shiny hair, the pearly sheen of her skin. So beautiful . . . so vulnerable. There was nothing he wouldn't do to keep her safe, or drive the fear from her eyes.

"Let's do it," MacAlister said. His hand rode possessively on the small of Rebecca's straight little back as he escorted her from the room. With one eye, he watched for trouble; the other enjoyed the subtle sway of her hips. Upstairs there was a room waiting for them, with two double beds. Still riding the emotional high from the fantastic day they'd shared, he was hoping they'd only need one of those beds tonight.

He'd promised not to push, and he wouldn't. But his feelings for her were perilously close to the surface tonight, tugging him in a dozen different directions until all he knew for certain was that he needed her. The ache went so deep, had been wound so tight by the hours talking to her, watching her and touching her, that he thought he might explode if he couldn't hold her. "Tired, honey?"

"A little, I guess," Rebecca admitted as they stepped into the hotel's foyer. "I enjoyed today... I don't want it to end."

"Nothing lasts forever."

Rebecca turned, pierced by the bleakness of his words. Looking up at him, she laid her hand on the center of his chest, willing him to understand, to reach out and feel. "Love does."

"I wouldn't know about that," he said roughly.

And you never will if you can't open yourself up to it. "My mother and father did. Even as a little girl, I could read it in their eyes when they looked at each other, or at me. That's what I want," she said softly.

The muscle in his jaw flexed, and his eyes narrowed slightly. "What if you never find it?"

I think I already have. Suddenly she needed to feel his arms around her. The music from the bar surged around them. Something dark and compelling. Snare drums and a sensual sax. "Dance with me, Gates," she murmured.

His hand tightened on her waist. "Here?"

Rebecca's pulse picked up, keeping pace with the unrestrained beat of the drums. "No... by the pool."

Neither of them spoke as he steered her toward the glassed-in courtyard at the back of the hotel.

"Yes..." Rebecca drew in a deep breath of warm, steamy air and turned slowly, taking in the glass dome that let in the moonlight, and then the pool with its thick fringe of jungle plants. "It's like something out of *Casablanca*." The piped-in music was slow and sensual, the room deserted. She lifted her arms to him, beckoning.

MacAlister gathered her close, her low, yielding sigh as she melted into him tearing at his already thin control. "God, you feel so good," he growled, running his hands up and down her back, caressing her through the thin layer of cashmere.

"I've been wanting this all day," she murmured, rocking against him, wrapped up in the sway of the music and the feel of his body. "Gates..." She slid her hands from his shoulders to frame his face and bring it down. "I need you," she whispered a heartbeat before she took his mouth with all the hunger he brought out in her.

MacAlister groaned like a dying man and met the darting edge of her tongue halfway. This was a side of her he'd never seen. The knowledge that she needed him enough to turn aggressor turned him inside out. Breathing heavily, he lifted his head.

"You know where this is leading?" Her eyes burned into his, and she nodded, making him tremble. "You're sure this is what you want?" he forced himself to ask, his voice raw with need.

"Very," she whispered. She knew it couldn't last forever, but she was willing to take what she could get.

"You have two choices, honey," he growled. "Either you let go long enough for us to get upstairs . . . or we find out if those lounge chairs are as comfortable as they look."

Their hotel room looked even more inviting than she'd remembered, all soft light and warm colors. It suited Rebecca's mood exactly. "Mmm. This is nice," she said softly as he locked the door.

"No, this is nice," MacAlister countered, huskily. Sweeping her up in his arms, he carried her to the bed. He set her down beside it, but kept her chained to him in a loose embrace. "Are you really sure about this, honey? I don't want you to have any regrets."

Rebecca smiled at the concern in his eyes. How could she have thought he was ruthless? "Yes, very sure."

"I'm glad." He sighed, his hands tightening possessively on her. "After the way things were between us today, the laughing, the talking . . ."

"The closeness . . ."

"Yeah. Most of all, the closeness." He drew in a deep, steadying breath. "Close isn't enough anymore. I need to be a part of you," he said raggedly, his head lowering.

Rebecca went up on her toes, arching into him as their mouths met, lingered. Her hands moved down to undo the buttons of his shirt. Slowly, she slid her fingers inside, flexed them on the naked, resilient flesh. "You're warm," she murmured, shivering as his lips explored her ear.

"Hot," MacAlister groaned. "Honey, just thinking about you makes me hot. Touching you..." As he spoke, his hands slipped up underneath her sweater, kneading her soft, satiny skin before stealing upward to loosen her bra. "Especially here..." His big hands gently cupped her breasts. "Feeling your nipples go all hard for me..." His thumbs brushed the peaks. "Drives me wild."

"Me, too." Sweet fire danced across her skin, burning, tingling. Rebecca swayed as his long fingers lifted and caressed her swelling breasts. Her nipples tightened in anticipation as he skimmed her sweater off and lifted one breast for his questing mouth. When he drew down on her, her knees buckled, and she would have fallen if he hadn't caught her.

"Sweet, sweet Becky. I nearly come apart when you melt for me. I need to touch all of you...." With quick, impatient movements, he stripped off the rest of her clothes, flicked back the spread and laid her down on the cool sheets. Then he set to work on his own clothes.

"Please." Rebecca stretched out her arms to him. "I wanted to do that."

"Too late." Naked, MacAlister tucked a foil packet under the pillow and came to her. He hadn't been prepared for their first time in Connecticut, but he was tonight. "Next time," he gasped. His mouth turned aggressor, his hands were urgent, control spiraling away even as he fought to keep it, fought to give her the time and the gentleness she deserved.

Rebecca tasted the greed on his kiss, and it fed her hunger. Blindly she reached for him, unbearably excited by the feel of his rough chest hair against her breasts, the strength of his smooth muscles under her fingers.

Through the dizzy whirlwind of passion and sensation, MacAlister felt her rise up to meet him, her mouth avid, her body tangling with his in an ancient dance. Stunned by the force of her response, he opened his eyes to drink in her beauty...her fiery hair spread across the pillows, her face flushed with newfound feminine power. She was all woman. His woman...if only for this moment.

Shuddering, he bent to tend the fire they'd built, his tongue swirling over her skin until Rebecca's pulse pounded, and her breath came in soft moans.

Wild and free. That's how his loving made her feel. Her body came alive with a will and a purpose all its own, the heat and the tension building inside her, coiling tighter and tighter. She moaned again, felt his answering groan as she shifted her hips, opening for his questing fingers like a flower seeking water. One finger eased inside her while his thumb teased her until the pleasure was almost pain. "Oh, Gates. I need you so."

He turned away only briefly, then with a low growl he moved over her, glorying in the soft sounds she made as he slid into her wet, silky heat. Home. Sinking into her was like coming home after a long absence. Then she arched sinuously under him, and all rational thought ended. The rest of the world faded away in the plunging fury of the gathering storm.

I love you... I love you so... The exquisite feeling poured through Rebecca as the storm broke. Pure sensation, pure pleasure, pure love. So intense, the words she'd locked inside her heart poured from her lips.

The electrifying tremors that shook Rebecca ripped through MacAlister like a chain lightning, snatching at his precious control. For an instant, he battled to regain it, but she was there for him, her words of love promising safe haven. With a desperate groan, he gathered her close, gave himself into her keeping, trusting as he never had before.

She didn't take from him; she opened to him, and he plunged deeper, meeting her, finding the other half of himself. They fit together as two halves of one whole. The wonder of it shook him to his soul. Pleasure so sharp it was both agony and ecstasy convulsed his body in a long, shattering release.

Minutes later, hours later, he didn't know which, Mac-Alister's mind kicked back into gear. They lay side by side, nestled like a matched set of silver spoons, the unsteady rasp of his breathing echoed in the rapid beat of Rebecca's heart beneath his hand where it rested between her breasts. "Are you all right?" he managed to whisper.

She sighed, stretched like a sinuous cat, then cuddled farther into the sheltering curve of his body. "More than all right," she murmured. "How about you?"

"I'd intended to be gentle...you deserve gentleness." He nuzzled her ear, stroked her warm silky skin from rib to hipbone and back.

"My fault, I think." She arched under his touch, her stomach muscles fluttering in anticipation. "I didn't know I could be so...wild, so..."

"Responsive?" he asked softly.

"'Greedy' covers it better," she said with a husky laugh. "And wanton, too."

"It's all this red hair." He chuckled, wrapping a curl around his fingers. "Where there's fire, there's passion." And laughter. Had he ever laughed in bed before?

"You knew I'd be passionate when you first met me?"

"No...I knew you'd be trouble." *I just didn't realize what kind, or how much.*

"Mmm. Too much trouble?" she purred, reaching back to run her hand over his stomach, chuckling at his quickly indrawn breath when her fingers drifted lower.

"Damn. I've created a monster."

"Complaints?"

Air hissed out between his teeth as she found him. "Not on your life, honey. But let me put out the cat before you have your wicked way with me, because I'll be lucky to have the strength to breathe when you get through with me."

Rebecca's gaze followed him possessively as he padded across the room. Though he seemed unconcerned by his nudity, she felt herself blush. Her giddiness suffered a slight setback when the "cat" turned out to be the deadly blue-gray gun he carefully tucked beneath his pillow.

"Sometimes, I can almost forget..."

"I know, honey, but *I* can't afford to forget that we won't be safe until this is all over." Recrossing the room, he moved to draw the drapes over the window.

"Wait...I've always dreamed of making love by moonlight," she said softly.

His head snapped around. "Yeah? With who?"

"With you . . . only I didn't know your name then."

MacAlister grinned like a fool, then sobered. "I know the window faces the garden, but we're on the first floor. I don't like leaving it open." It worried him that he'd forgotten to close it earlier, proved his theory that a woman was a dangerous distraction from an assignment.

"Please . . ."

Raking a hand through his hair, MacAlister reluctantly gave in and left the curtains open.

MacAlister woke up to find the moon, which had bathed them in silvery light while he and Becky made the kind of slow, lazy love he, too, had only dreamed about, had moved on, leaving the bedroom shadowed. At first he wasn't sure what had penetrated the haze of sleep.

Then he heard it. . . .

A soft whoosh. The whisper of fabric sliding.

The window was on Becky's side of the bed. As he looked over her, he sensed motion, caught the dull gleam of metal coming out of the darkness. Upraised. Threatening.

The gun was behind him, under the pillow. Becky was in front of him and vulnerable. He felt cold, tasted fear. He had only an instant to decide which way to roll.

Rebecca groaned, jerked from a deep sleep as a heavy weight crashed down on her. It passed swiftly, followed by a hard hand shoving her across the tangled sheets.

"Get the hell out of here, Becky," MacAlister shouted hoarsely. His words ended on a guttural grunt of pain.

He was hurt, Rebecca thought dimly. What had happened? Trembling, she scrambled to her knees at the edge of the bed, dragged the hair from her eyes.

Across the bed from her, MacAlister and a short, bulky man grappled for possession of something shiny.

A gun? A knife? Her heart thudded painfully against her ribs. MacAlister was strong, but he was wounded; she could see the dark, ominous trail running down his arm. As the thought formed, his opponent lashed out, his fist plowing into Mac-Alister's injured shoulder.

MacAlister grunted a curse, grabbed for the man's throat, and the two of them went down with a thud.

"No," Rebecca cried softly. Without being aware she'd moved, with no clear idea what she could do to help him, she started to crawl across the bed. Her hand slid under the pillow, touched something cold.

The gun. She grabbed it, clutched it as she moved again. Quickly this time, her breath catching in frantic little sobs.

They were on the floor beside the bed. MacAlister on the bottom, both hands braced to resist the downward thrust of the knife clutched in the fists of the man straddling his chest. She paused long enough to see the knife waver, then slowly begin to move down....

Rebecca jammed the barrel of the gun into the attacker's neck just below his ear. "Let go of the knife," she ordered in a calm, detached voice she couldn't believe was hers. When he hesitated, she spared a moment of regret that she didn't know if the safety was on or not, or even where it was.

In the end, it didn't matter. The gun made a satisfyingly ominous sound as her thumb brought the hammer back. "Now."

Chapter 11

"Are you sure you don't want me to drive?"

"I'm fine." MacAlister didn't take his eyes off the road, his face hard and dangerous in the green glow of the dash lights.

"Your shoulder...?"

"Relax, honey. I told you it was okay. You did a terrific job of bandaging it, and the aspirin took the edge off the pain." The edge of impatience in his voice warned her to back off.

Rebecca heaved a sigh. It was just after midnight, and they'd been on the road about fifteen minutes. Shaw was in the trunk, his hands and feet tied with pieces of the same sheet she'd torn to bind MacAlister's wound. She was unharmed physically, and MacAlister had assured her the knife had glanced off his collarbone, slicing a bloody line across his shoulder, but doing little real damage.

She shivered, suddenly cold despite the heat pumping through the car. "I was so scared...."

"Hey." He reached over, slid his warm hand under her hair and gently squeezed her neck. "You were terrific, sweetheart. If you hadn't stopped Shaw when you did, I'd have had another hole in me before I got the knife away from him." Jeez, he could kick himself for letting a punk like Shaw take him by surprise.

Rebecca leaned into his caress. "I couldn't have shot him. I didn't know enough to take the safety off," she said in a shaky whisper.

"It's the thought that counts, honey." He stroked his thumb along her jawline, then returned his right hand back to the steering wheel. He slowly lowered his left hand onto his thigh, stifling a groan as pain stabbed through his left shoulder.

Over the years, he'd been shot, gouged and bruised enough to know that although the wound wasn't serious, it would be sore and stiff for the next few days. *Damn.* He fought down a surge of angry frustration. Tomorrow he wouldn't be operating at one hundred percent when he went to the warehouse.

"You know the man," Rebecca said thoughtfully, her mind racing back over the evening's events, unable to settle down. "The man Shaw said had sent him."

"Yeah, I know Rousseau."

"Are you afraid of him?" She'd been surprised and a little frightened by the sudden flare of desperation in MacAlister's eyes when Shaw had finally yielded up the information.

Not for myself, princess, for you. "Rousseau's done some bad things," he said carefully. "He hurt someone I cared about," he added when he saw she wasn't going to be satisfied with that.

"Was it Lily?"

MacAlister's head snapped around. "What makes you say that?"

"Just...just the way you said it...as though you loved her."

"I didn't love her...that was the problem," he growled under his breath. "But, yeah, it was Lily. She's dead, and I think Rousseau was responsible. I still have nightmares about what happened to her, but I couldn't prove a thing at the time. And I still can't." Irritated, he started to rake his left hand into his hair, winced and let it drop back.

"Oh, Gates. Your shoulder is hurting you."

"It's not bad," he replied. He'd been expecting to hear the cold sting of jealousy in her voice, not the warmth of concern.

It carried a special, healing heat all its own. Exhaling softly as the pain receded, he slipped her a measuring glance.

"Were you expecting me to rant and rave?" She smiled faintly. "I may be naive...but I never thought I was the only woman you'd ever..." digging her nails into her palm, she carefully skirted the word love "...went to bed with."

"No, not the only one..." *But the only one who ever meant anything.* Suddenly, it seemed right that he tell her how it had been with Lily. Briefly, he sketched the case that had brought Lily into his life.

"There was a spark between us from the first, and it intensified after she moved in with me," he said bluntly. Steeling himself to ignore the pain in Rebecca's eyes, he pressed on. Better a small hurt now, than a big one farther down the road when she expected a commitment from him and he let her down as he had Lily. "Pretty soon things started to unravel. Lily was talking marriage—I was content to let things drift. She cried— I got mad. She threatened to leave—I let her walk."

His hand tightened on the steering wheel, knuckles turning white. "I let her walk," he said in an agonized whisper, "knowing that Rousseau wanted revenge because she had betrayed him to the Bureau and moved in with me after refusing to become his mistress."

"H-he killed her because she wouldn't sleep with him?"

MacAlister exhaled sharply. "No...not then, anyway. My partner, Jack Sabine, loaned her some money to get started in another city. I paid him back when I found out, and damned myself for not having thought she'd be in danger."

"You were hurt...."

"Hurt, hell," he growled on a wave of self-anger. "If I was, it was only my pride. I liked Lily, admired her courage, wanted her in my bed...but that was all I had to give her, and when that wasn't enough..." He shifted in the seat, his profile stark. "It was almost five years before I heard about her again. She was back in Cairo, singing in a fancy new nightclub Rousseau had just opened."

"She went to work for a man who wanted to kill her?" Rebecca knew she was prejudiced, but it seemed to her Lily hadn't acted very wisely...about a lot of things.

MacAlister checked the mirrors, then glanced over at Rebecca. Her quiet, patient curiosity shook him. Wasn't she drawing the parallel between his relationship with Lily and his affair with her? Because that's all it could be....

"I'm sorry she's dead," Rebecca said softly, longing to soothe his pain. If only he'd let her get close enough to try.

"I'm sorry, too. Rousseau saw to that," he added grimly. "The bastard's patient, I'll give him that. Over five years he waited to bring down the three of us... Jack, Lily and me. He knew I had called Lily and tried to convince her she was in danger. He also knew Jack and I were getting close to shutting him down, so he arranged an ambush. Jack and I got a message that Lily had information for us about Rousseau. When we went to meet her, Rousseau's men were waiting. They took Jack down right away, and I got two of them. By that time, our backup was pouring into the alley...." He dragged in a ragged breath.

Rebecca reached over to touch him, reassure him as he had done for her several times over the past few days. "You and Jack were close?"

"Yeah...." He stared out at the short stretch of black road illuminated by the headlights, but she sensed he was lost in the past. After a moment he shook himself and sighed. "I was up all night, grieving for Jack, searching for Lily. She was waiting for me when I finally got to the office...."

A chill moved over Rebecca's skin at the odd coldness in his voice. "Waiting...?" she forced herself to ask.

"Yeah.... There was a trunk with my name on it...." he said rawly, as though the words were being dragged from him. "And a note...'You can have her. I'm finished with her.'" A muscle in his jaw jumped as he grated his teeth. "Lily was inside the trunk...."

"In the... Oh, God..." Rebecca swallowed.

MacAlister nodded, grimly satisfied with the horror in her eyes. "Whatever you are imagining, the reality was worse. She didn't die easily," he added ominously, then sat back in the seat, feeling exhausted and disgusted with himself. "I'm not telling you this just to scare you, honey," he added more gently. "I want you to understand what kind of...monster...we're up against. Rousseau thought nothing of—'' *probably even enjoyed* ''—killing a woman who had scorned him and crossed him in a minor way. The book you took from your cousin's safe-deposit box is *very* important to him. If you stand in his way...''

"Oh, my God," Rebecca whispered. "What about Rose-anne?"

"What about her?"

"She's... When I talked to her, I heard a man..."

"I'm not surprised."

"A Frenchman...." she said hoarsely. "I couldn't hear what he was saying, but the accent was unmistakable."

MacAlister snapped to attention. "Did she mention his name? Tell you where she was?"

"No. But I still have the phone number. Maybe one of your friends at the Bureau could trace it."

"It's worth a try. I like the idea of going on the offensive, taking the battle to Rousseau's new little kingdom. Being on the run is beginning to get to me."

"Oh, I don't know," Rebecca said with a ghost of a smile. "You have to admit... it hasn't been all bad."

MacAlister chuckled in spite of himself and shot her a glance that made her blush. "No, it's been fantastic. Discounting the goons that have been chasing us, this has been the best—" He sobered suddenly, remembering that if something should happen to him, Amber would be all alone. "Ah, I need to ask you a favor...." he began hesitantly.

Rebecca's smile faded. A man like MacAlister didn't ask for favors unless he was desperate. "What?"

He guessed the best way to get through this was to blurt it out and hold his breath. "I have a daughter...."

"You do?" Rebecca was shocked. "Where is she? I didn't see any evidence at your apartment...."

"Amber lives with an Oriental couple in a house I rent outside New York City," he said gruffly. "Lily was her mother, but I didn't even know I had a daughter until a few days after Lily was dead when the couple—Lily's maternal aunt and uncle—came knocking on my door."

"Oh, Gates," Rebecca breathed, her emotions in chaos. 'Why . . . why doesn't she live with you?''

"It's better this way. She's had a lot of adjustments to make . . . her mother's death, living in a strange country, learning a new language. I'm a stranger to her, too, and I'm away a lot. . . ." His expression gave little away, yet Rebecca sensed confusion bordering on panic. Simply, he didn't know what to do with his daughter, any more than he knew what to do with Rebecca's love.

Rebecca ached for all three of them, but mostly for the boy who'd been forced to grow up too quickly and the man who couldn't trust himself to love. "How old is Amber?" she managed.

"Five," he said woodenly.

Five. Dear God. Rebecca felt a jolt of misery. It must have showed in her face, because MacAlister added, "She's well provided for, and her relatives are elderly, but . . ."

"Do they love Amber?" she pressed.

"They have a deep sense of family responsibility. And they're kind to her. I understand she really likes the bike I sent her."

Sent her, not gave her. Rebecca couldn't swallow her anger any longer. "MacAlister," she said sternly, turning in the seat to face him, demanding his attention. "You can't cut yourself off from your daughter like this. It isn't fair to you or to her. Take it from me . . . a shiny new bicycle—ten shiny new bicycles—can't replace a warm hug from someone who loves you."

He stared stonily at the road ahead, his lips compressed into a thin line. "It's better this way," he finally said. "This way, I won't let her down."

Like your father let you down, like you think you let Lily down, Rebecca thought with sudden insight. Her shoulders slumped with weariness and frustration. "No, it isn't better," she said quietly, but he didn't seem to hear her. Or if he did, he still wasn't ready to believe . . . or trust. "What was the favor you wanted from me?"

He glanced at her quickly with something that looked like regret. "I just wanted you to know about Amber."

Why was he lying? Rebecca turned the question over a few times before saying, "I think that's part of it. But I think you were going to ask me to look after Amber if anything . . . happened . . ." *To you.* The words stuck on the lump in her throat and she couldn't speak them.

"Nothing's going to happen." He said it like he meant it because a man who doubted his own abilities, even for an instant, was signing his own death warrant.

The agent's call rang through just as Rousseau's private jet was climbing into the early morning skies above the blue Caribbean ocean. "*Non*, we have not heard anything from Shaw," the Frenchman snapped into the receiver. "Have your operatives learned anything?"

"No. MacAlister's been too smart to use his credit card again, but we have people checking out the hotels and restaurants in the area."

"Let me know the minute you hear anything. I must get to him before your Bureau does."

"Understood." The agent paused. "There's been a slight complication. Charles Danforth received a call from his niece yesterday. He tried the number she'd left with his office and got the Fairmont Hotel. When they told him the room's occupants, a Mr. and Mrs. Johnson, had checked out, he went through the roof, called the Bureau and demanded action."

"I'm sure a man of Mr. Danforth's stature and, er, how shall we say, persuasiveness, got prompt results."

"He made Chief Crenshaw nervous," the agent growled. "The Chief told Danforth not to worry, told him his niece was in good hands . . . MacAlister used to be one of his best agents."

"What has this to do with us?"

"Danforth wasn't satisfied. He arrived here yesterday afternoon with six detectives he'd hired to search for his missing niece."

"So . . . the field becomes more crowded," Rousseau said with growing annoyance. "What if they find MacAlister and the girl before we do?"

"Crenshaw's trying to get a court order to bar Danforth's men from the area until the Bureau's investigation is complete by claiming this case is a matter of national security."

"Excellent," Rousseau said, settling back in the thickly padded leather seat.

"I don't know," the agent replied doubtfully. "Danforth went a little crazy when he heard, threatened to call the President if his niece wasn't found...yesterday...and the guy who'd abducted her strung up by his—"

"Strange...Danforth seemed unaffected when Roseanne disappeared after her husband's murder."

"Yeah. The guy's hard to figure."

"I will not waste time trying. All I want is the book."

The agent sighed. "I'm working on it...."

"Time is running out," Rousseau snapped impatiently. "If MacAlister has been able to decode the book, he will be at the Golden Circle warehouse tomorrow. Peck and some of my men will be waiting for him, of course, but if MacAlister should decide to bring in the authorities..."

"He'll turn to the Bureau, and I'll see to it he doesn't get any help."

MacAlister leaned his good shoulder against an old phone booth in a run-down little plaza just outside of San Francisco and waited for Theo to call back. He felt drained, and the two aspirin he'd taken a while ago hadn't touched the throbbing in his shoulder.

The car door opened, and Rebecca got out; she shoved her hands in the pockets of her coat as she shuffled stiffly toward him. In the harsh glare of a streetlight, her face was pale, her eyes dark and worried.

"There's more coffee. Sit in the car and drink it while I take a turn waiting for the call," she said quietly.

"No. You need the rest more than I do."

"Mmm. Determined to slay all the dragons yourself?" Her faint smile surprised the hell out of him.

"What dragons?"

"Never mind," she murmured, her smile turning soft and warm. She stood on tiptoe, brushed his mouth with hers. "I love you, Gates MacAlister, but if you don't sit down, I'm going to shoot you in the foot." Stepping back, she aimed the finger in her pocket at his boots.

"What?" he choked out. "This isn't a laughing matter."

"Sometimes that's when you need to laugh the most," she said soberly, then ruined it by smiling impishly. "Perhaps I should make it something you value more." She aimed her 'weapon' higher, threatening his...

"You are something else," he said, grinning and shaking his head.

She swaggered forward, raised her face to him. "You think so, do you?"

"I know so." He kissed her lightly, then walked the few steps to the car, wondering how he'd ever thought she was soft. The lady had a core of pure steel.

As he gingerly lowered himself into the car, eyes squeezed shut, lips contorted with pain, Rebecca felt tears burn the backs of her lids. Foolish, stubborn, wonderful man, she thought. He'd been wounded protecting her, then tried to convince her he was the kind of man who avoided commitment. *Baloney.* She'd seen the look on his face when he'd turned on the lights in the hotel room and asked if she was all right. Never mind the blood running down his chest, he'd been worried sick about her, refused to let her see to his wound until he was certain she was okay.

This was not the reaction of an uncaring man. Though telling her about Lily and Rousseau had been the act of a desperate one. He'd wanted to impress her with the seriousness of their situation. So, she was impressed. But he'd also been warning her away... from himself.

Maybe he was right, maybe he'd been scarred too deeply by his harsh childhood to ever learn to trust another human being. Maybe he could never love her the way she needed to be loved. Maybe by trying to reach him she was leaving herself open for a bad emotional fall.

For an hour, she waited in the chilly predawn air, thinking and watching the sky slowly lighten. There wasn't a sound out of Shaw in the trunk. MacAlister had reclined the seat and fallen asleep. She wondered where Roseanne was and if she was safe.

How complicated her neat, orderly life had gotten since Roseanne's fateful call. No matter how things looked, Rebecca couldn't believe her cousin had intended to harm her. Roseanne might be shallow, vain and selfish, but she wasn't a murderess.

The ringing of the phone jerked Rebecca around. She reached past the bifold door and snatched it up. The cold plastic chilled her ear. "H-hello," she stuttered.

"I, er, must have the wrong..."

"Theo? Don't hang up. This is Theo, isn't it?"

"Yeah. Who are you?"

MacAlister was beside her, taking the phone away before she could answer. "Theo?" he asked warily.

"Here. Was that the Danforth woman? Sounds nice...way too classy for you, old buddy."

MacAlister grunted something into the phone, then covered the receiver with his hand. "It's okay, honey. I'll take it from here." He gave Rebecca a gentle nudge in the direction of the car. She frowned up at him, her stubborn jaw set, and he was afraid she'd insist on listening to his end of the conversation. He touched her cheek in an unconscious gesture of appeal, grateful when she sighed, walked over to the car and got in.

"What did you find out?" he asked Theo as Rebecca shut the car door.

"My friend at the Bureau didn't have any luck tracing the number you gave me...said it switched and dead-ended into half the phone systems in the country. Whoever set it up is good."

MacAlister swore softly, thinking of the hundreds of tiny islands dotting the Caribbean. It could take months, maybe years, to find out which one Rousseau had bought. "Any luck finding out where Stone and the boys are?"

"Yeah. They've set up shop in one of the Sheratons." Theo gave him the address. "You going to call Stone?"

"I don't know." MacAlister said slowly.

"Arrange to meet him alone. You can trust Stone."

Can I? It was tempting as hell to think he could, because this job had gotten too big for one man to handle. Looking at the car through the cloudy glass of the phone booth, he made out Becky's pale face against the dark headrest. More than anything, he wished he could magically pull her out of this mess.

"Theo, could you hide someone for me for a few days?" he asked after a moment.

"The Danforth woman?" Theo guessed. "Sure. I'm meeting the guy who used to work for Deets in a couple of hours. After that, I'm available."

A warning fluttered in MacAlister's gut again. "Why?"

"He's got something more on Rousseau," Theo said excitedly. "Maybe we can nail the bastard this time."

"Don't go, Theo. I've got a bad feeling about this."

"Hey, the guy just wants to help out. Hell, he's even getting close to uncovering Rousseau's Bureau connection . . . says it's someone you've known a long time."

Damn. That meant it had to be either Stone or Thatcher. "I don't like it," MacAlister growled. "If this guy knew so much, he'd have gone to Crenshaw instead of leaking information to you and trying to set up a meet with me."

Theo hesitated. "Maybe you're right . . . but I'd do anything to help you get Rousseau."

"And if your guy is Rousseau's plant, he knows that. Stall him for a couple of days, lay low until you hear from me. If things work out here, we may be able to put Rousseau away without his help."

"Sounds good to me. What about the woman?"

MacAlister sighed. "She stays with me." For better, or for worse.

The motel was a dozen grades below any they'd stayed in, just one in a string of cheap, faceless motels near the waterfront where rooms could be rented by the week, the day . . . or even by the hour.

"Sorry, honey, I know it's not what you're used to," MacAlister said grimly as he ushered her into the small, dingy motel room.

Rebecca looked around at the drab walls, stained carpeting and scarred furniture. Though the bed was only a double, it took up most of the room, and the faded orange spread accentuated the lumps in the mattress. "It's only for one night," she replied, suppressing a shudder.

"You're going to have to stay here tomorrow while I'm gone," he reminded her. Slinging the duffel bag onto the bed, he closed the door and locked it. She sighed and nodded, but she looked so forlorn he had to jam his hands into his pockets to keep from gathering her close. "I'll get you some books while I'm out."

"Can I go with you?" Rebecca asked hopefully. At his curt negative, she started to protest.

"This isn't a pleasure trip, honey." His expression was cool, his voice crisp, devoid of the gentleness he'd shown her. "I've got to get rid of Shaw and—"

Rebecca gasped in shock. "Oh, my God . . ."

"I'm not going to kill him." Hurt glittered briefly in his eyes, and she felt ashamed to have doubted him. "I'm going to see to it he's out of commission for a day or so and ditch the rental car. Why don't you get some sleep. When I come back, we'll get something to eat and something for you to read."

After he left, Rebecca paced the dingy room, wondering how she was going to get through the next day and a half without going out of her mind from boredom and worry. Finally, exhaustion overcame her. She lay down on the uncomfortable bed without any real hope of sleeping, yet the next thing she knew, someone was calling her name and shaking her awake.

"What?" She opened her eyes, looking up groggily at the man who stood beside the bed.

It wasn't MacAlister.

Rebecca's heart kicked into double time, her mind whirling with possibilities. Fear and flight were the only ones to take root. Instinctively, she rolled to the other side of the room and bolted for the bathroom. There was a small window there. If she could lock the door . . .

"Easy, honey. It's me," came MacAlister's voice.

One hand on the bathroom door, she hesitated. Eyes narrowing, she stared at the tall blond hippy waiting on the other side of the bed.

His hands rested on the waist of the formfitting dark gray coveralls he wore. The cap worn low on his head shadowed his eyes. The build was right . . . broad, powerful shoulders, deep chest, lean hips and muscular legs . . . the scuffed boots even looked vaguely familiar. But the hair sweeping his collar was blond, and the matching taffy beard hid most of his face.

"See anything you like, princess?" he drawled.

"M-MacAlister?"

Behind the fringe of yellow hair, his lips curled up. "Ever kiss a guy with a beard before?"

"Oh . . . you rat. You took ten years off my life." Rebecca seethed as she stomped around the bed. According to the name stitched across his left breast pocket, the man she was about to punch was Steve.

"Hey. Remember I'm a wounded man," he declared, catching her right hook in one hand and easily drawing her up against his chest despite her resistance. Below the bill of his cap, his eyes danced wickedly.

"MacAlister," she warned through clenched teeth.

"Steve," he corrected, grinning. "And I didn't intend to scare you, honest. It just sort of . . . happened. If you hadn't scooted off the bed so fast . . ."

"Conditioned response," she replied tightly.

MacAlister's grin faded. "It'll be all over tomorrow, honey," he said softly as he folded her close. He'd promised himself he wouldn't touch her again, but he just couldn't seem to do what was right, what was noble. He needed her too damn much. By tomorrow, he'd have to find the strength to walk out of her life and not look back.

Rebecca sighed and melted into his embrace, nuzzling into the hollow above his heart. Its strong, sure beat steadied her own. "Will everything be all right tomorrow?"

"I promise nothing will happen to you, honey."

"That wasn't what I wanted to know." She lifted her face, searched his eyes. Something in them told her he was far more worried about her than he was about himself. "This is the disguise you're wearing to the warehouse."

He nodded solemnly. "There really is a Steve Sarcoff working for Golden Circle in New York." He drew a picture ID from his pocket. The man in the blurry photo had long blond hair and a full beard. "I got a duplicate copy of this when I decided to come out here. Steve is shorter than I am and heavier, but it should work. He transferred out here from New York last week, but he's not due to start work until next Monday. Shouldn't seem strange if he comes in a few days early to take a look around."

Rebecca nodded, her stomach already churning with the fear she was certain would have it tied in knots by the next morning. Much as she wanted to scream and cry and beg him not to go, she forced herself to stay calm. She needed to be strong so he could concentrate on his job.

"What does a girl have to do to get fed around here?" she asked softly.

She had to wear a pair of oversize sunglasses and a short brown wig, Rebecca discovered. MacAlister exchanged the Golden Circle overalls for black jeans and a sweatshirt, but left on the rest of his disguise.

They ate at a McDonald's, shopped for books and a deck of cards at a discount store, then walked along the wharf for a couple of hours before returning to the motel. There was no TV, so they sat cross-legged on the bed and played cards listening to a jazz station on the portable radio bolted to the headboard above the bed.

The atmosphere was companionable, yet beneath its surface ran a current of sensual awareness that flowed hotter and faster every time their eyes met. Rebecca could almost imagine they were a pair of runaway lovers, hiding from her irate relatives. Goodness knows, Uncle Charles would have been more than irate if he knew where she was.

For once in her life, Rebecca didn't care. She made no attempt to hide her feelings, put every spark of the hunger burning inside her into the glances she slanted his way. When he laid down a card, she made sure her fingers were there to caress the back of his hand or touch his arm.

In the middle of the third hand, MacAlister suddenly threw down his cards and tumbled her onto the pillows. "Witch, you've been tormenting me all night," he growled, his mouth hot on her ear, her throat.

"Yes, I have." All day she'd sensed him moving away from her emotionally, and she was determined to bind him to her any way she could. She refused to let him remove their clothes, merely opening and pushing aside what was necessary until he had her where she wanted him. The homeward thrust was swift, the journey wild and fiercely urgent, the climax mutually explosive.

"The next time is going to be gentle, lazy and last for hours," MacAlister promised huskily as she lay spent and breathless in his arms. He removed her clothes slowly, then kept his promise with such tenderness it brought tears to her eyes.

MacAlister had visited all the Golden Circle Import/Export Company's warehouses before concluding his deal with Deets. Some changes had been made at the San Francisco facility since then. Changes Deets hadn't bothered to tell his partner about. Like the strings of barbed wire ringing the building, the sophisticated new security system and the pairs of guards armed with Uzi submachine guns patrolling inside as well as out.

There was definitely something more valuable than electrical components, wine, furniture and decorative geegaws passing through here, MacAlister thought as he settled in behind a row of crates containing Mexican glazed pottery. They sat atop a double-decker skid rack near the loading docks. The shadows were deeper atop the stack, and from this vantage point he had an unrestricted view of the pair of large overhead doors in shipping and receiving, as well as the warehouse's main aisles.

It was nearly ten at night, yet the last shipment of the day—Indian jewelry from somewhere in Arizona—still hadn't come in. He wasn't leaving until it did.

He'd been here since eight this morning. The guards at the front gate had checked him out thoroughly, even called personnel to verify his story. But once he'd gotten inside, he'd ambled around without attracting much attention.

Then he got lucky. They were shorthanded in shipping and receiving. Naturally, he'd offered to help, and while the supervisor's back was turned, MacAlister had flipped through the list of shipments expected in. Mentally comparing them to the points of origin from the New York warehouse, he'd found two definite matches—Salt Lake City and Baltimore, Maryland—and one possible. It was the possible that caught his attention.

Though the shipment due in from Arizona today didn't originate from the same town as the one on the New York manifest, both were small Arizona towns he'd never heard of. It was definitely worth checking out. They kind of went together...drug deals and out-of-the-way places, a different one each time.

At closing time, it had been a cinch to hide in the warehouse. Waiting until everyone left but the guards, he snuck around and opened the cartons that had come in earlier in the day from Salt Lake and Baltimore, just in case his hunch about Arizona didn't pan out. It had been slow, dangerous work opening the boxes and sorting through the contents very carefully, knowing the slightest noise would bring the guards running.

In the end, he found nothing in either shipment. The ice had to be coming in from Arizona.

MacAlister settled back to wait, trying not to think about Becky alone in the run-down motel. Alone and frightened. If the last glimpse of her pale, set features as she closed the door behind him was any indication, she'd spend the day worrying about him.

"Please be careful," she'd whispered, looking up at him through eyes wide with fear, shimmering with tears she fought to keep back. "If you're not back by tonight, what should I do?"

"Nothing, honey. It may take me all night to search the warehouse. You've got enough food here to last until tomorrow. Don't go outside, don't open the door to anyone. I'll be back for you as quick as I can." He slipped his arms around her and gathered her close, buried his face in her hair, breathing in the light floral scent of shampoo and Becky, strangely strengthened by the feel of her softness wrapping around him.

She trembled, and he tightened his grip. "Hang on just a little longer, brave lady," he murmured. He kissed her hard, tasted the desperation on her lips, and the tears.

The sudden ringing of the dock bell jerked MacAlister back to the warehouse, and his heart kicked into high gear. Someone outside the big overhead doors wanted in.

A pair of guards trotted down the aisle, guns cradled in the crooks of their arms. They fanned out on either side of the door, guns at the ready, and one of them depressed a button on the wall. Overhead, a switch clicked on, and the heavy steel door began to move up.

Adrenaline surged through MacAlister, driving out the ache of cramped muscles. Peeking around a crate, he watched a half-ton truck back up to the dock. Below him, he heard the pounding of booted feet as four more guards jogged down the aisles and into view.

"Great," he muttered to himself. Six against one, and who knew how many men were in the truck. He had two guns, his own and the one he'd taken from Harvey Shaw, but they were no match for the guard's semiautomatic weapons and assault rifles.

The truck's doors swung open, and two men in olive-green uniforms hopped up onto the loading platform.

"You guys are early," drawled a voice MacAlister knew only too well. *Enos Peck.*

A tremor shook MacAlister as he watched Rousseau's personal bodyguard saunter into view. Jack and Lily were dead by Rousseau's order, but it was a sure thing Peck had fired the shot that had killed Jack, and the slime had probably taken even more pleasure in beating Lily to death. Peck had this thing about women.

Looks-wise, the guy hadn't changed a bit in the past few months. He still resembled something that had crawled out from under a rock. Short, thickset and white as a fish's underbelly. The Slug, Jack used to call him.

There were two more guards with Peck, but MacAlister wasn't figuring the odds, he was fighting the urge to plant a bullet in the middle of Peck's wide white forehead. And the hell with everything else.

Chapter 12

Rebecca had spent the day pacing, too keyed up to read more than a few pages of a novel, too nervous to eat the fruit and cheese in the cooler. By nine that night, her nerves were stretched so tight she wanted to scream, and her imagination was running wild.

In her mind, she saw MacAlister lying hurt somewhere, and felt powerless to help. There wasn't even a phone in the room. He couldn't call if he needed her. Neither could the hospital. . . .

Rebecca's stomach clenched, every instinct warning her MacAlister was in trouble. Damn, why hadn't she followed him? Turning from the window, she rifled frantically through the dresser drawers, looking for a phone book. She'd get the address of the Golden Circle warehouse and . . .

Her shoulders slumped as she realized that no phone meant no phone book. And what could she do, anyway? She was only one, untrained woman. This Rousseau probably had dozens of men at the warehouse, hired killers like Harvey Shaw. What MacAlister needed was help from professionals like Thatcher and Stone.

Shivering, Rebecca closed the bottom dresser drawer and straightened slowly. She wrapped her arms around her body and paced back to the window. What should she do? The longer she considered MacAlister's reasons for not involving the Bureau, the more convinced she became that he'd made a mistake. Admittedly the best way for MacAlister to clear his name was to capture the real drug dealers. But he couldn't do it alone.

MacAlister thinks there's an informant at the Bureau, but he trusts Stone, she reasoned. And he'd told her where his former boss was staying. Maybe MacAlister had meant for her to go to Stone if anything went wrong.

That's not what he said, and you know it. He'll be furious if you leave.

Better furious than dead.

Rebecca jammed the wig on her head and stuffed her curls up under it, hoping she had enough money for a cab ride to the downtown Sheraton.

"Any luck tracing the shipment back?" Peck demanded of the truck driver.

"Naw. The bastard must've known we had guys waitin' on the ground to tail him. He sent the stuff in a helo this time." The driver's thin face twisted into a grimace. "Looks like this'll be the last shipment."

Peck swore, his voice flat and hard. "Rousseau's working on that. Now get busy unloading the stuff."

MacAlister could have hugged himself. Theo had been right. Rousseau didn't know who Deets's supplier was. There was always a chance the Iceman knew who Rousseau was, but MacAlister bet Deets had kept that a secret, too. They'd be out of business after this shipment.

Of course, the Iceman could set himself up another distributor, MacAlister thought, his smile fading. Damn, he wished Deets had been more specific. What the hell was a *seadot?* Once this was over, maybe the Bureau's computer experts could figure it out.

Down below, the forklift growled to life, and two men started to unload the truck. The other four fanned out, Uzis and AK47s poised and ready in case there was trouble.

MacAlister ducked back behind the crates. *Okay, hotshot, what now?* He needed to be three men. One to stay here and watch the boxes until someone came to pick them up. Another to follow these guys . . . hopefully back to Rousseau. A third to get Peck.

Damn. If he'd trusted Stone, MacAlister would have called the Sheraton for reinforcements. Hell. If he'd trusted Stone, the agents would be here now, waiting with him in the shadows to make the bust.

"Get those crates of pottery down here and we'll start packing the stuff into them," Peck ordered.

"What the hell..." MacAlister muttered under his breath as the skid rack he was sitting on rocked. The hair rose on his nape as he saw the large steel prongs of the forklift slide under the first crate in the line. Instantly, he shifted as far to the left as he could, half behind, half beside the fourth carton. *Damn.* If they took down all four, he'd be totally exposed.

Quickly he scanned the neat rows of boxes ten feet below him. *Hell.* If he stayed where he was, he'd be a sitting duck. If he jumped, he'd be vulnerable for the few seconds it took him to land, get his bearings and scramble for cover. But that was exactly what he was going to do, MacAlister decided, because there was no way in hell he was sitting still.

One gone.

Then two. The sweat beaded on his upper lip.

Three.

He checked the chambers on his 9 mm revolver as the forklift lumbered back for the fourth crate. His pulse was jumping, but the adrenaline pumping through him kept his mind clear and his nerves steady. Already, he'd picked out the carton farthest from the door and made the leap a dozen times in his head. He'd be okay...if he didn't break something when he landed.

The operator switched the forklift to neutral and pulled the lever to raise the fork.

MacAlister's hand tightened around the gun.

"Drop your weapons." Stone's harsh voice, boosted by a bullhorn, rang off the rafters.

MacAlister froze, expecting to have his head blown off any second. He felt no fear, only a deep sadness that Stone had been the one after all.

"You men on the loading dock," Stone shouted. "Drop your weapons. Federal Bureau of . . ."

You men on the dock . . . Not him. MacAlister let out the breath he'd been holding.

From the open bay door, a guard's Uzi spat fire at the men slithering down the warehouse's main aisle. A man screamed.

MacAlister didn't wait to see who was hit. Whipping up, his body shielded by the last crate, he pulled the trigger once and the guard flew back, a crimson splotch blossoming in the center of his chest.

The forklift operator abandoned his machine and sprinted for the open back of the truck. A spray of bullets raked the floor ahead of him and he screeched to a halt, hands over his head.

"Don't shoot. . . ." The other guards began tossing their weapons aside and lifting their hands.

As the area filled with men in bullet-proof vests and helmets, MacAlister caught a flash of someone moving outside. The man opened the door to a dark car parked beside the truck. The harsh beam of the dome light burnished pale hair and the sickly white face below for an instant before the man pulled the door shut. *Peck.*

"Peck . . . He's getting away," MacAlister shouted. He jammed his gun into the waist of his jeans and got ready to jump, but the car took off, tires squealing.

"Damn." MacAlister slammed his fist into the crate.

"MacAlister? You okay?" Stone shouted.

"Never mind me, Peck's getting away."

The wail of sirens cut through the night, and a pair of squad cars raced off in the direction Peck had gone, but MacAlister knew they'd never catch him. He took his anger out on Stone. "What the hell are you doing here?" he growled. Hands on hips, he glared down at his former boss.

"Saving your ass, from the looks of things." Stone glanced over his shoulder at the agents who were cuffing the guards and reading them their rights, then back at MacAlister. "Or were you planning on becoming invisible before they picked up the last crate?"

MacAlister stepped onto the forks of the electric truck. Legs braced, fists and jaw tightly clenched, he rode them down while one of Stone's men worked the controls.

"What I was planning on doing," MacAlister snarled when he reached the ground, "was tracing these guys back to Rousseau. Thanks to you, all we've got are his gofers...and you let Peck get away." "Sorry about Peck...I know how much you wanted him," Stone said, drawing in a deep breath and exhaling in exasperation. "But we both know you didn't stand a chance in hell of tracing these guys anywhere once they spotted you up there...and you had no place to hide."

Rage glinted in MacAlister's eyes for an instant, then muted to frustration. "Yeah, I know." *Damn. He'd come so close....*

"We'll get him next time," Stone said tersely.

"There won't be a *next time*. This was the last shipment." Stone muttered a pungent oath, and MacAlister nodded in agreement. The only good thing to come of this was that he no longer thought Stone was working with Rousseau. "Did you have the warehouse staked out? Or did you just happen to show up at the right time?"

"Nope. Rebecca Danforth told me where to find you."

MacAlister's mouth dropped open. "Becky...Rebecca? But she was supposed to keep out of sight."

"She was worried about you." Stone smiled knowingly.

MacAlister swore softly, half angry because she'd disobeyed his instructions, half pleased because she cared about him. *Cared, hell.* She'd said she loved him...more than once. The tangle of emotions inside him tightened. "She should have stayed put," he said gruffly.

"She's safe," Stone assured him. "I left her back at the hotel under guard until her uncle can come for her."

"Her uncle's here?" MacAlister's heart sunk. *It was over.* Rebecca would be going back to her life...and so would he. So why did he feel as though the rug had been suddenly pulled out from under him?

Stone grimaced. "Yup...I'll be glad to get him off my back. Charles Danforth's been raising holy hell over his niece's whereabouts." He clapped MacAlister on the back. "Now that this is over, mind telling me what's really been going on?"

MacAlister drew in a deep breath to ease the tightness in his chest, then exhaled slowly. "Deets kept a record of the ice shipments. That's how I knew the stuff was coming in tonight," he began. Turning toward the cartons, he saw Newcomber and Anderson busily cataloging the ice they'd seized. Something nagged at him, but he couldn't figure out what. There was something he hadn't done....

"Did Deets name his supplier?" Stone asked excitedly.

"Not really." MacAlister frowned. While he told Stone what Theo had found out, a part of him wrestled with the gut-level feeling something was wrong. "Theo confirmed my suspicion about the leak at... Oh, God." He spun around, eyes frantically searching the warehouse. "Where are Sanchez and Thatcher?"

"Sanchez is taking care of things outside. I left Thatcher back at the hotel. Miss Danforth knew him, and I thought she'd be more comfortable— Where the hell are you going?" Stone demanded as MacAlister swore and took off.

"To the hotel," MacAlister shouted over his shoulder, his eyes glittering wildly. "If you aren't the one, then Thatcher's the leak. He'll turn her over to Rousseau...."

MacAlister raced out of the warehouse with Stone at his heels. They commandeered a police escort and careened up and down the San Francisco hills, sirens wailing. But they arrived to find Thatcher and Becky gone from the hotel suite the Bureau had turned into a temporary command post.

For an instant, MacAlister wanted to smash everything in sight. His body trembled with impotent rage and fear. Through a red haze, he heard Stone swear and make a quick call to Charles Danforth at the Mark Hopkins.

"Danforth hasn't heard from her or from anyone at the Bureau," Stone said wearily when he finally got off the phone. "And he's hopping mad. There goes my chances of making

Chief...not that it matters right now," he hastily assured MacAlister.

MacAlister grunted. His fingers and jaw were clenched so tightly they ached. He took a deep breath and forced the muscles to relax as he had countless times before. Only this time it was harder to pretend this was just another assignment and Rebecca Danforth nothing more than a woman who needed his help.

"Why would they take the Danforth woman?" Stone asked.

"My guess is they'll want to trade her for the book I found in Deets's bank box," MacAlister said slowly.

Stone's eyes narrowed. "You never mentioned a book."

"It's your own fault, Stone," MacAlister snapped, temper fraying. "You were acting so screwy I thought *you* might be in with Rousseau."

"*Me?* Hell, I thought you might have been part of Deets's drug operation," Stone shot back.

That hurt. MacAlister swallowed his anger. "Then you asked me to tail Roseanne...I mean, Rebecca...because you thought I'd lead you to Rousseau?"

"Sort of." Stone dragged a hand through his hair and sighed. "Only we didn't know Rousseau was behind this ice ring. After the way you left the Bureau, Crenshaw was out to prove you were Deets's partner in everything. I didn't believe it, but knowing you'd go through the roof...maybe do something more stupid than you did when you quit the Bureau...I figured the best way to clear this up was to let you work with us."

"Thanks...I think," MacAlister grumbled. "But if you'd trusted me all the way, I'd have turned Deets's stuff over to you the minute I got my hands on it."

"Don't remind me," Stone snapped. "What was in the book, anyway?"

MacAlister frowned, ran a hand over his jaw. "Not much, and that's been bothering me. The code was pretty simple—I cracked it in an hour...decoded the whole book in two. But your guys should look at it. Maybe I missed something." His scowl deepened. "The shipping dates were there, my name, and a reference to this iceman, but no clue to his identity. Frankly,

I can't see why the damn thing was important enough to kill for."

Stone pursed his lips. "Why do you suppose Deets wrote your name in the book?"

"Maybe he wanted to frame me...."

"Or lead you to his killer," Stone mused. "What about the other stuff?"

MacAlister shook his head. "The money's not marked. I looked it over with a magnifying glass I bought. And the ring's...ordinary. I don't know why a rich guy like Deets bothered storing it in his safe-deposit box."

"Maybe it had sentimental value."

"Not likely," MacAlister scoffed. "Deets wasn't the sentimental type. I'm betting your lab boys find something scratched into the metal...maybe directions to another box somewhere, or a safe in his house."

"Right," Stone said briskly. "Do you have the stuff with you?"

MacAlister hesitated, carefully weighing the things Stone had said. They had the ring of truth, he decided. Besides, he'd have made a bargain with the devil to get Becky out safely.

"I'll tell you where to find them, but if I need the book to get Be—Rebecca out, I want your word you'll let me take it." At Stone's nod, MacAlister told him how he'd wrapped the ring and book in a square of the gauze Becky had bought to dress his wound. Then, while she was showering, he'd removed the heating grate in their cheap motel room and fastened the packet inside the duct with some of the adhesive tape.

When MacAlister had finished giving him the details, Stone sent four guys to get the stuff, and MacAlister drew a chair up to the window and settled in to wait for Rousseau's call. With dark, brooding eyes he watched the lights of the Golden Gate Bridge dance in the choppy water of the Bay and tried not to wonder where Becky was, or if she was hurt or scared.

The ringing of the phone jerked MacAlister upright. Lunging across the room, he picked up one extension just as Stone got on the other, and a technician began the complex procedure of tracing the call.

"Stone here," growled the agent.

"We've got the girl," came the raspy response.

Peck, MacAlister mouthed, his lips twisting as he remembered what Lily had looked like when Peck got done with her. If he touched one hair on Becky's head . . .

"I'm listening," Stone said evenly, his eyes shooting MacAlister a warning to keep quiet.

"I figured you might want her . . . since her uncle's been riding you pretty hard about finding her."

"I'm still listening." Stone had one eye on the clock, the other on the technician.

"And stalling, but it's not going to work," Peck snarled. "I'm calling from a phone booth around the corner. I'll give you the girl in exchange for Deets's black book. And I want MacAlister to deliver it."

MacAlister and Stone exchanged startled glances. "Why?"

"Rousseau has a few things to settle with him," Peck said with soft menace. "Do we have a deal?"

Stone covered the mouthpiece with the receiver. "I'll tell him I don't know where you are."

"No. If we cross him, he might hurt Rebecca."

"If you go, he'll kill you."

"He'll try." MacAlister flashed him a grim smile. "It doesn't matter. I'm going after her."

"Deal," Stone reluctantly told Peck.

"Good. Chinatown. Phone booth at the corner of Sacramento and Powell. Ten minutes. You'll get a call telling you where to go next. Oh, and, MacAlister, remember . . . the girl will be waiting with *me.*" His low laugh made MacAlister's stomach roll over.

"I want you to wear this," Stone said a few minutes later.

MacAlister looked up from putting his boots back on to see Stone holding out a watch.

"It's a tracking device. Pull out this stem and it activates a silent beeper."

Nodding, MacAlister checked the stiletto in his boot, straightened and exchanged his own watch for Stone's.

"Peck'll find the knife," Stone warned grimly.

"I'm counting on it," MacAlister said calmly. "He'll expect me to have something hidden—if he finds the knife, maybe he won't look too closely at the watch."

"Always thinking." A faint smile tugged at Stone's mouth, then faded as he walked MacAlister to the elevator. "Rousseau's going to be very unhappy when you show up without the book."

MacAlister shrugged. "He should know I'm not stupid enough to walk in and hand him my only bargaining chip. We'll argue about it for a while..."

"We'll be there as quick as we can," Stone assured him. "I'll put a tail on you, too... because Peck'll expect it."

Peck not only expected a tail, he spotted it right away. "What the hell!" he shouted. Turning in the passenger seat of the van that had just picked MacAlister up, Peck cuffed MacAlister in the side of the head.

With his hands taped behind his back, MacAlister had no way to brace himself. He slid off the seat and groaned as his bad shoulder struck the floor of the speeding van.

"Lose that guy in the green sedan," Peck ordered the driver.

MacAlister gritted his teeth against the pain as the van bounded through the hilly city. A rough twenty minutes later, the van rocked to a stop. From his position on the floor, MacAlister could make out the top of a wrought-iron gate. Once past the gate, they drove through a forest.

When the van stopped again, Peck turned around in the seat. "That pretty little girl is going to be real disappointed you didn't hold up your end of the bargain and bring the book," he drawled. A sly half smile twisted across his pallid face. In his hand he held MacAlister's wallet, knife and watch.

Ah, hell, MacAlister thought, groaning inwardly. The stem had been pushed in... cutting off the beeper's signal.

"'Course, I'm real glad you didn't...." Peck went on, his smile turning into a leer for MacAlister's benefit.

MacAlister forced himself to shrug off Peck's insinuation. "I discuss the book with Rousseau... not the hired help."

Peck's pale eyes narrowed. "Teach this guy some manners while I go tell Rousseau we're here."

* * *

The bedroom they'd locked Rebecca in was situated on the second floor of a gray stone mansion that looked more castle than house. The room jutted out over the ocean, and with the exception of a narrow stone ledge running the length of the structure, it was a straight shot from the window to the moon-lit rocks some forty feet below.

Looking down made Rebecca's head spin, her stomach roll, and she quickly turned away. She wasn't desperate enough to escape that way...yet. Besides, that vile Peck had warned her that he had dogs patrolling the grounds.

It took fourteen steps to reach the bed midway across the room. Funny, she thought, idly stroking the heavy peach satin spread as she looked around, how fear and the locked door had made the large, luxurious chamber seem more cramped and dismal than the cheap motel room she'd left a few hours ago.

The air sighed out between her teeth as she sat down on the antique Spanish four-poster bed. According to the exquisite gold clock on the matching dresser, it was just past one in the morning. She'd been here only a few hours, but it felt like days. Lord, she was tired, and hungry, and scared. But mostly she felt guilty. If she hadn't disobeyed MacAlister, she wouldn't be Rousseau's prisoner, and Thatcher wouldn't be...

Don't think about it, she warned, squeezing her eyes shut to block out the memories. Thatcher was one of them. He'd told her so, turning on her shortly after Stone and the others had gone.

At first she'd refused to believe the Thatcher who had played cards and joked with her in the kitchen of the safehouse could be her enemy. But the gun leveled at her head and the hard look in his eyes had quickly convinced her he was serious.

Rousseau had been more subtle when he'd questioned her a short time later, but the menace underlying his tone had reminded her of the terrible things MacAlister had told her about this man.

"You have caused me a great deal of trouble these past weeks," he'd said. "Now tell me where Deets's book is."

"I don't know," she replied firmly, head high despite her apprehension. "And I wouldn't tell you if I did."

"A foolish, empty promise," Rousseau said coolly, his gaze pinning her to the chair. "I want to know where you and MacAlister have been staying." He signaled to one of the guards. "Otto, I believe Miss Danforth needs a lesson."

The burly Otto stepped from behind the chair Rebecca was sitting in, grabbed her left wrist and bent it back until the tendons screamed and so did she. Dizzy with pain, she gave him the address and dug the key out of her shoe where she'd hidden it. So much for her show of bravery.

They'd waited in Rousseau's study for his men to search the motel room and report back. While Rebecca held her throbbing wrist in a pan of ice brought by the same man who'd nearly broken it, Rousseau sat across the desk from her, calmly reading computer reports and signing letters.

Business as usual, she thought, glumly regarding the bruises developing on her swollen wrist. But Rousseau's calm veneer developed a crack when the men called to say the book wasn't in the motel room.

"Search again. Take the furniture apart.... I don't care what you have done, do it all again." A vein throbbed at Rousseau's temple as he hung up. Beneath his bronzed tan, his skin was flushed with rage.

Rousseau glared at Rebecca. "MacAlister must have it with him," he said in a voice cold with fury. "I will—"

The study door opened, and a pale, chunky man burst into the room. He had an automatic weapon slung over his shoulder and a look on his face that would have peeled paint. "They got the shipment...." he snarled.

"What?" Rousseau catapulted out of his chair. "Who took it, Peck? Was it MacAlister?"

"No. The Bureau..." Peck detoured by an antique sideboard, filled a crystal glass from the decanter marked "Vodka," drained it and refilled it again before walking over to the desk. His eyes flickered briefly over Rebecca and returned to Rousseau's angry face. "But MacAlister was there."

Rousseau said something, but Rebecca barely heard him, her mind still reeling from the impact of seeing Peck. He was the man she'd seen the night of Lucien's murder. She would have recognized those eyes anywhere. They were...inhuman. Nearly colorless, they glittered like shards of glass. Cold. Hard. Watchful. A predatory kind of anticipation had kindled in them when he'd looked at her.

Peck knew she'd seen him bending over Lucien's dead body, and he'd enjoy seeing to it she never told anyone.

Rebecca wrapped her arm around the bedpost and leaned against it for support. She was going to need all she could get. If MacAlister followed Rousseau's instructions, he should be arriving shortly with the book. He'd be furious with her, and rightly so. She took small comfort from the knowledge that he'd found the drugs at the warehouse. They were both in danger, and it was all her fault. Part of her hoped he wouldn't come . . .

Her head came up as the door opened.

Rousseau paused on the threshold, wearing the same dark business suit he'd had on when she was brought here. "It's time," he said in a deep, rich voice, so low-key he might have been announcing dinner. He looked so polished and urbane she had a hard time equating this handsome man with his crimes. It was easy to see why Lily had been fooled into going to work for him.

And what about Roseanne? Had her cousin been taken in by him, too? No, she couldn't believe Roseanne was part of this.

Numbly, Rebecca rose and went with Rousseau. For a drug dealer he had excellent taste, she thought, catching glimpses of expensive furniture and tasteful accent pieces, artfully arranged, as he led her through the house. Admiring them took her mind from the dull ache in her wrist and the cold knot of fear in her stomach.

As Rousseau opened the door to his study, Rebecca suppressed a shudder and unconsciously stepped back.

"No need to be afraid. If you cooperate, you will be reunited with your uncle shortly," he assured her smoothly. His hand on the small of her back urged her into the room.

Rebecca pretended to believe him, but she doubted he would let her go. She'd seen too much. What puzzled her was why he still seemed to need her when MacAlister was bringing the book.

From across the room, she saw Peck watch her approach the familiar straight-backed chair in front of the desk, his expression smug, his anticipation more obvious.

"Ah, I see you've noticed Peck," Rousseau drawled. "But you haven't said hello to MacAlister."

Every nerve in Rebecca's body jumped to attention. *MacAlister was here.* She turned in the direction Rousseau was pointing, saw a big man sprawled in the leather wing chair before the fire.

MacAlister wore black jeans and a gray sweatshirt, and he'd removed the blond wig and beard. His hands, bunched into fists, were taped together at the wrists, the knuckles scraped and bloody. The dark wetness on his shoulder indicated his wound had reopened. There was blood trickling from his split lip, too, and from a cut above his left eye, which was swollen. More bruises discolored his cheekbone and jaw. His eyes were closed, and he was so still Rebecca feared he was unconscious, or dead.

Shock alone kept her from running to him.

"MacAlister. You are being rude to the lady. Open your eyes and greet her," Rousseau prodded silkily.

MacAlister's eyes opened, narrowed slightly with pain, then looked at her as though she were a stranger. The breath stuck in Rebecca's throat, and a chill crept down her backbone. He'd worn that same shuttered look when they'd first met.

The wounded man in the chair was not her Gates; he was a cold-blooded professional . . . a man with a mission. Emotions washed through Rebecca like small, choppy waves. Why was he doing this?

"Mornin'. . .princess," MacAlister mumbled around his split lower lip.

Princess? Rebecca frowned. He only called her that when he wanted to upset her. . .or make her angry. Suddenly grateful her back was to Rousseau and Peck, Rebecca struggled to understand the message she thought MacAlister was sending her. He wanted her angry so she wouldn't be afraid; he wanted to distance himself from her . . . so Rousseau wouldn't suspect something. Wouldn't suspect they . . . cared . . . for each other?

Okay. She'd play along. "I do hope you've brought the stupid book so we can leave," she grumbled in a princessly tone.

Something flickered very briefly in his amber eyes. She thought—hoped—it was satisfaction.

"Regretfully for all of us, MacAlister claims he doesn't have the book," Rousseau said tersely.

Give me a clue, she silently asked MacAlister. How was she supposed to act? To Rousseau, she said, "What do you expect me to do if you weren't able to beat it out of him?"

Peck stepped into view, smiling faintly. "You and me are goin' to play a few games. . . ." He cupped her chin in his cool, clammy fingers and squeezed until her lips pursed. "I like your mouth . . . think I'll start there."

"No." Rebecca jerked free and took a step backward. She was trembling, and she longed to run to MacAlister. But Peck looked like he'd relish the chance to chase her. "Mac-Alister . . ." she sobbed.

MacAlister sighed. He'd hoped to drag this out. The harder Rousseau had to work to get the information from him, the more likely he was to believe what MacAlister told him. But Becky was going to get hurt if he screwed around much longer. "Okay." Groaning, MacAlister dragged himself upright in the chair and scowled at Rousseau. "I mailed the book to myself . . ."

"Where?" Rousseau demanded.

"I sent it to the hotel . . . certified mail."

Rousseau eyed him with suspicion. "Which hotel?"

"Let the girl go," MacAlister countered because it was expected, not because he had any hope Rousseau would do it.

"Non. . . ."

MacAlister's next move was a stubborn glare.

"I'll get it out of him," Peck promised darkly.

"Non." Rousseau rose from behind the desk, the hostility in his eyes nearly palpable. "I have had my fill of this. You will tell us which hotel, and you will accompany Peck there . . . to ensure there is no difficulty in getting the package . . . or the girl dies. There will be no discussion, no delays."

"If I do what you want, you'll let her go?"

Rousseau smiled thinly. "But of course."

He's lying, he can't afford to let me go, Rebecca wanted to shout. But she kept quiet because she suspected MacAlister already knew that.

"Okay," MacAlister muttered. "But obviously I won't give you the name of the hotel until we leave tomorrow."

Rousseau scowled, then nodded curtly. "All right."

MacAlister let out the breath he'd been holding. Covertly, he eyed the watch sitting atop the pile of things Peck had placed on the corner of Rousseau's desk. The stem was still pushed in. If they kept him in this room, he'd find a way to activate the beeper. Stone and the cavalry would be here in thirty minutes, maybe less.

"Return the girl to her room and put MacAlister in the other one," Rousseau told Peck. "I want four guards in the hallway outside his room."

MacAlister's hopes plummeted. Knowing he might not see Becky again until morning, and then, only if he was lucky and Rousseau decided to be generous, he cast a sidelong glance at her. She was staring at him, her eyes filled with the same sadness and longing he felt. If only she hadn't seen Peck bending over Deets's body, he might have struck a bargain to save her life.

The door swung open, and Rebecca gasped as her cousin walked into the room, followed closely by a hard-faced man carrying a gun. Rose wore high-heeled black satin slippers and an elegant nightgown, the black chiffon so sheer it left little to the imagination. Her red-blond hair tumbled down her back in wild disarray, but her makeup was impeccable and she looked more angry than frightened.

"Brenner, what's the meaning of this?" Rousseau demanded.

"She picked the lock on her door...I caught up with her out in the hallway."

Roseanne reached Rousseau's side and looped her arm through his. "*Cheri,* why was I locked in . . . ?"

"I didn't want you to be disturbed." His tone remained even, but his full mouth twisted with annoyance.

"By whom?" Roseanne asked, seemingly oblivious to his mood. Then she noticed Rebecca, and her eyes widened. "Rebecca? Why are you here? Did she bring the book you wanted, darling?'' she asked Rousseau.

Stunned at finding her cousin here, and apparently on good terms with Rousseau, Rebecca struggled to find her tongue. "R-Rose, why are you here with him?''

"Where else would I be but here, with my fiancé,'' Rose-anne said, looking up adoringly at the scowling Rousseau.

"F-fiancé…?'' Rebecca choked out. From the corner of her eye, she saw MacAlister stiffen, knew they were both wondering if Roseanne had helped plan Lucien's death.

"Otto, take MacAlister and Miss Danforth upstairs while I escort Roseanne back to our room,'' Rousseau said coldly, turning Roseanne toward the door.

Roseanne dug her heels in, her frown deepening. "I don't understand. You said nothing about Rebecca coming here.''

"It is a business matter….''

With everyone's attention focused on Roseanne, MacAlister sidled a step closer to the desk and his watch. Otto's bulky body still stood between him and his goal, but if something happened to distract the man, he wanted to be in position.…

"I don't want her here,'' Roseanne cried.

"Your jealous outburst is unnecessary,'' Rousseau said, the set of his jaw the only clue that he was upset. "Your cousin will be leaving us tomorrow…as soon as I get the book.'' His tone turned steely. "Otto, you have your orders.''

Otto grabbed Rebecca's arm and ungently herded her and MacAlister toward the door. His touch broke through her paralysis. "Rose … you can't stay here. He's—''

The usually nimble MacAlister stumbled into her and stepped down hard on her toe. "Quiet,'' he hissed under her startled cry.

"She's in danger,'' Rebecca whispered.

"Aren't we all,'' mumbled MacAlister.

"No talking,'' Otto ordered, shoving his gun into Rebecca's back to emphasize the point.

"Jean-Claude … promise me she isn't staying,'' Roseanne wheedled, drawing Rebecca's eye back to the pair.

"I assure you your cousin will not be staying with us,'' Rousseau said firmly.

To Rebecca, the pointed look he gave her made things very clear. Whether or not he got the book, he intended to kill her. A chill ran down her spine.

Chapter 13

Groaning, Rebecca flopped over on her back and dragged the tangled curls from her eyes. She barely remembered walking back to her bedroom/prison, wasn't even sure how long she'd been here. She'd cried a little because she was afraid for MacAlister and herself, and for Roseanne, who seemed unaware of the danger she was in. Then she'd dozed, but something had penetrated the protective haze she'd sought to hide in.

There it was again. A faint click that seemed to come from the next room. Sitting up, she frowned at the wall as though she might suddenly develop X-ray vision. Had Rousseau said something about putting MacAlister in there? She slid off the bed and crossed the room, put her ear to the wall. Nothing.

She rapped softly with her knuckle. Then listened again. Still nothing. But behind her, she heard the whisper of denim. As she turned to look, two hard arms wrapped around her, and a hand closed over her mouth.

"Jeez . . . Stop pounding on the wall. You want to bring the whole rat pack in here?" rasped a beloved voice.

MacAlister. Rebecca melted against him, a sigh of relief shuddering through her. "How did you get free?"

"There was an antique lamp in the room they put me in. I smothered the glass under a pillow, broke it and used the edge to cut the tape."

"You agent-types certainly are resourceful." Rebecca gave his hands a grateful squeeze.

"Easy, honey. Even my hands aren't up to much hugging right now." As he dropped his hands, she spun around and got a close look at the damage Peck had inflicted.

"Oh, Gates," she whispered, framing his poor battered face with her palms. "Come into the bathroom and let me see what I can do...."

"No time." He hugged her as tightly as his bruised ribs would allow. "Ah, honey," he breathed into her hair, smoothing one hand down her back.

The neck of his sweatshirt had been torn. The exposed V of skin was hot and sleek beneath her cheek, the beat of his pulse fast yet reassuring. "I know you're probably mad at me," she said in a shaky voice.

"Mad as hell." The kiss he brushed across her temple robbed the words of their sting. "When I get you home, I'm going to paddle your cute little butt."

The "home" part had a nice ring to it. "Then you didn't need Stone's help."

"I'd have been in serious trouble if he hadn't shown up when he did," MacAlister reluctantly admitted.

Rebecca's eyes widened. "Really?"

"Yeah." The uninjured side of his mouth quirked up. "But I'm still mad at you."

"Me, too. You got all ... this ..." she gestured helplessly at his injuries " ... because I didn't stay put."

MacAlister sighed and rested his forehead against hers. "Rousseau would have come after me sooner or later, but I didn't want you mixed up in this."

"I'm not too crazy about it myself."

MacAlister drew back enough to see her eyes without letting go of her. "We stand a real good chance of getting out of this if I can get downstairs and activate the tracking device Stone gave me."

Rebecca nodded. "There's a but, isn't there?"

"Yeah. We can't take on the four guys in the hall, so we'll have to go out the window and walk along the ledge."

"That tiny little ledge outside?" she croaked.

"It's safe enough if you go slow. That's how I got in here."

She peeked cautiously around him and spotted the half-open window. "It must be forty feet down...." she protested.

More like fifty, and I hate this every bit as much as you do, babe. "Only here on the corner where this pile of rock overhangs the bank. Further down the building, it's only a story...twelve feet or so."

"'Only,'" Rebecca sputtered, her mouth dry just remembering what it had been like to look out the window. "I can't do it. You go on, and I'll wait...."

"No." His hands tightened briefly on her back. "It'll be light soon...and there's no telling when Peck will decide to come for us. I want to pick up the beeper and hide in the woods until Stone can get here."

Rebecca shuddered.

"What is it, honey?"

"Peck is the one I saw at Lucien's."

MacAlister's expression hardened. "All the more reason to get you out of here."

"What about Roseanne? I won't leave my cousin here," Rebecca said firmly.

Protecting you is my first priority. "Roseanne's been safe enough here so far." He tried for reasonable, came off sounding as angry as he felt. "She obviously knows how to stay on Rousseau's good side," he added, thinking about the nearly transparent black nightgown. It had looked good on Roseanne; it would have looked terrific on Becky.

"But you said yourself that Rousseau was a monster."

Now he was sorry he had. "They may be two of a kind. Hell, she used you, honey. Think back to what she did and said the night Deets was murdered, and you'll realize she was probably in on the whole damn thing."

Despite the set of her chin, her lower lip wobbled. "I don't think so. And even if I did, she's still my cousin...part of my family. And you heard her say she'd been locked in...."

"I also heard her say she was planning to marry Rousseau."

Rebecca sighed deeply. "You don't seriously think he means to marry her, do you?"

"No," he said, sighing when her shoulders slumped. "But I could be wrong. For now, our first priority is letting Stone know where we are. Once the cavalry gets here, we'll sort things out. If we try to find Roseanne now, we could get caught. Or she could betray us. Don't forget, she's very likely one of them."

"S-so was Thatcher, and they killed him."

MacAlister swore. "Thatcher was a good agent, once."

"I was shocked, too. He... he was so nice to me," Rebecca said quietly, a dazed look in her eyes. "On the way here, he apologized...said he'd fallen in love with an Egyptian woman while he was living in Cairo. Unfortunately, she worked for the Soviets, and Rousseau found out...."

"Blackmail." MacAlister's jaw tightened.

"I feel sorry..."

"Don't. He's the one who got us into this mess."

"I know. But he paid...." Rebecca shivered, remembering the sickening *thunk* as the bullet cut Thatcher down.

"You are one brave lady," MacAlister said softly. "I was afraid you'd panic when you first saw me and do something foolish."

"Like faint? Or throw myself at you?" She smiled wryly. "Don't think I wasn't tempted. But I was in shock for a moment, and then you called me 'princess'...."

"Mmm. I hoped that would put you on guard." It was a good thing nobody but him had seen her face when she turned and noticed him. The love and the yearning there had taken his breath away. He'd never expected anyone would ever look at him that way. Now that someone had, he wasn't sure what to do about it, except that he had to get Rebecca away from here. He'd concentrate on that and take the rest as it came. "We have to leave, honey. I know you're afraid," he added when she opened her mouth to protest, "but the fog's come in, so you can't see the ground."

"I remember how far down it is," she said weakly.

"I'll keep you safe... remember that instead."

"After you activate this device, can we at least look for Roseanne?" she asked hesitantly.

His expression turned grim again. "No promises. With any luck, Stone and the boys will catch Rousseau off guard, and the only danger she'll face is a lot of pointed questions about her part in Deets's death."

"Yes, I'd almost forgotten about that part of it," Rebecca said, thinking how devastated her aunt, and especially her uncle, would be if their daughter were indicted for murder.

MacAlister stepped out onto the ledge first, then reached back for her. Rebecca winced when his hand closed over her left wrist. "What happened?" he muttered, scowling at the swelling he could feel, the bruises he could just make out in the dim light.

"Rousseau told Otto to make certain I didn't know where the book was."

He nodded grimly and adjusted his grip to her forearm, his mouth thinning to a flat line. "Ease yourself over the sill," he instructed. Keeping one hand under her arm, he guided her over it, steadied her as she climbed down onto the ledge. "Stand still." His hand brushed across her stomach as he reached around her to push the window shut.

Rebecca had no problem following that order. She pressed her back tightly against the house, expecting a smooth surface, surprised to find huge stones, beveled on the edges and held together by thick strips of mortar. *Great.* Curving her fingers around the stones, she found some security in clinging to the faceted surfaces.

"Okay... start moving," MacAlister murmured in her ear.

Rebecca swallowed. "I—I don't think I can."

"Just do it, honey. We don't have time to be scared."

She shot him a frightened glance, saw his face in the half-light, a mask of bruises and dried blood. He'd be dead...they'd both be dead...if she didn't conquer her fear. Trembling, she nodded, took the hand he extended to her and shuffled toward him, careful not to look down.

"Honey," he said gently. "Take a quick look at the ledge so you'll know how much room you have."

Another tremor shook her, but she glanced down. The stone ledge was a little wider than her foot. Beyond the tips of her loafers, she saw thick white clouds. "What is it?"

"Fog," MacAlister whispered, smiling at her. "It's a life-saver for people like us...can't be afraid of heights if you can't see the ground."

"Well..."

"Come on," he said briskly, tugging on her hand to get her moving before she had a chance to examine his reasoning.

Rebecca picked up one foot, then the other, keeping her eyes on MacAlister's shoulder ahead of her, and her body as close as possible to the stone wall. The fear hadn't left her, but the ledge beneath her feet felt sturdy, and MacAlister was right. It was harder to fear what you couldn't see. Still, her mouth was dry, her palms wet by the time they reached the next corner.

"Hang on to this," he murmured, showing her a small metal ladder going up the outside of the building.

Gratefully she grabbed on with both hands, thinking it must be for maintenance or washing all those nasty multi-paned windows. "What now?" she whispered.

MacAlister gestured for her to be quiet, and below them Rebecca heard the crunch of gravel and the faint jingling of something metal.

When she cocked her brow at him, MacAlister mouthed the word *guard*. She shivered, and he was glad he hadn't told her about the dog.

As soon as the guard and his companion had walked off, MacAlister knelt on the ledge. Feeling along the underside, he located the ladder going down to the ground.

"How did you know that was here?" she whispered.

"I walked the ledge this far before going back to get you," he replied in a low voice. "I want you to wait here while I go down and take a look around."

"Why can't I go with you?"

"I can cover more ground on my own," he said evenly.

She shivered. "What if the guard comes back?"

"He won't be able to see you in the fog."

"What if the fog lifts?"

"Dammit, Becky. I won't be gone that long...unless you keep me standing here all morning."

Rebecca didn't like it, but she nodded. He *could* move more quickly and more quietly without her.

MacAlister didn't have much trouble getting in. He crept around the outside of the house, checking windows until he found one that wasn't latched, then crawled in, finding himself in the kitchen. The house was dark, and no one was around to see him slink past the dining room full of tall, stately furniture and into the entry hall they'd used when Peck had brought him here. He remembered the way to Rousseau's study and got there without running into anyone.

So far, so good, he thought.

Opening the door a crack, MacAlister peeked in. Dark and empty. His heart tripping against his ribs, he cat-walked over to the desk, activated the beeper on the watch and slipped it on. Then he grabbed up the stiletto and tucked it into his boot. It wouldn't do much against the Uzi or the AK47 the guard was probably packing, but armed was better than unarmed any day.

Thoughts of Rousseau sleeping upstairs somewhere, alone...unless Roseanne was with him...and probably unarmed, tempted MacAlister to take the stairs to his right as he came out of the study. But the need to get Becky to safety while they waited for Stone was stronger. They'd get Rousseau, it was just a matter of time now.

How much time? MacAlister wondered as he crept back to the kitchen. In his mind, he imagined a Bureau technician at the Sheraton picking up the silent transmissions from the watch and rousing the troops. According to Stone's watch, it was just after four in the morning. There shouldn't be much traffic. In twenty to thirty minutes the cavalry should be storming Rousseau's castle.

MacAlister figured he and Becky could stay out of sight for that long. He also decided using the kitchen door would be easier on his abused ribs than crawling through the small window over the sink had been.

But his luck had run out. As he opened the door, he set off an alarm.

*   *   *

Rebecca nearly fell off the ledge when the unearthly wailing noise abruptly started up.

An alarm of some kind. Had MacAlister gotten caught?

She squinted into the swirling fog below, her heart thumping against her ribs like a trapped bird. After a moment's panicked indecision, she decided to climb down. If the guards came up the ladder, she'd have no place to hide.

As her foot touched the ground, MacAlister suddenly barreled out of the fog. For an instant, he stared at her, his expression hard and determined. Then Rebecca stepped forward and threw her arms around his waist.

"Oh, God. When I heard the siren, I thought Rousseau had caught you," she said shakily.

MacAlister ground out a particularly ripe oath. "I got careless. I'm glad you had the sense to climb down. I was afraid I might have to come up after you." He gave her a quick hug, then reached for her hand. "Come on, we can't stay here."

With MacAlister in the lead, they ran back the way he'd come, the sharp leaves of the chest-high holly bushes along the foundation tearing at their hands and clothes. Ahead and to the right, Rebecca heard the thud of running feet and slowed instinctively.

MacAlister grabbed her around the waist, took her down to the cold, slick ground with him, shoving her into the leafy cavity between two of the large bushes where it was darker and wetter still. Shivering, she caught the glint of naked steel in his hand before he backed in after her, effectively shielding her with his body.

Over the uneven rasp of her own breathing, Rebecca heard several sets of feet pound past them. When the sounds faded away, she slowly let the air out of her lungs. "Close," she whispered.

"Yeah. We got lucky." *No dogs.* "We'll rest here. Chances are it will be a while before they come back this way." Behind him, MacAlister heard Becky's grateful sigh. Peeling back the sleeve of his sweatshirt, he checked the time. It had been ten minutes since he activated the beeper. Another twenty before he could reasonably expect help.

They crouched motionless in the bushes, muscles cramping, ears straining for some sign their pursuers were close by. The tension was the worst, Rebecca thought, the strain of not knowing from one heartbeat to the next whether you were safe. "Did you do this often when you worked for the Bureau?" she murmured.

Too often. He heard the fear in her voice, wished he could hold her and promise her everything would be all right, but he couldn't afford the distraction. "No talking, honey," he said as gently as he could.

Originally, MacAlister had planned to hide in the woods rimming Rousseau's castle, but reaching them now was too risky. Besides, that was the first place Peck would send the guards . . . and the dogs. Damn the dogs. In this fog, he and Becky could hide from the guards until doomsday, but the dogs didn't need to *see* them. Just as soon as they'd finished checking the woods, the dogs would be back.

"Do we just sit here and wait?" Rebecca asked. Her hand touched his back, and he could feel her shaking.

"We're safest here, for the moment."

The faint, excited bark of a dog rolled over Rebecca's hushed reply. "Oh . . . I forgot about the dogs."

"Now we go." MacAlister grabbed her hand and dragged her out of the bushes. He trotted along the side of the building with Rebecca right behind him.

"Th-they're coming faster," she whispered after a moment.

"Don't think about them . . . just keep moving," he hissed.

A second later, MacAlister slammed into a wall, and Rebecca careened into him, jarring his injured shoulder. Swearing softly, he steadied her with one arm and felt his way up the wall with one hand. It ended just above his head. This must be the courtyard off the dining room.

The barking of the dogs was closer now . . . more frantic.

"MacAlister . . ."

"Steady, honey. We're going over this wall. Put your foot in my hands, and I'll give you a boost." Even as he spoke, he took her foot, and Rebecca was forced to grab his shoulders to keep her balance. "Easy on that left one," he whispered as he stood, hoisting her with him. "When you get to the top, swing your legs over to the other side and sit tight until I come up."

The stone was cold and slippery under her hands. As Rebecca attempted to pull herself onto the top of the wall, a sharp pain jolted her left wrist, and she would have fallen if MacAlister hadn't given her an extra push up the last few inches to the top of the wall.

Dazed and frightened, she sat there gulping air. The fog hadn't penetrated the inner courtyard, and she could make out the dark shapes of tall palms and lacy ferns. She heard the dogs more clearly and, under their excited yelps, the deep voices of men urging them on.

MacAlister rose out of the mist like a whale sounding and landed beside her with a thud that shook the wall. "Damn shoulder," he muttered hoarsely.

"Are you all right?" Rebecca reached out to touch him, but he didn't sit still that long. Catching her around the waist, he launched them both off the wall.

Rebecca was too shocked to scream....

One minute she was flying, the next she was sprawled on the cold, damp ground, her body reverberating from the jolt of landing, her lungs aching for air.

"Stand up, Becky, we have to get going," MacAlister hissed.

Blinking her eyes open, she scowled up at him. "Stand...I can't even breathe," she croaked. Over her rasping gasps, she heard the dogs pass by on the other side of the wall.

"Ah, we fooled them." He pulled her to her feet, steadied her when she swayed. "With any luck, it'll take them awhile to decide we aren't outside."

She licked her lips. "Where are we going?"

"Back inside the house. They've turned off the alarm system, and Stone should be here in ten minutes or so. It should take Peck and his goons at least that long to search the grounds, and there'll be lots of places to hide in a house this size. All we have to do is find one and stay put." His grin was probably meant to inspire confidence. Unfortunately, the bruises and split lip made him look like a guy who'd already lost one round.

Rebecca smiled back, anyway. What the heck. MacAlister was good for more than one round. Crouching beside him, she watched as he slipped the knife from his boot and pried open the lock on the French doors leading inside.

Heavy draperies swirled around them as they stepped into a formal dining room. Thick carpeting muffled their steps, and overhead an impressive chandelier tinkled in the breeze. Pale moonbeams followed them inside to be caught and split into a rainbow of colors by the delicate crystal drops, then reflected and magnified the length of the room by mirrored walls.

Rebecca turned in a slow circle, captivated for a moment by the way the light played around her, breathing in the mingled scents of lemon-oil polish and roses in the bowl at the center of the massive old table.

She sighed when MacAlister soundlessly closed the door and pulled the drapes shut, effectively ending the brief light show. "Rousseau doesn't deserve all this."

"And I mean to see he doesn't get to keep it," MacAlister muttered. Taking her arm, he hustled her past the dark, bulky furniture. If he had to make a stand, it wouldn't be here. This room made him as nervous as a cat in a room full of rocking chairs. Nothing to hide behind but the table, and the mirrors reflected every movement.

As MacAlister steered Rebecca through the doorway, Roseanne abruptly stepped in front of her.

"What are you doing here?" Roseanne demanded with her usual arrogance. She'd put on an ankle-length green satin robe, and her hands were splayed at her waist, the long, red-tipped nails drumming impatiently against her hipbone.

"Ah, hell," MacAlister muttered.

"Rose . . . you have to come with us," Rebecca said, stepping up to her cousin. "Rousseau is—"

"Are you trying to ruin everything?" Roseanne exclaimed. "Just when I finally found someone I really love."

"But Rose, he's an evil man. . . ."

"It isn't enough that you invaded my house . . . turned my parents against me . . . Now you want Jean-Claude. . . ."

Rebecca flinched. "Roseanne . . . you can shout at me later, but we aren't safe here. Come with us."

Ignoring Rebecca's outstretched hand, Roseanne tossed her hair back, eyes blazing with bitter fury. "Well, you won't get him as easily as you got this—'' Lunging forward, she grabbed the chain around Rebecca's neck and yanked it off. ''This was mine . . . mine, and they gave it to you because your father had died and they felt sorry for you,'' she cried, dangling the diamond and gold initials in Rebecca's face.

''I—I didn't ask for it,'' she whispered.

MacAlister snapped out a succinct oath and grabbed control of the situation. ''We're going.'' Taking Rebecca's icy hand in his, he started to brush by Roseanne, but a movement behind her stopped him cold.

Peck materialized out of the shadows, a revolver in one hand, a lazy smile splitting his pale, round face. ''You're not going anywhere, MacAlister.''

MacAlister moved so quickly Rebecca didn't have time to gasp before he shoved her backward. She sprawled across the carpet, cracking her head so hard on a chair leg it brought tears to her eyes. Over the ringing in her ears, she heard the bark of Peck's gun, a woman's scream, then a guttural grunt.

Two thuds—one small, one large—followed as she scrambled to her knees. Blinking back tears, Rebecca swayed where she crouched, saw Roseanne lying on the floor in the doorway and MacAlister just beyond bending over Peck.

''Roseanne . . .'' Rebecca crawled to her, turned her over gently. Her cousin stared back, eyes wide, mouth open as though something had surprised her.

''Oh, God . . .'' Rebecca moaned. There was blood, so much blood. She had to stop the bleeding, she thought dimly, and started to open Roseanne's robe, but MacAlister's hands closed over hers.

''Don't look. . . . She's gone,'' he said softly.

''No.'' Rebecca raised her head, saw the compassion in his gaze and started to shake. It was true.

''She panicked and ran into the bullet Peck meant for me,'' MacAlister said, drawing Rebecca to her feet and holding her by the upper arms to keep her from collapsing.

In a way, Roseanne had saved their lives, MacAlister thought, buying him the precious seconds needed to bury his knife dead center in Peck's throat. He almost hated her for the things she'd said to hurt Rebecca, but he would have saved

Roseanne if he'd had the chance. "We have to get out of here, honey," he murmured.

Rebecca nodded, but he thought she was too dazed to realize they were still in danger. "A-and Peck?"

"He's dead, too." *Much quicker and far easier than he deserved, but at least he was dead.* MacAlister picked Rebecca up, stepped over Roseanne's body, then past Peck's.

Rebecca struggled feebly in his arms. "I . . . There are things I must do for her."

Ignoring the pleading in her eyes and the pain in his shoulder, MacAlister started down the hallway. "I know the timing stinks, but your grieving'll have to wait. That shot will draw Rousseau and the guards into the house."

He was right, of course. Rebecca swallowed hard, battling to marshal what little reserves she had left. "Put me down," she said a moment later. "You'll need both hands free."

MacAlister nodded his approval and kept her close beside him as they crept through the darkened house. Her knees were shaking so badly she thought they'd give out. At every corner, she flinched, expecting Rousseau or Otto to step out and shoot them.

Behind them, MacAlister heard shouts, guessed the guards had found Peck and Roseanne. Time was running out. Where the hell was Stone? "Stay behind me, be ready to move," he whispered as they approached the door to Rousseau's study. Logically, this was the last place anyone should expect to find them.

MacAlister lifted his hand to the knob. . . .

"By all means . . . let us go in," drawled a dark voice.

Whipping around, MacAlister confronted his worst nightmare. Rousseau, with a mocking smile on his face and the end of a small revolver pressed to Rebecca's throat. She was white with shock, her lips trembling.

An anguished cry clawed through MacAlister, and his body went rigid with impotent fury.

"After you," Rousseau said silkily.

Somehow MacAlister got the door open and took the chair Rousseau indicated. Outwardly, he guessed he appeared calm because Rousseau looked disappointed in his reaction. Inside, he fought to keep the awesome rush of fear and adrenaline under control when what he really wanted to do was leap up and tear out Rousseau's throat for daring to threaten his Becky.

Out of the corner of his eye, MacAlister watched Rousseau walk around the desk. He propelled Becky ahead of him with one hand, the gun still trained on her, but from a little distance, as though he felt comfortably in charge. Enough moonlight filtered in for MacAlister to see that confidence reflected in Rousseau's glittering black eyes as he stared smugly back at him.

If they were going to act, MacAlister thought, it had to be now, before Rousseau tied them up or separated them. His gaze shifted to see how Rebecca was bearing up.

MacAlister needed her help. Rebecca realized that in the split second she looked up and their eyes met. But how? Rousseau had relieved MacAlister of Peck's gun....

"You have caused me a great deal of trouble, MacAlister, but you are going to begin paying for that now," Rousseau said with soft savagery.

Rebecca took one look at the curve of Rousseau's tanned throat, vulnerable as he leaned forward to light the small Tiffany lamp on the desk, and she knew her moment had come. Closing her teeth over her bottom lip, she bent her arm and jabbed her elbow into his throat as hard as she could.

There was a strangled gurgle as her blow connected, then a triumphant shout as MacAlister vaulted over the desk, shoving her clear and slamming Rousseau up against the wall with enough force to ring another hoarse cry from the Frenchman.

"Your timing was just about perfect, honey," MacAlister growled cheerfully.

Rebecca sat up, rubbing the shoulder she'd bruised when she landed. "Is it really over?"

"Yeah." MacAlister smiled grimly and pressed the small handgun he'd confiscated a little tighter against the Frenchman's ear, enjoying the long-overdue leap of fear in the dark eyes that had mocked him for over six years. In the distance, he heard the faint sound of sirens and Stone's voice bellowing orders through a bullhorn. "Looks like the cavalry's arrived...."

* * *

Stone took charge of the cleanup, and Charles Danforth took charge of Rebecca. It was embarrassing, really, to have him fussing over her bruises and sprained wrist when his own daughter lay dead a few doors away. She supposed it was his way of dealing with the stress and sorrow, by giving her the care his daughter was beyond needing.

"I'm fine, really," Rebecca told the young physician her uncle had brought with him. "MacAlister is the one who needs medical attention."

Uncle Charles's eyes narrowed to angry green slits. "Is he the one who kidnapped you?"

Rebecca winced. "Ah, actually... I went with him...."

"Why?"

Conscious of MacAlister lounging against one wall of the study, she hesitated. So much remained unsettled between them, and she didn't want to discuss any of it with her uncle glowering over them like a storm cloud.

Stone walked in just then, his expression grave. "Your niece can't talk about the case until she's been debriefed by my people," he said coolly.

"We'll see what your superior has to say about that," Charles snapped.

Stone sighed. "Yes, I expect we will, sir." He glanced briefly at MacAlister, then added, "I know you've been under a terrible strain, Mr. Danforth, but the mortuary people you called have arrived. And, Doctor, if you're through here, one of my men could use your help."

The doctor snapped his bag shut and left the tension-charged room with obvious relief.

Charles followed more slowly. At the door, he paused, turned to stare at Rebecca, his gaze sharp. An instant later, he transferred his attention to MacAlister. His nostrils flared like a hound scenting a stranger poaching in his territory.

"Rebecca." Her uncle punctuated the command by extending his hand to her.

"I'll be along in a moment, Uncle," she said gently.

"What do you suppose that was all about?" she asked MacAlister when Stone and her uncle were gone.

"He doesn't like leaving you alone with me."

"That's silly ... we've been alone together for days."

"Yeah. And it bothers him ... a lot." Which shouldn't have surprised him. Danforth was exactly the sort of rich guy he despised ... the kind who'd buy a Ming vase from him but wouldn't want him dating his daughter. Or, in this case, his precious niece. MacAlister understood that. What bothered him was his gut instinct that despite the wealth and polish, Charles Danforth was a dangerous man.

"Will you come back with us?" Rebecca asked, wearily brushing the hair off her forehead as she walked over to him.

He avoided looking at her. He had to. "Your uncle doesn't want me along...."

"I do," she said quickly. She sensed him withdrawing from her, slipping back behind the barricades he'd erected to shield himself from feeling, from hurting, and she wanted to cry.

"I'm not done here. Stone has a pile of questions for me, and I want to stick around until his technicians finish decoding the book."

"I ... understand...." she murmured.

MacAlister felt the pain radiating from her and couldn't bear to be near her another second, but he couldn't make himself leave her yet, either, knowing he wouldn't be seeing her again after today.

Pushing away from the wall, he walked over to the window. The sun had burned off the fog, revealing immaculately manicured green lawns stretching from the house to the dark forest beyond. Scattered across it were beds of pink and white flowers and a small pond with a lacy white gazebo. It was beautiful here, and peaceful. "You were right, Rousseau didn't deserve a place like this," he said slowly. But Rebecca did, and a man to share it with, and babies. *God.* It hurt, thinking of her married to another man, having his children....

"MacAlister?" She'd followed him, knowing he didn't want her to, but determined to make one last try. "I—I wanted you to know that I meant it...."

"Meant what?"

She wished he'd turn and look at her when she said the words, because if he did, he'd see the truth, and the love, shining in her eyes. "I love you."

He shuddered as though she'd struck him, his knuckles popping out white where he gripped the window frame. "Wrong guy," he said hoarsely. "I can't give you what you want."

"Can't? Or won't let yourself," Rebecca demanded. His refusal even to try made her angry and frustrated.

"There's no difference...."

"Yes, there is, dammit." Rebecca grabbed his arm and pulled him around.

"Well, I don't see it." The cold certainty in his eyes chilled her; the bitterness in them made her heart ache for him ... for them.

"You could try," she said in a small, desperate voice.

"If I can't make a commitment to my own daughter, how the hell do you expect me to make one to you?" He raked a trembling hand through his sweat-darkened hair. "Hell. I know what you want me to say, but I can't even say the words, much less understand what they mean."

Weariness washed over Rebecca, or was it resignation? "I want so much for us to be together, but my loving and my wanting aren't enough.... I know that, but I thought ... we could try." Her eyes filled with tears, but she refused to have his last memory of her be ruined by tears. Blinking them back, she straightened her shoulders. "You're right. It would only work if you wanted it, too."

MacAlister watched her cross the room, her back stiff, her head high. He felt like he'd been run down by something. Inside, he was a mass of throbbing emotions, open, vulnerable and scared.

Dammit, why did he have to fall for someone like Rebecca when it was too late to change the way he was?

Chapter 14

Rebecca buckled her seat belt and leaned her head against the headrest as Danforth Pharmaceutical's company jet taxied down the runway at San Francisco International Airport. Stars were just beginning to pop out of the night sky, and below them as the plane climbed she could see the fog that had delayed their departure until 7:00 p.m.

One of several delays. Her uncle had chafed at each one. First the mortuary had taken longer than he thought necessary to prepare Roseanne's body for transport. Then Rebecca had insisted on answering Stone's questions.

She had been half relieved, half disappointed when Stone had showed up at her uncle's hotel suite without MacAlister. It had only been a few hours since they'd parted, and she already missed him so much her whole body ached with longing. Having to talk about what they'd been through together made it even worse.

"You've had an eventful couple of weeks," Stone said when Rebecca finished filling him in.

"Yes. I'm just glad it's over." It was a lie, but she'd cried herself dry an hour ago when she was supposedly taking a nap, so she told the tale without breaking down whenever she was forced to mention MacAlister's name.

"Do you think Roseanne was involved in Lucien's murder?" Rebecca asked hesitantly.

Stone sighed and dragged a hand through his hair. "I really don't know. Your statement clearly puts the blame on Peck. We *think* he was acting on Rousseau's orders. Naturally, Rousseau says he knows nothing about Deets's death, and with your cousin and Peck both dead..."

"You're out of witnesses." Maybe it was better not knowing; then she could go on thinking Roseanne had simply fallen in love with the wrong man...again. "What about Theo's informant?"

"Gone. Vanished without a trace. We're pretty sure he worked for Rousseau and was trying to trap MacAlister. Rousseau may have had him killed, but we're still hoping to find him and uncover the name of Deets's mysterious ice supplier."

"That would be something, anyway. You've all worked so hard on this, with very little to show for it."

"We got the two of you out alive." They were sitting side by side on the couch, and he reached to pat her hand. "I have two of my best men working on Deets's book...along with MacAlister."

"M-MacAlister is...still here?"

Stone's expression gentled, and she knew he'd felt her tremble at the mention of MacAlister's name. His next words confirmed that he knew, or guessed, she'd been involved with his former agent. "Deep down inside, MacAlister's really a sensitive, caring guy. He just doesn't want anyone to realize it. Including himself."

"I know," Rebecca said bleakly.

He squeezed her hand again. "Give him time."

How much? A lifetime? It chilled her to think about getting through the coming days without him, to say nothing of the empty weeks, months and years to follow. She sighed dispiritedly. "He knows where I'll be."

"MacAlister went through some tough times when he was young, and most of the people he met while working for the

Bureau were the sort he couldn't afford to trust. He needs to learn how all over again.''

Rebecca nodded and changed the subject before she cried again. ''You'll let me know if you find out anything? I mean, I feel as though the man who made those drugs is responsible for Roseanne's death, and Lucien's, too.''

''We'll get him. Take care of yourself, Miss Danforth. And I *am* sorry about your cousin.'' Stone turned and walked away, and with him had gone Rebecca's last contact with Mac-Alister.

''Underway at last,'' her uncle grumbled as the small jet leveled off.

Rebecca glanced up as her uncle sat down on the couch beside her. His features were composed now, thankfully. He had been so upset over the flight's postponement, that Rebecca had feared he'd have a stroke. She surmised that it was the weight of Roseanne's death that had made him uncharacteristically edgy.

Rebecca felt a pang of guilt as she thought about the expensive coffin resting in the hold of the plane. Unconsciously fingering the diamond necklace in her pocket, she replayed Roseanne's last spiteful comments. Though she'd known her cousin resented her, Rebecca hadn't realized how much. Logically, she knew she couldn't have prevented Roseanne's death, but . . .

''Stop torturing yourself, Rebecca,'' her uncle sternly ordered. ''Roseanne started down the path to self-destruction years ago. There was nothing you could have done to save her.''

''I should have tried. . . .'' Dear Lord, she hadn't even realized Roseanne needed saving. All her life, she'd envied her cousin's beauty and self-confidence, while silently condemning the wildness in her that upset Aunt Margaret and infuriated Uncle Charles. Never once had she stopped to think her cousin's tactics might have been a cry for love and attention. Certainly, she'd never guessed Roseanne might have been jealous of *her*.

''Roseanne was weak . . . like her mother.''

The coldness in his voice surprised Rebecca. Vainly, she groped for something positive to say.

"Have I told you how much you remind me of your mother?" Charles asked suddenly, leaning forward to balance his elbows on his knees.

Stunned as much by his wistful tone as by the change of subject, Rebecca shook her head. "My mother had dark hair, and her eyes were..."

"As blue as a summer's sky. You resemble her in the only way that counts.... Like you, she was beautiful on the inside...so pure and innocent." He looked through Rebecca to some distant memory that made his face glow.

As flattering as his words were, particularly after MacAlister's rejection, Uncle Charles was beginning to worry her. He wasn't acting like himself. Why, he almost sounded as though he'd been in love with her mother.

Mentally, Rebecca shook herself. The strain must be making her imagine things. "I think I'll take a nap."

As her uncle's eyes refocused on her, he smiled. "Yes...a nap is just what you need. When you awaken, we'll have arrived."

Rebecca forced an answering smile. "Well, I don't intend to sleep all the way to Connecticut."

His smile turned cryptic. "We shall see."

Oblivious to the activity going on in Stone's suite, MacAlister leaned back in the couch, put his feet up on the coffee table and brooded. Peck was dead and Rousseau faced federal charges for kidnapping and attempted murder...which would put him away for a very long time, even if Stone didn't succeed in making the drug charges stick.

With Lily's and Jack's deaths avenged, he should have felt on top of the world. Instead, he felt itchy, tense and just plain lousy, MacAlister thought morosely. What was Becky doing now? Was she still blaming herself for Roseanne's death? Was she thinking about him, missing him as much as he missed her? His fist clenched. *Dammit, don't think about her.*

Maybe he'd get rip-roaring drunk or start a knock-down, drag-out fight. He'd never drunk much because of his father, and he hadn't hit anyone in years...except in the line of duty. Just now, either alternative sounded better than sitting around thinking about Becky and cursing himself for being too scared to take what she'd offered.

"You haven't lost your touch, MacAlister," Stone said, dropping down on the other end of the couch. "We found three pieces of microfilm under the stone in Deets's ring."

Across the room, MacAlister saw the technician hunched over a sophisticated viewer. "Seadot... See dot... Microfilm...of course. Find anything useful?"

"Don't know yet." Stone took a sip of the tepid coffee, grimaced and set it down. "Where do you go from here?"

MacAlister shrugged. "See what I can salvage out of this mess, I guess," he said unenthusiastically. "Providing you boys don't close me down and seize my assets."

"Why don't you come back to work for the Bureau?"

"I'm through with fieldwork...." MacAlister shuddered. "Permanently."

"Not fieldwork." Stone leaned forward. "How would you like my job?"

"Your job?" MacAlister echoed, his brows raised. "What happened—did they fire you over this?"

"No. Though for a while I was afraid this case was going to queer any chance I had for the job, they promoted me...into Crenshaw's job."

MacAlister's smile was genuine. "So, you're the new Chief. Congratulations...it's about time. You've worked damned hard, and you're the best man for the job."

Stone's granite face cracked into a smile that went from ear to ear. "I've asked them to name you to succeed me."

"Me? I quit the Bureau, and up until yesterday, you suspected I'd helped Deets pedal his designer drugs."

Stone rubbed the back of his neck. "Yeah. Crenshaw thinks I'm a little crazy."

"I know you are." MacAlister sobered. Drawing in a deep breath, he said, "Thanks, Stone. I appreciate the vote of confidence, but I've got a few things to clean up in my personal life before I take on anything more."

"Like what?"

"I've got to decide what happens to my business..." *And my daughter.*

As Stone opened his mouth to counter MacAlister's objection, the technician called his name.

"There's something here I think you should see," the young man said, pushing his glasses up on his nose. "The first two pages of microfilm were Photostats of documents, showing kickbacks to a dozen important people . . . including two senators and a governor."

"Blackmail?" Stone queried.

"Looks like it, sir," the technician said quickly, turning to shove another piece of film under the lens. "The third page was divided into three columns. Names, dates, names again. I ran the names in the first column through the Bureau files. They're all dead, sir. Each one died on the date recorded here."

MacAlister swore under his breath, not liking the sounds of this at all. "What did they die of?" he asked, walking over to the table for a closer look.

"It wasn't old age. Some died in car accidents, three died in fires of 'suspicious origin.' The crash of a private plane took five guys at once. One guy drowned in his own pool, another died in a laboratory explosion."

Stone frowned. "Sounds like a hit man's scorecard."

"Theo said Deets had been involved in some pretty rough stuff a few years ago," MacAlister said thoughtfully. "What about the second column of names?"

"Oh, they're all alive. Some of the names even appear several times on the list." The technician smiled as Sanchez and Anderson joined them, obviously enjoying his moment in the limelight. "I ran these names through the computers, too, and turned up three who have records."

Newcomber whistled through his buck teeth. "Looks like Deets kept a list of his victims and his customers."

"And I think he may have been blackmailing some of his, er, clients," the technician said excitedly. "There are handwritten notations next to some of their names. Dollar amounts and frequencies of payments." He rattled off examples until Stone called a halt. "But I haven't gotten to the really interesting part," he protested.

"Okay. Spit it out, then we'll get busy seeing if we can link the clients to the victims," Stone replied.

The technician nodded. "You remember I mentioned a lab explosion. Well, the man who was killed was Stephen Danforth. And the man who apparently ordered him killed was his brother... Charles Danforth."

"What!" MacAlister nudged the technician out of the way and scanned the microfilm. "Jeez... the kid's right," he growled. "Only it wasn't money Deets wanted from Danforth. There isn't a dollar amount next to Danforth's name, just a word... *ice.*"

The air hissed out between Stone's teeth. "Danforth is Deets's Iceman. It makes sense. Danforth owns a drug company. He could easily get the ingredients and the equipment. But why would he pay Deets to kill his own brother in the first place?"

"Greed. Jealousy. Who knows," MacAlister muttered, pacing now. Those traits seemed to run in Charles's side of the family, he thought darkly. "Damn. I didn't like him when I met him, but I thought it was just habit. Now Danforth's gone, and he's got Rebecca with him."

Damn. He should have known something was wrong. His stomach had been queasy all day, but he'd chalked that up to the pain of letting Rebecca go.

"Sanchez, call the San Francisco tower and get the details on Danforth's flight plan," Stone ordered.

Fighting fear and his runaway imagination, MacAlister stood over Sanchez while the agent waited for the tower's reply. "Danforth's not flying straight through to Connecticut," the agent reported. "He's scheduled to stop in Winslow, Arizona."

MacAlister swore savagely. "That's got to be where Danforth's lab is. The ice shipments were coming out of small towns in Arizona."

"Why would he be stopping there now?" Stone demanded.

"I don't know...." Dread made MacAlister's heart pound, raised gooseflesh on his arms. "But I've got to get to Winslow," he growled, heading for the door.

Stone was with him every step of the way. "There's an airforce jet at Alameda that can have us there thirty minutes after it leaves the ground."

"Half an hour to the airport . . . another thirty to Winslow. It's too long." MacAlister wrenched open the door.

"Hang on a sec, MacAlister," Stone said, putting a hand on his arm. "You'll get there quicker if you come with us. Newcomber," he called over his shoulder. "Get us a police escort. Anderson. Order up that jet. Sanchez. Call whatever passes for the law in Winslow. Find out if there's a Danforth Pharmaceuticals lab there, and have them stake out the airport. But tell them not to move in until we get there," Stone added as MacAlister took off, running.

Rebecca woke up when the plane touched down. At first, she couldn't believe she'd slept all the way home, then she spied the small terminal building that the jet was taxiing toward. This wasn't the airport her uncle usually used. Disoriented, she glanced around and found him staring at her. "Where are we, Uncle Charles?"

"Winslow . . . Arizona."

Her eyes widened as she recognized the name. Her uncle made twice-monthly trips to the Danforth Pharmaceuticals labs here. Surely he wasn't planning on conducting business at a time like this. "Why are we stopping in Winslow?"

"There's something I have to take care of," Charles replied, unbuckling his seat belt and standing.

"Now?" Rebecca's raw nerves stretched a little tighter. Smiling faintly, Charles unfastened her seat belt and held out his hand to her. "Yes. I'm afraid my unfinished business will not wait."

Rebecca sighed. How like him to put business before anything, even grief. Rising stiffly, she took his hand and allowed him to guide her down the jet's narrow metal steps.

Night had fallen, yet the air was still hot from the sun that had baked it all day. There was a car waiting to whisk them away to the plant. The long, shiny black limousine looked out of place in a barren desert dominated by piles of sand, rugged rocks and scrubby cacti.

As the dark car sped along the flat, dusty road, Rebecca settled back in the plush seat and tried not to compare the desolate landscape to her own bleak future.

"I presume MacAlister turned Deets's book over to Stone," her uncle said conversationally.

Rebecca flinched. MacAlister was the last person she wanted to discuss with her disapproving uncle. "Probably."

"Pity," Charles murmured. He shifted his gaze to the dark window. Neither of them spoke again until the car had stopped.

"Is that the plant?" Rebecca asked, squinting up at an unlit, two-story stone building that blended so perfectly with the surrounding rocks it was nearly invisible. "It doesn't look like anyone's here."

"I gave them today and tomorrow off... because of Roseanne." Depressing a button, he rolled down the window separating them from the driver. "We may be inside for some time... I'll call down when we're ready to leave."

Uncle Charles's second-floor office, like his office at Danforth's corporate headquarters, reminded Rebecca of the man himself...cool, reserved, expensive. One whole wall was floor-to-ceiling windows. He opened some of them, letting in the warm, fragrant desert air. A flick of a switch turned on a bank of floodlights, illuminating the courtyard below.

"What do you think?" he inquired, one hand resting lightly on her shoulder.

Rebecca resisted the urge to fling off his hand, and managed to murmur a polite reply.

"You're far too tense, my dear. Sit down and I'll get us something to drink."

Rebecca didn't want to sit, or drink. She wanted to be at home, in her own bed, with the covers pulled over her head and all of the unpleasantness yet to come out of the way. Still, her uncle had been through a lot, and the news of Roseanne's death would probably launch Aunt Margaret on a drinking binge, leaving the poor man to cope with everything himself.

Sighing, Rebecca seated herself on a nearby couch. The least she could do was give in to his wishes. After a moment, she relaxed, lulled by the sounds of a light breeze ruffling the palms and the gurgle of water falling in the fountain below.

"Wine?"

Rebecca started. Covering her surprise, she reached for one of the two glasses of white wine he carried. She was even more astonished when he sat down beside her instead of returning to his desk to work on whatever business had brought them here.

"What do you think?" he asked, quietly.

"It's very..." *Romantic* popped into her mind, reminded her of MacAlister, and she shied away from the word. "Nice," she ended, lamely.

"I loved her, you know," he murmured.

Rebecca nodded sadly. "I loved Roseanne, too, even though..."

"Not Roseanne—Elizabeth ... I loved Elizabeth."

Elizabeth ... her mother? Suddenly Rebecca felt chilled.

"She was everything I wanted in a wife...strong, beautiful, cultured." His lips curled slightly. "Everything Margaret was not. If I had met Elizabeth before Stephen did, I know she would have chosen me instead."

"W-why are you telling me this?"

"Because I want you to understand." He looked through her, his gaze focused on the past. "In the beginning, I thought that if I built Danforth Pharmaceuticals into something really big, she would leave Stephen for me. So I took some chances...made some deals.... But success came too late...." He sucked in air, his eyes glazed with pain. "She died before I was ready."

"Yes, she did," Rebecca murmured, her voice thick.

Charles exhaled sharply. "Your loss was nothing compared to mine. You were young, and I saw to it you had everything money could buy. But I had nothing.... Elizabeth was gone, and I was in way over my head with the wrong people. Do you understand?" he asked, turning on her suddenly, his eyes glittering, intense.

Dazed, Rebecca shook her head.

Charles smiled that strange, sad little smile again. "You are so beautiful...like your mother. But you have the Danforth brains, and you're moralistic, like your father was. In time, you would figure what I had done and hate me for it just as Stephen did."

"W-what are you saying?"

"I borrowed the money to expand Danforth Pharmaceuticals from an...unconventional...source. The company was doing well, but the interest he demanded was exorbitant. When I complained, said he was ruining me, my, er, associate offered to take goods instead...things a man in my position could easily get."

"Drugs?" The word hissed out between Rebecca's lips.

"Close...the components to make them." Charles sighed deeply. "Eventually, Stephen found out, of course. I have never seen him so furious. He threatened to go to the authorities. I tried to tell him you could not simply stop working for dangerous people like my associate, but Stephen refused to believe me. What could I do?"

"Y-you killed my father."

"Of course not," he cried, clearly appalled. "What kind of man kills his own brother? But when I told Deets what Stephen was planning to do..."

Rebecca shuddered. "Lucien Deets killed my father?"

"Yes," Charles said softly. "The explosion in the lab was no accident."

"Oh, my God. Why didn't you go to the police?"

Charles paled. "I couldn't...Deets would have implicated me. And with Stephen gone, he expected even more from me. No longer was he satisfied with the ingredients to manufacture his own drugs, he wanted me to develop new ones for him. I was a fine chemist once, but I became his personal drug designer." He grimaced, then looked at Rebecca. "I hated giving in, but I—I had no choice...."

"Oh, Uncle Charles." Dizzy with grief, Rebecca closed her eyes. She felt her uncle's arm hesitantly slide around her shoulders and knew that he was finally offering the love and comfort he'd perhaps been too ashamed to give before. But she was too heartsick, too overcome by the emotions that churned inside her to respond to his unspoken apology. *He had allowed her father to be killed.*

And Roseanne, too. Rebecca shuddered. *Dear God.* In a way, he had been responsible for his own daughter's death. The pain and sorrow clenched deep inside her, and she shuddered again.

Feeling her movement, Charles drew in a ragged sigh and released her. "Here, drink some of the wine."

Rebecca took the glass. The cool wine felt good sliding down her parched throat. She attributed its slightly metallic taste to her own bitterness. "You must stop making the drugs and tell Mr. Stone—"

"No." Taking her empty glass, he set it on the coffee table beside his and grabbed both of her hands. "The scandal would be too great."

"The scandal. Two members of our family are dead...along with countless other people who used the drugs you made...and you are worried about your reputation?"

Charles's eyes narrowed. "It was not my fault. All I did was borrow money from Deets. If he hadn't been so greedy..."

"Oh," Rebecca exclaimed as a new thought intruded. "The Bureau has Deets's book. If you were his supplier, your name will be in it. How can you avoid...?"

"Not avoid...escape...by killing myself...and you."

"Me?" Rebecca gasped. His calm expression told her he was quite serious. The feverish glint in his eye made her wonder if he was mad. "I don't want to die...I don't want you to, either."

"I could not bear to lose everything I have worked so hard to build," he whispered, a grimace of distaste twisting his features. "To be held up to public humiliation, to suffer the indignities of prison."

He shook his head. "Impossible. Nor could I stand living with your hatred." There was deep sadness and regret in the gaze he turned on her. "I'm afraid we have no choice."

He glanced pointedly at her empty wineglass, and Rebecca gasped. *Poison. He would have access to oceans of it.* "No," she screamed, trying frantically to free her hands. Already she could feel a strange languor stealing over her.

"Rebecca. Stop this." He gave her a little shake. "You won't feel a thing, I promise. I'll wait until you're asleep before I shoot you."

"Sh-shoot? Th-then it's n-not p-poison?" The words slurred together.

"Believe me, poison is painful. And I do not want you to suffer any more than you already have." Pushing her back against the cushions, he produced a gun from his pocket.

His image was beginning to blur together. "H-how would I—
I suffer?"

"The scandal…they'd take everything…you'd be poor…"
He said it as though he couldn't imagine anything worse. "I
can't let Elizabeth's daughter suffer."

Rebecca tried to lift her arm to push the gun away, but her
muscles refused to work. She searched frantically for something to say that would stay his hand. "I—I'd r-rather be alive
and p-poor than d-dead . . ."

"Your father and I grew up dirt poor. Believe me, you would
be miserable if you had to live like that."

No. No, I wouldn't. Disjointed memories flickered through
her fogged brain. MacAlister, telling her he'd been poor.
MacAlister, listening to her plans for the house and restaurant. MacAlister, making love to her with unexpected gentleness. MacAlister, rescuing her once…twice…. She loved him
so much, and now she wouldn't be around when he realized
that he loved her, too.

MacAlister. I need you. Where are you? Hanging on to consciousness by a thread, Rebecca sobbed his name as her eyes
drifted shut.

Suddenly there was a terrible explosion . . . and men yelling,
then another explosion. The acrid smell of gunpowder drifted
over Rebecca. But there was no pain. Only darkness and more
voices, men shouting, a woman weeping.

Hard hands gripped her shoulder and shook her eyes open.
MacAlister's face swam into view. He looked grim and worried. "Becky? Are you all right?"

"MacAlister . . . you came back," she whispered.

"Ah, honey." He hugged her so tightly she couldn't breathe,
then released her before she was ready to be free of him. "It's
all over…really all over, this time." He stood to make way for
the ambulance personnel, his eyes remote, his lips tight.

No. Don't leave me. Rebecca fought the effects of the drug,
struggled to call him back. But as she watched him slip away
from her, Rebecca dimly realized he hadn't just been speaking
about the danger, he had been speaking about *them*.

Epilogue

"And you sign right here also, Miss Danforth."

Rebecca obediently moved her pen to the line beside her lawyer's pudgy finger and scrawled her name for the twentieth, and last, time. Discrete applause broke out around the conference table as she set the pen down.

The accountants beamed.

The lawyers beamed.

The two Belamy brothers, Danforth Pharmaceuticals's new owners, beamed.

Rebecca managed a small smile and tried not to think about the deaths of her father, her cousin and her uncle...after three months, the pain was still too fresh.

She had accomplished a lot in three months, Rebecca reflected as she shook hands with the lawyers and declined the Belamys' offer of dinner and drinks. The new owners accepted her refusal with identical brisk nods and left with the accountants and lawyers in tow.

According to her investigation, the Belamys were progressive, honest and good to work for. Her management and board of directors had expressed regret at her decision to sell Danforth. But she'd been adamant, wanting nothing more to do with the business that had cost her so much. Bowing to her wishes, Danforth's employees had pulled together to impress the prospective buyers. The Winslow plant had been dismantled and sold separately to a firm that made face powders.

Back in her office, Rebecca picked up the phone and dialed her aunt's number. The bright, cheery voice that answered brought a smile to her lips. "It's done, Aunt Margaret . . . I've just signed the papers."

"Wonderful, dear. I know that's a load off your mind. Now you can relax and pamper yourself."

"Now I can devote myself to turning Le Petit Gourmet into a restaurant," Rebecca countered.

"Rebecca . . . you know you should begin taking it easy," her aunt warned.

"I'm feeling fine." Rebecca smoothed a hand over the small bulge concealed by her long, tunic-style jacket. Thankfully, current fashion trended towards the loose and flowing. Not that she was ashamed to be carrying MacAlister's baby under her heart. She was overjoyed . . . but she wanted to conclude the sale of Danforth Pharmaceuticals before going public with her secret.

"Well, I still say you need more rest," her aunt said. "And we should do something to celebrate."

"Yes." Rebecca thought of champagne, then immediately rejected it. She wasn't drinking, and her aunt hadn't touched a drop since returning from the clinic. The quick, energetic woman Rebecca had brought home from the facility bore no resemblance to the vague, shaky woman who had signed herself into the rehab center two months before.

"What shall we do?" her aunt asked briskly.

There was such strength in her aunt these days. Rebecca tried not to think Charles's passion for Elizabeth and his disdain for his own wife had led to Margaret's illness. She tried to concentrate on the positive, on the renovation of her house, the expansion plans for the restaurant and the birth of her child. If only she could stop missing MacAlister, she just might succeed.

"It's too late to ask Anna to prepare something special," Rebecca mused. "Shall we go out?"

"That would be lovely, dear. But could we make it tomorrow? Mr. Oberlander, the president of my garden club, is coming over to repot orchids this evening...and I'd hate to cut short our dinner to rush back."

Rebecca chuckled to herself at the breathlessness in her aunt's voice. Mr. Oberlander had been a regular visitor for the last month. "Tomorrow it is. I think I'll drive over and see how the repairs are coming on my house...."

"No. I mean, er, aren't you too tired to drive all the way over there?"

"It's been six weeks since I've seen the place." It had been more convenient to live at her aunt's while she was working at Danforth. "How do I know that the workmen you hired are doing a good job?"

"They are," Margaret said quickly. "I—I was there yesterday. You should wait until next week before going over. They're working on the electrical, and there are wires all over the place. You wouldn't want to fall, would you?" she added.

"No, of course not. But I do feel like taking a drive. Maybe I'll stop at Le Petit Gourmet for a minute." *And then I'll drive by and take a peek at the house.*

It was dark and snowing lightly by the time Rebecca pulled into her driveway. For a moment, she stood by the car, oblivious to the flakes drifting around her.

From the outside, the place looked great. The roof no longer sagged, the shutters were straight, even the back porch looked strong and sturdy.

Smiling, she inched around the car and crept up the back steps. Her boots provided good traction, but she wasn't taking any chances. She unlocked the door, stepped inside and closed it before flicking the wall switch.

Nothing happened.

Maybe the workmen had the electricity turned off, she reasoned. Beside her, something moved. *She wasn't alone.*

A scream welling up in her throat, Rebecca groped behind her for the doorknob.

A callused, sawdust-covered hand closed over her mouth. "Easy, honey. It's me." The hand slipped away.

"MacAlister." Rebecca sagged against the door, a thousand thoughts spinning through her mind. Confusion. Disbelief. Joy. "Th-the lights don't work."

"I turned the electricity off." He was standing so close she could feel the heat from his body, smell the scent that was uniquely his.

"W-why?" she murmured.

"So I could rerun a few circuits. Some of the wiring in the walls was frayed . . . it can be hazardous."

It took a few seconds for his words to sink in, for her to wonder why he was in her house, running wires and checking circuits. "What are you doing here?"

"Your aunt hired me."

"But . . . what about the Golden Circle?"

"I decided on a career change."

A career change? She remembered MacAlister saying he'd inherited his father's carpentry skills. But why was he here, working on her house? "Did . . . did Aunt Margaret call you?" she asked shakily.

His hand skimmed over her hair, and she realized he was trembling, too.

"No," he said softly. "I called her. I had to make certain you were all right."

Anger took the chill from her cheeks. "You could have called and asked *me.*"

"You've had enough to deal with these past couple of months." His voice was deep, rough. "And there were things I had to do, things I needed to understand before we talked. Only I didn't know where to begin until after I'd spoken to your aunt. Then I realized there was something I could do for you, something of myself I could give you."

Rebecca nearly giggled despite the ache in her throat. *If he only knew.* Thankfully, her aunt hadn't said anything about the baby, and she wasn't going to tell him, either . . . not until she knew how he felt. She'd handed him her love once and had it thrown back in her face. Selling Danforth had taught her the fine art of negotiating from a position of strength.

MacAlister's sigh was ragged. She felt him move, could almost see him dragging his hand through his hair. "Damn. I thought I'd have another week or so..."

"Before what?"

"Daddy." A child's high, frightened voice punctuated the tense pause.

"Don't move." Giving Rebecca's hand a quick squeeze, he rushed from the room with the easy assurance of a cat. "I'm here, baby," she heard him say, his voice light and full of reassurance. A tiny, sleepy voice gave a teary reply.

Daddy. Rebecca fumbled in her purse for a box of the souvenir matches she was always taking from restaurants. By its dim light, she stepped over coils of wire and assorted tools, following the sounds of voices to the upstairs guest room.

By the light of a lantern set on a nearby dresser, she watched MacAlister soothe his daughter's fears and try to tuck her into bed. His back was to Rebecca, but the little girl saw her immediately.

"Hello," she said, popping up like a jack-in-the-box. "Are you the lady who lives here?"

The tang of the Orient still flavored Amber's rounded *l*'s and slurred *r*'s, but Rebecca had no trouble understanding her. "Yes, I am." She divided a smile between the two pairs of identical amber eyes illuminated by the soft light. One set curious... the other wary.

"We're fixing it for you," Amber proudly announced. "My daddy lets me help."

The tears Rebecca had been so careful to suppress were suddenly swimming in her eyes, making the figures on the bed blur. He'd listened to her, he'd made a place in his life for his child. Maybe... just maybe... there would be room in his heart for another.

"Bed now, Amber," MacAlister said firmly.

Amber's lip came out. "But, Daddy... we've been waiting for her to come live with us...."

The shadows in MacAlister's eyes deepened. "Amber..."

"I've been waiting to meet you, too, Amber." Rebecca walked over and knelt beside the bed. Brushing back a lock of shiny black hair, she tucked it behind Amber's ear. "If your daddy says it's okay, I'll tell you a short story."

MacAlister was looking out the living room window, both hands stuck in his back pockets, when Rebecca came downstairs. Turning, he watched her cross to stand beside him, memories washing over him. Her expression told him nothing, and he looked away, fearing memories might be all he would ever have. "I'm sorry she put you on the spot."

He looked bigger than she'd remembered. Bigger and rougher. But beneath the strength, there was such gentleness, such compassion, such pain, it made her heart ache.

He was more vulnerable than she was. The realization gave her the courage to take the most important gamble of her life. "She didn't put me on the spot. I . . ."

"I'd figured I'd have the house done before you found out we were here," he said in a rush, as though he was afraid to hear what she had to say. "But now that you know . . . Well, Amber and I can move into a motel until I'm done, if it bothers you."

"It would bother me to have you and Amber staying at a motel," she said quietly.

His hand tightened on the window frame. "Maybe you'd rather get someone else to finish the work."

"That would bother me more."

"It would?" A spark of something that might have been hope kindled in his eyes. "Why?"

"You understand how much this house means to me. . . ."

He smiled raggedly. "Yeah, you were right about this place. Even a guy like me can feel the warmth . . . the . . ." he swallowed, as though his throat was as full as hers was " . . . the love . . ."

"Yes, love," Rebecca whispered, looking deep into his eyes. "Why are you here?" she asked again.

"Because I wanted to do something for you . . . ." He stopped, shook his head. "No, that's only part of it. I'm here because I love you. I've never said those words to anyone else, and what I feel for you scares me half to death, but it's true. I love you."

When she didn't say anything, just continued to stare up at him in amazement, he lightly touched her hair. "It's too late, isn't it?"

Rebecca smiled. "No, it isn't too late...it'll never be too late. I'll always love you...."

She squeaked as he swept her off her feet and folded her into his arms, fiercely, hungrily. "Oh, honey. I love you so much. God, I was so afraid." His words were interspersed with a dozen quick kisses, planted on her ear, her jaw, her cheek. "I wasn't thinking straight the last time we were together. I was scared I'd let you down like I did Lily, but after I left you, I realized you'd become so much a part of me, changed me in so many ways, that I couldn't live without you."

"Oh, Gates," she murmured as his mouth closed over hers. From the strength of his embrace, she'd been prepared for greed, desperation. Instead, the incredible tenderness of his kiss melted the coldness inside her.

She touched his cheek, and he shuddered. The tension in his arms eased as he stroked her arms, her shoulders, her throat, then, finally, cradled her face in his palms.

"Marry me." It was more demand than question.

Rebecca smiled. His eyes were clear and unshuttered. In them, she saw the reflection of her own love. "Yes. Oh, yes."

"I love you," he murmured. "So damn much." He slid one hand down her side and up under her tunic, zeroing in on the front closure of her bra. Along the way, he brushed across the slight fullness of her stomach.

Rebecca held her breath, wondering if he'd notice.

The strangest look came over his face, and his hand reversed course, touched lightly. A muscle jumped in his cheek as his fingers splayed over their unborn child like a shield. Eyes closed, he leaned his forehead against hers.

"Oh, baby," he breathed with such heartfelt wonder that her whole body tingled, and her eyes filled with tears again.

"Yes, it is," Rebecca agreed shakily.

"Why didn't you tell me?"

"I didn't want to."

His head came up, his eyes blazing under lowered lids. "You're sorry it happened."

"Not a bit," she said, defensively.

"Easy, honey. Neither am I...except that you were alone when you found out." As prickly as she was about this, he was damned glad he'd asked her to marry him before he found out about the baby. "Were you scared?"

"No."

"Then why didn't you get in touch with me?" he demanded.

"I thought if you knew, you'd feel obligated to provide for her, or him, and I have the resources..."

"Yeah," he growled. Obviously, the differences in their finances was still a sore point.

"If it matters," Rebecca snapped, "Aunt Margaret and I have sold Danforth Pharmaceuticals and used the money to set up scholarships for gifted chemists and endow a library at my father's and uncle's alma mater. As of two o'clock this afternoon, I'm just a struggling bakery owner."

His arms tightened around her. "I've got more than enough to provide for you, honey. We can even open that restaurant you wanted, and I may try my hand at restoring antiques. But the money doesn't matter anymore. Nothing matters as long as you still need me," he said softly.

"I need you. I'll always need you." Standing on tiptoe, she pulled his mouth down and showed him how much.

When she let him up for air, MacAlister buried his face in her hair, dragging in her scent, wondering how he'd ever thought he could live without her. "You better be sure, honey. Because, princess or no...I'll never let you go."

"Mmm. I was never surer of anything in my life. Does that mean I won't be driving back to my aunt's house tonight?" she asked, playfully running her fingers down his chest.

He groaned, picked her up and headed for the stairs. "Not tonight or any other night, honey."

*   *   *   *   *

COMING NEXT MONTH

#487 COLD, COLD HEART—Ann Williams
Rescuing kidnapped children no longer interested rugged
American Hero Jake Frost, but to save her daughter,
Rachel Dryden was determined to change his mind. Could
Rachel warm his heart to her cause . . . and herself?

#488 OBSESSED!—Amanda Stevens
Both shy cartoonist Laura Valentine and undercover FBI agent
Richard Gentry were pretending to be something they weren't. But
complications *really* arose when they realized their passion wasn't
a fake. . . .

#489 TWO AGAINST THE WORLD—Many Anne Wilson
All Alicia Sullivan wanted was a little peace—and *maybe* a nice,
normal, sane man. Instead, she found herself stranded with
secretive Steven Rider, whose mysterious nature was far from safe.

#490 SHERIFF'S LADY—Dani Criss
Fleeing cross-country from a powerful criminal, C. J. Dillon
couldn't afford to trust anyone. But when Sheriff Chris Riker
offered his assistance, C.J. longed to confide in the virile lawman.

#491 STILL MARRIED—Diana Whitney
Desperately worried about her missing sister-in-law, Kelsey Manning
sought out her estranged husband, Luke Sontag. But as they
joined forces on the search, could they find the strength to save
their marriage?

#492 MAN OF THE HOUR—Maura Seger
Years ago, fast cars, cold beer and easy women had been bad boy
Mark Fletcher's style. But he'd changed. Now his only trouble
came in the form of single mother Lisa Morley.

INTIMATE MOMENTS®

10TH Anniversary

Celebrate our anniversary with a fabulous collection of firsts....

The first Intimate Moments titles written by three of your favorite authors:

NIGHT MOVES   Heather Graham Pozzessere
LADY OF THE NIGHT Emilie Richards
A STRANGER'S SMILE Kathleen Korbel

Silhouette Intimate Moments is proud to present a FREE hardbound collection of our authors' firsts—titles that you will treasure in the years to come from some of the line's founding members.

This collection will not be sold in retail stores and is available only through this exclusive offer. Look for details in Silhouette Intimate Moments titles available in retail stores in May, June and July.

Take 4 bestselling love stories FREE

Plus get a FREE surprise gift!

Silhouette Books
is proud to present
our best authors,
their best books...
and the best in
your reading pleasure!

Throughout 1993, look for exciting books
by these top names in contemporary
romance:

CATHERINE COULTER—
Aftershocks in February

FERN MICHAELS—
Nightstar in March

DIANA PALMER—
Heather's Song in March

ELIZABETH LOWELL
Love Song for a Raven in April

SANDRA BROWN
(previously published under
the pseudonym Erin St. Claire)—
Led Astray in April

LINDA HOWARD—
All That Glitters in May

When it comes to passion,
we wrote the book.